# Jay — The Arrival

The night chill was more than he had expected, and he hoped that he will survive until he found a nice warm place to stay for the night. Jay hoped that this wish for shelter was impending, because the threadbare brown robe he wore over his diaphanous white toga was not doing the trick. And it did not help matters that he had chosen to wear his hand made sandals for this unforgiving climate.

Where he had just come from, home, was always nice and warm, and so he really did not put much thought into wearing his bearskin coat and boots. "Mmm . . ." Jay wanted to kick himself, but his toes would fall off. He continued to drudge onward and forward, constantly looking for somewhere suitable to get some warmth, and rest his tired soul. Though already tired and weary from his travels, Jay kept his cold feet moving, until the cars that passed him on the highway finally started to dissipate. He stopped for a moment to go into his leather satchel he carried, and bring out his deerskin flask. "I am so thirsty!" You could hear him gulping down the lukewarm water from miles around. Once semi-refreshed, Jay commenced on his trek to nowhere. He decided to turn off at the next junction he saw, and kept walking until he saw an old black lady standing by the side of the road. She was standing in front of a metal stall which had smoke emanating out of it. Jay could now smell the aromatic food that she was cooking and selling. *I'm starving!* The smell of the spiced cooked meat and fishes was making his stomach scream out in capitulation. At this late hour of the day, the old black lady was still serving quite a few customers, and Jay went over to investigate.

When he stepped up after the previous person had been served, the old black lady asked "How can I help ya today, mister?"

Well . . ."

The old black woman looked at him impatiently, "Well what do ya want?"

"Everything," was Jay's veritable reply. "I'm hungry."

"Everything." This made the old black lady laugh, and Jay could see that she had lost most of her teeth. "Well mister, I'll sell ya the whole cart for a measly $500.00."

There was no reply. "Look mister, all I have is . . . The fish is good, and if you put it in between two thick slices of my hard-dough bread, ya won't be hungry for another week." As she spoke, Jay saw that she was already putting *his* order in a brown paper bag. "Are you going to eat it now," she asked.

"No my child, I will take it with me." Then Jay realized that he did not have any money, except what he had brought with him. "My child, I don't have any of *your* money."

"Ya what," asked the now truculent old black woman? She pulled the package back toward her ample drooping breasts. "Well what do ya have, mister?" With eyes that seemed to have glaucoma, she looked through him, and this made Jay feel rather uncomfortable.

"I've got a few gold coins," said Jay quickly as he went into his leather satchel and pulled out a cloth bag, which was tied at the top. Jay untied the bag, and pulled out one of the gold coins inside and passed it over to the old black woman. Her mouth was open, and she was lucky that it wasn't summer tim3, or she'd have an open grill full of flying insects. "This isn't *our* president," her toothless mouth was saying. She continued to turn the coin over in her frail and arthritic hand, "And this isn't our damn president."

"No," said Jay passively, "it's Julius Caesar."

Still scrutinizing the gold coin, with one glaucoma eye on Jay, the old black woman finally said, "Ya can't spend this Monopoly money around here, boy. What da hell is wrong with ya? Where ya from anyway, Sunshine?"

"I come from a distant place." The old black woman was now trembling at the sound of his ominous voice. The voice he now spoke with had the old black woman wanting to bow down and kiss his sordid cold feet. *There's something about him,* she told herself. *The way he was dressed, his manner, the ancient coin she still held in her hand.* It was as if she knew that he was once here, as someone that deserved reverence.

The clothes, the long hair and beard had her now shaking from within. Once again she found the nerve to chance another look up into his innocent and bearded face, and then gulped audibly. The old black woman no longer wanted to look into those deep blue eyes of his, so she kept her head bowed, and stared at the ground in front of her.

"Sorry Sir." Her attitude had now changed, diametrically. "Please, take this food. It's on me, and here is a ginger beer to wash it down with. She quickly wrapped

# Contents

# A Friend Named Jay

To: Irene

God bless...

Enjoy

Michael Atkinson

# A Friend Named Jay

## Michael Atkinson

Rev. date: 07/11/2013

**To order additional copies of this book, contact:**
Xlibris LLC
0-800-056-3182
www.xlibrispublishing.co.uk
Orders@xlibrispublishing.co.uk
307214

the food for the stranger, and decided to give him an extra fish. "This is for you also."

"Well thank you my child," said a surprised, but delighted Jay. "May God bless you?"

"Sorry," she said, her head still bowed.

"Why are you sorry, child?"

Shoving the food and ginger beer into Jay's hands, the old black woman said, "Because I feel I disrespected you in the way I spoke to you." Jay noticed that she was rapidly busying herself cleaning up, while she continued to speak to him, with her head down. He watched as she put her food away, closed the food cart, and before he could say "Farewell," she was off, pushing the cart down the street. He watched as the food cart moved as if it had an electric motor on it.

The person who was patiently waiting to be served in line behind Jay screamed, "A, old lady, what about me, ya old bat?" There was no reply, because there was no there to reply to the angry dreadlocked man who was now scowling at Jay, and then at the bag of food in his hand. Jay did not move, not even his blue eyes, which were fixed on the dreadlocked man. The man walked off. *Not pleased at all,* thought Jay.

# Drug Addict

Michael sat there frozen, waiting and thinking, in Randy's living room, along with the others. They had all finished what they had brought into the apartment, and was now waiting, in a state of daze and confusion. Some of Rand's patrons looked like fold fishes, and some looked like reptiles, eyes roving around the vicinity for some more crack cocaine that may have fallen on the sordid apartment floor by mistake, or fall out of the paint cracked and damp ceiling. The "Gold Fishers" were just holding their breath in their lungs for as long as possible, just before their lungs burst. Their ultimate and pathetic goal was to hold the cocaine fumes for as long as they could as possible, which caused the ugly gold fish look on the sordid and sleep deprived faces. All of Randy's patrons had that scrawny face look, because they had all been smoking their drug of choice for years, and it showed in their wide as a flying saucer eye and the bones that forced their way through their diaphanous tight skins.

Randy's living room was dark, because none of his patrons either couldn't stand the light or wanted it on. The room that Randy rented out to drug addicts that wanted to take their hits was already defiled with excrements indescribable. As Michael looked on with his own gold fish eyes at the despicable and grimy filth that surrounded him, he wondered which one of them was going to give him his desperately needed next hit of crack.

Randy's apartment was one of the many "Base Houses" around the neighbourhood where he could have gone, but tonight Michael had decided to come here to smoke his nickel vial of crack. Just as all the other "Base Houses" he has been to, this one had strangers, and people he knew, coming in and going out of it constantly, bringing in whatever drugs they had, but mostly crack cocaine.

Using drugs in a "Base House" was much better, and somewhat warmer, than trying to smoke your drugs in some cold and sordid alley in the streets of New York. Plus the owner of the apartment, in this case Randy only asked for a small fee to use their apartment. The price to enter was a measly piece of what you had.

With the hundreds of people coming through his apartment every day, Randy was guaranteed to be in the state of oblivion on a daily basis. *The boy hasn't slept in weeks,* thought Michael as he watched Randy's reptilian eyes flash around his skeletal face.

Though Randy looked like a homeless bum, Michael knew better. The boy had become an entrepreneur by selling lighters, glass stems, metal screens, and coat hangers on the side for his patrons. The only reason Randy wasn't rich by now Michael knew, was because he had fell victim to the new invention called Crack Cocaine, like the rest of them in his squalid apartment.

# JAY — CREATING A HOME OF PEACE

Worn out, just like his tired feet and sandals, Jay was more than glad to spot a dilapidated farm house off the dusty road of Suffolk County. Looking around at the barren land it was not a hard decision to make for him. It was a good a place as any to stay for now, out of a choice of one. After making sure that the deserted farm house was truly abandoned, Jay divagated over to the small dilapidated stable across from it.

Though the stable was a much smaller building than the big farm house across the dusty and unkempt field, it was exactly what he needed right now. I *don't need to sleep in a seven room mansion,* he told himself with a wry smile on his face. *My cup runneth over . . .*

After getting himself settled, kicking off his worn and sordid sandals and then throwing the food and satchel on the floor of hay, Jay commenced to move around a few bales of hay to make the stable more comfortable for his stay. How long that it will be, he did not know.

Inside the stable was not as small as it appeared to the naked eye on the outside, especially now that he had strategically moved around the bales of hay to make a half decent living room for himself. It was perfect for what he wanted, and that was a little rest.

Here Jay knew that he would also be able to listen out for any unwanted intruders through the plethora of holes in the stables walls. He commenced to make a comfortable bed in the corner, using his tattered brown robe as a blanket.

Sitting crossed legged on the ground, Jay commenced to un-wrap the food the old black lady had given him, before she hastily rushed off. The aroma of the fresh steamed fishes had him dizzy, but he continued to open the rest of the package. The hard-dough bread was still tepid, because he had them sitting in the bag next to the fishes, and the ginger beer was still semi-cold because he had put it separately inside his leather satchel.

The aromatic smell reminded him that he hadn't eaten a thing all day, and that was why he felt so tired and weak, and was now ready to feast. Once Jay flung one of the large sized carps, unceremoniously in between the two slices of hard-dough bread, he found that his jaw could not open wide enough for him to wrap his salivating mouth around the dense sandwich. This only made him hungrier, and more determined to attack and destroy his food. "Even if it takes me a couple of days," jay told himself, "I will finish this sandwich."

After nibbling around the edges of the hard-dough bread teasingly, Jay opened his jaw as far as the hinges allowed, and took his first beautiful bite. The taste of the fish made Jay's eyes go back into his head – *Heaven!* He then went into his leather satchel and pulled out the can of ginger beer. Wiping his lips with the sleeve of his robe, Jay gave thanks, already regretting that he forgot to say grace before eating. "Thank you, Father. My cup runneth over!"

After he washed his late night meal down with the "Olde Jamaican ginger beer, he burped loud enough for the wooden slates of the stable wall to quiver. After this, since he knew that he shouldn't go to sleep straight after eating, he decided to get up and stretch his legs. His stomach was full, and he castigated himself for being so greedy and eating so fast. Standing in the doorway of the stable, Jay stood there and looked around the vast waste land that once used to be a farm, a land that used to bring forth life and food. W*hat a waste,* he thought. He then perked up his ears, and listened to the sounds of modern earth. The unfamiliar mechanical noises coming from the highways over the hills seemed so incongruous to this vast open plain he now called home. The sky he knew was filled with beautiful stars could not be seen because of all the dense smoke, smog and pollution blanketing it. He could also smell the stench of death, as it made its way toward him. After stretching his weary bones and muscles, Jay inhaled deeply, and sighed. He then went back into the stable, and made himself comfortable on his new straw bed. W*ho needs a "Memory Foam" mattress?*

Using his tattered brown robe as a blanket, Jay lay on his back, and looked up at the stars through the holes in the rotted ceiling. Jay began to talk to *his* father. Speaking with his father did not last too long though, because after uttering several words, sleep hit Jay like an Iron Mike Tyson upper-cut. Lights out! He dreamt of his last conversation that he had with his father, before he had decided to come *here.*

"The good people of the world have lost their way," Jay had said, as his father watched his son pack some food and a deerskin wine flask. "It is only because they are in the wrong environment father," he insisted. His father had been sitting in his throne silently, but Jay knew that he was being watched studiously.

Jay also knew that his regal father was only silent because he really did not have anything more to say to his son about *his* self-proclaimed mission.

"I need to go out and save them, father." Though he disagreed with his son's fatuous decision to leave home, to go and help *his* fellow brothers and sisters, again, Yahweh was quite proud that his son still wanted to do something for his ungrateful brethren's.

Yahweh sat there fiddling with his crown, knowing that he had already given the world enough warnings, and chances, to correct their despicable and insolent behaviour. They had failed, miserably. T*hey must be doing it on purpose,* thought a disconsolate Yahweh.

"Father," his thoughts were interrupted, "you know that you cannot plant a good seed in a field full of weeds. The superfluous amount of bad weeds will just grow, and choke the few good seeds."

This had Yahweh scratching his right temple with his baroque staff. His mouth was wide open, but there was nothing emanating from it. After all, he was the one that had told his son all these things. After a long time thinking about what his precious son was saying, he told him, "Son, after all you have seen, and what *they* have done to you, you still see fit to try and save *them,* again?"

"Yes father," was Jay's succinct reply. "Some of them, can be saved, and deserved to be saved."

Jay knew that all people were born as innocent as a new born baby, but as they grew up in *this* soiled, insidious world, they became hardened of heart. *Evil is rife down there.*

Tossing and turning in his deep sleep, Jay's subconscious turned to the work he had to do. It was going to be an arduous task he knew, maybe even harder than the first time around. Nothing had gotten better after the sacrifice he had made for them, yet there were still people out there that he knew still believed in him, slightly, and could be saved, possibly.

# RANDY'S PIT

Before he had arrived at Randy's snake pit of an apartment, Michael had bought himself two nickel vials of crack with his last $10.00. Now his drugs had inevitably finished, and he now had to face the down side of being a drug addict, when you had no more.

Like all the other drug fiends in Randy's squalid apartment, Michael had been through the motion of pushing the small diaphanous screens back and forth through the glass stem so that he could collect the left over oily residue which was produced after every hit on the glass stem. When that avenue was exhausted that was when every professional crack head had to admit to him or herself that the session was completely and utterly over. *What a bummer!*

The end of a sessions was the dread of every *crack-head*, any drug user for that matter. At first they are over-joyed with anticipation with getting the first hit, and then the inevitable ending came, which made them feel that they had left heaven on the express Otis elevator to hell.

"Pass that empty crack pipe Majestic," announced a very scrawny and sordid Patrice as he entered the room. He looked like a filthy rat that just crept up from the sewers, with a large piece for cheddar. "If ya gonna finger f*ck it all night, you might as well pass it over to someone that can make good use of it."

Patrice was a well-known burglar and petty thief, a successful one by his presence here alone. Everyone in the Randy's "Crack Den," even with brains half fried, wondered why Patrice was not strapped to an electric chair by now. They all snapped out of their pitiful fugue once they realized that there were some fresh drugs about to be introduced to this dead man's party.

"Patrice my man," asked a half-naked Debbie with the sexiest voice available in her large selection. Now getting up off the floor, brushing off her over used knees, and putting her clothes back on, she quickly presented herself to Patrice. "Hi ya, honey. Can I get a piece?"

"A piece of what, Debbie?"

"You know, Pee. A hit off one of them large rocks there in the bag." "Damn girl," screamed a disgusted Patrice. "Can't a fella take off his coat first, before you start slobbering all over him?"

"I'll do anything you want me to, Patrice."

"No thank you, Debbie. You sucking my d*ck is not a priority right now. Now leave me the f*ck along, so I can get my groove on."

"Please Patrice . . ."

"Debbie, can I get a hit of my own first. Please child, stop f*cking with me." Everyone in Randy's pit was tense, already bracing themselves for the sound of a slap to Debbie's jaw, but it did not come. Reluctantly, Michael passed the empty glass stem over to Patrice, who after throwing his coat in the general direction of the floor, made himself comfortable on the worn out leather couch, between Dirty Debbie and Avarice Angela. He reached over, and threw a brown bag of stolen groceries behind the couch, and there in front of his wide eyed audience, he displayed a Ziploc bag full of nickel vials of crack. The room was now illuminated by eyes as bright as lighthouse beacons. As bright and wide as their eyes were, their mouths were wide and dark as the Harlem tunnel, spewing out drool.

Patrice could read their minds, as if he could see right through their foreheads. He wished that some of these low life punks had the audacity to rob him. While fumbling to get his first hit into the well-used and cracked stem, Patrice was praying that someone tried something stupid tonight. The new stolen dagger he had in his waist was ready to be christened, and he wouldn't mind using it on the first idiot that stopped him from getting his first hit.

It was as if they could all in turn read Patrice's mind. They could all see the anxiety and desperation in his face, and this made them all afraid of him tonight. Patrice was known to them as a violent person, but it seemed that he only bullied the weak ones; the ones he knew were too scared of him. They usually all saw him after his ass has been kicked and humiliated in public. They have all witnessed Patrice getting his ass kicked by drug dealers, store owners, and people chasing him out of their homes, after they had all been robbed. Tonight Michael thought that it looked as if Patrice has had enough of the beat downs, and wanted desperately to be the one bringing forth blood.

Michael watched the macabre scene in slow motion from his three legged chair in the corner of the room. He was positioned where he could see everyone that came and left Randy's pit. He could see clearly that as much as Patrice wanted to smoke his crack, he wanted a fight, and was wishing for someone brave enough to rob him. If it weren't for these drug session he frequently had during the day, Patrice would be out on the streets either robbing or bullying someone. *Thank God for drugs,* fear creeping into his body. He was scared of Patrice, and people like him, who thought nothing of taking your life because it was a fun thing to do at the time.

Inside Randy's pit, Patrice was now the man of the moment, and all the other crack fiends in the room would do anything for him. He knew all this, but not right now. Right now he wanted his first hit of the day. The best hit of any session.

Avarice Angela had her hand slowly sneaking up his right knee and crawling up toward his open crotch. Patrice snapped his knees closed, almost breaking her skeletal hand.

It wasn't about having sex right now, though he did want to make love to both Debbie and Angela, but that will have to be later, because it was all about getting a hit, a very good one at this moment in time. Patrice ignored Avarice Angela's shock at almost having her scrawny hand crushed, and commenced to put a lovely sized white rock on top of the screen in the stem. As soon as he put the lighter to it, the sizzling and crackling of the crack cocaine had everyone in Randy's pit the salivating. Once again murder, robbery, and jealously crossed their devious minds. Out of all the despicable thoughts running through their fried brains, only jealousy was the conclusion. They all wished that it was they who were lighting up that irresistible rock that Patrice was now frying and inhaling. Even Randy, who stood by the door, was transfixed with the loud sizzling sound and smoke slowly making its way down the stem to Patrice's dry and cracked lips. He had already been paid by Patrice at his front door, just like the rest of them in here, but now he wanted more, just like everyone else. . Michael saw the look that Randy and the rest of the crowd had, and thought, "With this damn drug, *you will always want more, even if you had just smoked a whole kilo.*"

They watched as the smoke was swirling slowly around in the glass stem, and shot into Patrice's lungs as he inhaled deeply. Patrice's eyes went up into his forehead, and he was now in Utopia, where everybody in "The Pit" wanted to join him. U*topia is a good thing!*

Michael looked around at the others, and for once asked himself, *what am I doing here?*

*You're a f\*cking scum bag low life like the rest of your colleagues,* said a triumphant Brainz.

*F\*ck you!*

*No, Mike. F\*ck you, ass hole!*

*This is not the time or place Brainz,* pleaded Michael.

*Well I am your Brain, and I know more than you, and I'm telling you to get out of this rat hole now. You don't belong here!*

*But . . .*

*But nothing, Mike. We could be doing much better than this. We can go back to just drinking beer and having fun.*

Brainz was right. Was this the Utopia that he had dreamt of? He knew that answer, but capitulated immediately once Patrice offered (tempted) him the glass pipe. "Thanks Pee," was all he said as he reached for the apparatus that will take him . . . Out of here.

*You're such an idiot, and I would like to leave you now, and go live with someone else with more intelligence, like a rodent!*

Brainz was making Michael feel guilty, as it always does, but he was able to ignore it once he started to inhale on the fresh little white rock that Patrice had put in the broken stem for him. While he eased back in his three legged chair, Michael's thoughts drifted to the man who held all the cards and power in Randy's pit tonight.

# HOME WITH THE PATKINSON'S

"If you don't stop doing drugs and destroying your life Michael," his tear-filled mother was saying, "you're going to have to get out of *my* house!" Why was she screaming into his brain cells? His mother's piercing shriek had always crept in and haunted him, even entering his dreams.

"Son, we love you," she always ended up saying, after making him feel like she should have aborted him. Both his mother and father were standing over him in his bedroom, while he stirred and tried to get rid of his mother's high pitched voice inside his head. When he finally realized that it wasn't a dream, and blinked his eyes to focus on the two silhouettes standing in front of him, all he could think was, *Oh sh\*t.*

*This can't be happening!*

Michael slowly wiped the rest of the crust out of his eyes, but instantly wished he hadn't, because he could now see the pity in theirs lucidly. Looking into their flooded eyes felt like a Ginsu knife, straight through the heart. "Son," said his father, his words choking in the back of his throat. "I can't stand seeing you like this."

*Like what,* thought Michael?

"This is not the loving, and caring person that we know and raised."

"It's the drugs Ken," interjected his mother. "It's turning him into a vile and maleficent person."

"Err . . ." Was all Michael had to say? As per-usual, when they made him feel as if they wished that he had never been born, or was related to them. He was an embarrassment to *his* parents, especially his Christian mother, who had to listen to the torrid and acidic gossip of the loquacious church members and her neighbourhood associates. Michael knew that his mother *will not* be humiliated by him, or spoken about in a derogatory way because of him. *If he wants to do drugs, he could do it in another state, or country.*

He could imagine all of their so-called church friends talking about them behind their backs, *do you know Gossipiah, that the Parkinson's eldest son is a drug addict. He-he . . .*

He felt sorry for his mother, seeing her this way, almost. If you wanted to know what pure sadness was, all you had to do was look into his mother's eyes right now. Michael knew how much it meant for her to be able to hold her head up in church and around the neighbourhood, but still . . . She just had to handle it, because it was his life, not hers. Still, she must feel as if she had failed him in some way, her quivering shoulders told him so. Though she may feel as if she has been an inadequate mother, which Michael knew was far from the truth, neither of them could exactly argue the point right now, not with the pathetic evidence lying in his bed right in front of them.

*Yikes*, said Brains!

*F\*ck you*, replied Michael.

*I tried to tell ya, but would ya listen to little ole me?*

Michael tried to fix himself up as best he could in front of his parents, but there was not much he could do with his parents standing over him. He felt more than rancid now that he was being scrutinized. They looked at him as if he had just failed a garbage inspection. *Shame, said Brainz!*

"Are you really going to throw me out," asked a nervous Michael, £ "into the sordid and grimy streets, ma?"

"What's the difference Michael," stuttered his inconsolable mother. "It seems that you live there anyway."

"Michael, we can't take it anymore," said the sad and deep Barry White voice of his father. "We don't even know who you are anymore."

"It's me dad, word up. I'm still your loving and caring son."

They both turned their backs on him, and while walking out of his bedroom, "You used to be," they both replied in unison.

"What's up, Pee?" Michael had spotted Patrice first, and had thought twice about calling the villain. But Patrice was an okay guy sometimes, like last night when he shared his drugs with everybody in Randy's pit. "Yo, Majestic. It's funny how we're both out this early in the morning. Did you get any sleep?"

"Just a little, Pee. What time did we leave Randy's?"

"I don't know Majestic; all I know is that the sun was out when we left a few hours ago."

"Have you been home, yet?"

"Home, Majestic. I am home. The streets are my home?"

Right then Michael thanked God for all he had, which looked like nothing, but he realized that it could be much worse.

Michael has known Patrice for over a decade now. They had grown up together, had went to high school together, but since this crack epidemic came along, they were practically strangers. Their paths only seem to cross when they ended up in one of the many base houses, like Randy's pit, around the neighbourhood.

No one around here could have ever thought that a creation like crack cocaine would ever be invented and then take over lives like a plague. This cocaine based substance had made long standing friends and family members, surplus to requirements.

"Where ya heading to then?"

"I'm gonna make some more money, honey." Patrice was laughing his scrawny little head off, and Michael did not like it at all. "Same Bat time, Majestic?"

"Err . . . I don't have any loot."

"Well come along with me, and I'll show ya how to make some loot, Majestic."

"Err . . . No thank you, Pee. I'm okay."

It was now Patrice's turn to securitize Michael. "So how do you make your money, Majestic? You're not a thief, mugger, drug dealer, or a murderer. What's your game, Majestic?"

"Err . . . I just do people small favours like going to the store for them, go along and help them out with their shopping. You know."

"Yeah, Majestic. I know. We all know that's how you have all these elder ladies buy you beer and giving you enough loot to buy your crack. You're like the neighbourhood Escort Service."

Though Michael has heard the rumour about himself, it wasn't the truth. Nobody wanted to hear the truth, not without it being embellished tenfold. *Tell the people what they want, and they'll go away happy!*

He had heard this saying on a show called the "Persuaders" staring Roger Moore and Tony Curtis. It was so true.

"Yeah, Pee. You're looking at a regular pimp supreme." This had them both laughing their head off, and that was a rarity for a crack head.

"Okay Majestic, have it your way, like Burger King." With that said, Patrice was ghost, leaving Michael to his own devices.

As he headed to Lincoln Terrace, his favourite place on the planet, Michael thought of all the people he hung out with lately. Anyone one of which Michael knew would not hesitate to slit their mother's meaty throats for just one hit of crack, if they haven't done it already.

His old friend Patrice has gone on to become a violent little thief, and news on the street had it that he was becoming more violent by the day in his quest for crack.

There were a lot of people that asked him if he had seen Patrice, and Michael knew that they only wanted to find his old friend to break his legs, have his throat crushed, and better . . . Patrice has obviously created a lot of enemies, and Michael did not want to be around him when the inevitable came.

# THE CLOUD

Not taking too much pleasure in it, Michael knew he was a little bit better than all the other crack addicts he rolled with. He always made sure now that he kept a little money for the next day, even though he fought with every ounce of free will each time. The next day Michael knew that he would want, need some cigarettes and beer. He had experienced it on too many occasions, and it wasn't a good thing to feel low after a session, and feel even lower still when you couldn't light up a morning cigarette, or take a swig of refreshing beer.

As he casually walked down the big slab steps of Lincoln Terrace Park, Michael took a lovely swig of his liquid breakfast. He thanked God silently, making a sign of the cross with his 40o/z of Private Stock in hand. *At least Lord, I'm not like the majority of thieving and heartless scum around here. Not yet anyway.*

Since migrating from England to America in his early years, it still amazed him how *his* race were so un-unified, and discombobulated. It was everyone for him and herself.

It was so ludicrous to Michael, and it also made him quite angry when he thought about it, how his race made it so easy for their superiors, suppressors to manipulate them. Even before the invention of the pernicious crack cocaine, *his* race was selling their mothers for a slice of pizza and a can of coke. It hurt him that his race was so materialistic, and would do anything to have the latest in brand name merchandise, even if they didn't need it, or it didn't fit them. *F\*cking amazing!*

He stopped on his way down to the duck pond, only to light up a Newport cigarette, the bad thoughts still running through his head like a track star on steroids. The thoughts were making him even more depressed than he should feel after a drug session has ended. Though his race lived in filth, with the rodents and insects, and had hearts of stone statues, they had to look good, no matter what.

*By any means necessary!*
*Whatever, Malcolm.*

Michael pulled up the hood of green snorkel, because the morning wind was starting to cut through the three layers of clothing he had on. Though it was quite chilly this morning, Michael was glad to see the early morning sun rays flickering in and out of the clouds. It made the sordid and vile Brooklyn that he called home look better than the war zone it actually was.

As he wandered deeper down into Lincoln Terrace his thoughts changed from his pathetic race to his mother. He knew that though she was disgraced, she was more worried about him. Right now though, he did not care about his mother's feelings, because it was her despicable decision to bring him, and the rest of the family here to New York.

"How the hell could you bring us from a civilized country like England ma, and plant us in the middle of Crooklyn New York?" He and his younger brother Floyd were confused, because they thought as young teens that they were living the life of Riley back in England. They had their friends, both at school and at home, were good at playing soccer, each one playing for their school teams.

"What the hell were you thinking ma," they had both asked?"

Her guilt ridden platitude answer was always, "This is the land of opportunity," the words not even convincing their dad. "We'll have a better chance of making a good life for ourselves here. Trust me!"

Well Michael was sick of the opportunity to live an impecuniously life in the shanty towns of the United States, where he was constantly harassed by *their* racist cop, and that was if he wasn't a mugging victim. "They treat us like step children over here ma," he acidly told his mother one day. "Truly ma, f*ck America!"

The green wooden park bench in front of the pond was his favourite, and Michael made himself comfortable, and watched the colourful mallards play with each other. Some of them were already coming out of the pond, flapping their mosaic wings, toward him. It was as if they thought, demanded, that he had brought some bread with him to give them. *You inconsiderate fat b*stard!*

He sighed and went into his black Jansport back pack, and opened a plastic bag full of stale bread, which he had got from Patrice's discarded grocery bag from behind the couch at Randy's pit.

He put his 40o/z of beer down beside him on the bench; long enough to tear the bread up into bite size pieces for the mallards, and started flinging them toward the pond. "Everyone's gotta eat, ya'll."

*That's strange,* thought Michael who was now looking up and watching one of the white puffy clouds, shaped like a heart, floating toward earth. "Look ya'll," he said to the colourful mallards jokingly, "God is sending down his love." The heart shaped cloud looked as if it were descending, now coming toward him.

Michael quickly wiped his eyes, and then looked at his 40o/z of Private Stock. "No way. It can't be." He lit another Newport, and commenced to gulp down as much of the barley water as he could. The mallards were now nipping at his old black and white Nike sneakers, because they wanted his attention back to feeding them, and not on the sky.

He tried shooing the mallards away, while trying to keep his eyes on the heart-shaped and descending cloud, but he failed, and lost sight of it. "Damn ducks," he moaned at them. "You made me miss the cloud."

*"Quack" – Just feed us asshole!*

Between a half swig of his beer, and trying to blow a smoke ring into the wind, Michael could now hear someone's voice in the distance. It sounded as if it was coming from beyond the bushes, behind the duck pond. Where ever it was, it sounded close by. He stopped what he was doing, along with the pretty coloured mallards, and they all listened intently. Michael looked around the area, but could not see anyone around him, not even the local muggers or crack heads.

After not seeing anything, the mallards and Michael went back to what they were all doing, before they all stopped once again. This time it sounded as if the mysterious voice was singing. The sound of the person's voice was much more lucid now.

Michael looked down at the mallards in front of him, just to make sure that it was not one of them pulling a fast one, and then swivelled his head on his shoulders, as if he were Linda Blair in the Exorcist. Still . . . He could not see anyone or anything out of place, not immediately in front of him, so he knew that it was time to move his lazy ass, and start an investigation.

The singing was becoming louder as he walked around the duck pond, and neared the bushes. "Hey," he shouted with no conviction. "Is anyone there?" Fear was now creeping into him, and Michael was conscience of it. Of course there was no reply, but he could still hear the seraphic bass voice singing . . . "Shit!"

*Isn't this where I get killed by the three headed monster,* thought a very nervous Michael? *Maybe the cloud I saw is a spaceship in disguise, and it dropped off it.* Michael laughed nervously at his own idiocy.

"Hello, anybody there," he was practically screeching now?" He took a deep breath, and ventured forward like an idiot in a horror movie.

In the middle of the small meadow beyond the bushes, Michael could see a person sitting there, crossed legged in the grass. The person had his or her back turned to him. It was hard to tell the gender, because the person sitting there had very long and flowing brown hair down to his or her back. From what

Michael could see, as he approached the person stealthily from behind, was that the person was popping off the tops of the flowers in the meadow, and throwing them into his/her mouth?

*What the f\*ck?* As he continued to creep up on the person, Michael could now hear the person start singing again, merrily.

*Why am I jealous,* Michael asked himself?

He knew the answer, but did not like it. Michael truly wished that it was he that was sitting in the middle of the meadow, singing to himself, with not a care in the world. All he has ever wanted in his life was a little peace, and this person had it. The person sitting before him seemed to have it all, without having to find his or her happiness inside a 40o/z of beer or through a glass stem.

*This cat must be on some sort of Acid trip,* thought a mischievous Michael. *Why else would anyone be sitting in the middle of Lincoln Terrace, early on a cold morning, singing to themselves and eating flowers?*

Whatever the person's drug of choice was, a now depressed Michael knew for certain that it was not one of the soul destroying variety. He commenced with his prudent steps, until he was almost upon the person. As reticently as his deep voice could utter, Michael asked, "Is everything okay, Duke?"

"My name is not Duke," the stranger said succinctly, without even turning around.

*Okay,* thought Michael. Now he did not know what to say in reply to the stranger. *This guy,* thought Michael, *may not want to be bothered by an intruder?*

Before he could turn around and leave, Michael noticed that the singing had stopped again, and hoped it was not because he had invaded the man's personally space. "Sorry . . ."

Turning from whence he came, Michael started his journey back to the duck pond. He knew that the man must have come down here to be with his private thoughts. I *can understand that.* It was the same reason that he always came down here, to get away from the vile and over populated thieves, back stabbers, and snakes outside the parks wrought iron fence. *Maybe the guy was just anti-social,* mused Michael.

Well Michael was not anti-social; as a matter of fact anyone that knew him would tell you that Michael was more than an affable and effervescent person. He liked meeting and speaking to people, so he turned back to the stranger in white, and gave it one more try. *If this guy doesn't want to be bothered,* Michael told himself, *I'll just be on my way.* "My name's Michael."

"I know."

"You know?" The sharp edged reply made Michael back up a couple of steps, as if he had been pushed forcibly in the chest. "You know what," asked a shocked Michael?"

"I know who you are, Michael."

"You do. And who the hell are you?" Michael was visibly shaken now. The man could not even see him, he still had his back turned.

"My friends call me, Jay." Michael was now visibly trembling, but at least this strange man, Jay, was now speaking to him. He took a deep breath, and felt more relaxed. The earthquake in his body was subsiding, but his bowels were telling him different.

"Well . . . Hello Jay." The man was silent again, sitting there, picking off the heads of flowers, and eating them. "Can I ask you a question, Jay?"

"Go right ahead, Michael." *The man spoke as if he had just graduated from Harvard University,* thought Michael. *This Jay* character *sounded so damn proper, like a university professor. He sure isn't from around here,* was Michael's final conclusion.

"You said before, that you know me. Have we met before?"

"I've heard a lot about you, Michael." The fear came back instantly, and Michael felt as if he were going to empty his bowels. "Well whatever you heard Jay," mumbled Michael, "they're lying."

A boisterous explosion of laughter burst out of Jay's chest cavity. It sounded like thunder. It was still reverberating throughout the vast park a few minutes later, and although Michael wanted to join Jay in his laughter, he didn't think that anything he had just said was that damn funny. He didn't even know that Jay had heard him mumbling. He sure wasn't meant to have heard. Michael nervously walked around so he could see Jay's face. "You okay, Jay?"

The man could not stop laughing, and this frightened Michael even more. *The man's in hysterics!*

"Do you want some of my 40o/z, to wash down those dry seeds you're eating?"

After Jay finally stopped laughing, he looked up at Michael still wearing a smile on his face. "Thanks, Michael. Much appreciated." Michael watched as this long haired, bearded, and scruffy looking hippie almost downed half his Private Stock. "Well damn Jay, you were really thirsty."

"I've come a long way to be here, Michael."

"Err . . . Why. And from where?"

"Why?"

"Yes, why," asked a determined Michael.

"I came to help."

"Help who, Jay?"

"My fellow man."

*Okay. That's it. This guy is a total nut job,* thought Michael, *and I need to get the f\*ck outta here.* For some unknown reason though, Michael couldn't get himself to move away from the stranger. It was as if they were magnetically linked together somehow. *Brainz, help me out here,* pleaded Michael.

*Err . . . F\*ck you.*

*Thanks, Brainz. I can always depend on you. B\*stard.*

He liked the way Jay spoke as if he were a child or a drunken person, unable to lie, unable to say what you want him to say. Anyway, helping people, especially people with special needs, was what he did best. *I guess I'll play along,* Michael told himself. *I have nothing better to do with my pathetic life. Anyway, this could get very interesting, indeed.*

After a long period of silence between them, Michael just watching as Jay started popping off the tops of flowers again, and eating them.

"Are you hungry Jay, asked a facetious Michael?" As per-usual, there was no reply. Michael continued to watch as Jay continued to feast on his plants. "I don't have much loot Jay," said Michael as he searched in his pockets, "but I'm sure I can buy you something more substantial to eat than flowers."

"Thank you Michael, but I'm okay." They looked at each other for a while. "Truly Michael," Jay finally said, "I'm okay. Thank you for your kindness." Afterward, Jay reached out his hand and asked Michael, "Is it okay if I can have some more of your beer?" Immediately Michael passed the remaining liquid in the 40o/z bottle over to this new and crazy looking friend. Michael watched as the man gulped down the beer. *The man obviously needs the barley water more than me,* thought a concerned Michael. Michael looked at the diaphanous clothes that Jay was wearing. "Do you need some warm clothes, Jay? It's pretty cold out this morning, and I could get you some warm clothes at my house?"

Instead of answering, Jay tipped the large green bottle of beer to his chapped and cracked lips, and guzzled down another copious amount of the brown liquid. Michael's precious barley water seemed to flow down Jay's dry throat; as if it was being absorbed into the man's every dry pore. The beer seemed to have made Jay larger and stronger, as he sat crossed legged on the patch of grass. It was as if Jay needed the beer, as Popeye needed spinach. The smirk could have been seen on Michael's face, if Jay had chanced a glace up, but he hadn't. Out of nowhere, there was a voluminous burp that emanated out of Jay's chest cavity, and just like his laughter, his burp shook the very ground they stood on.

"I've been drinking that beer all my life," said a shocked, but giggling little Michael, and I've never gave out an earth shattering burp like that."

When Jay returned the bottle of 40o/z beer to Michael, there was nothing in it but suds. "Err . . . What the hell am I supposed to do with this, Jay?"

"Drink up my friend."

"Drink up. The bottles empty my new friend?"

"I left you more than you gave me, Michael."

"What. Excuse me Jay; are them seeds you're eating getting you high or something?"

"High?"

"Yeah Jay, high as in sniffing glue, smoking weed, or injecting heroin. High, as in a jet in the sky. Bugging out type of high. What part of "High" don't you understand Jay, because I'm willing to run it pass ya again."

"You mean transcendental meditation high?"

"What. I don't know what you've just said Jay, but it better be good. No. I mean bugging out high."

"What is this bugging out, Michael?"

An exasperated Michael said, "Never mind, Jay." He then commenced to relieve the 40o/z bottle he was holding of its suds, but immediately started to gag and choke. It was true, Jay had left more beer in the bottle than he had thought, and now he found himself choking on the plethora of liquid that overflowed in his throat. Even his chin and the collar of his green Enyce Snorkel were sharing some of the beer.

Jay just watched on, trying his best to stifle the laugh that wanted to erupt and blow the trees off their roots.

After Michael stopped gagging and sputtering, he looked at the 40o/z bottle, and saw that it was still filled to the top, as if it had been untouched. He looked studiously at Jay, who seemed to be feigning ignorance. Michael wasn't having any of it from this stranger, "How Jay," he asked, the astonishment still in his voice. "I saw you guzzle down everything, with my own eyes. I saw you empty the bottle, Jay?"

"May be your eyes are playing tricks on you, Michael. You cannot believe everything you see. This is how magicians are able to trick you."

"I don't think so, Jay . . . This was no illusion." As soon as the words were out of his mouth, Michael thought about the descending cloud. *Maybe I have burnt out my brain cells, drinking, and smoking that sh\*t?*

Now trying to dry his chin and Encye snorkel with his sleeves, Michael changed the subject, because the thought of him losing his mind in front of this stranger was a no-no. "Anyway Jay, you said that you came from somewhere far."

"Yes I did."

"Well . . ."

"I come from a place far away, a place that you would not know of, Michael."

"Try me, Jay." Michael was now getting a little agitated with constantly fighting for a direct answer from this character. And Jay was definitely a character. Getting a straight answer out of him was like pulling teeth. Everyone else he knew were not only loquacious, but talked some much sh*t, they believed it themselves.

Though Jay spoke eloquently, as if he were a pompous erudite from some Ivy League college, Michael did believe that this man was telling the truth. It was up to him to figure out what the hell the man was trying to say. What's with all this speaking in riddles? *Far off place, my mother f*cking ass,* thought Michael.

Jay could see the impatience of Michael, and hear the tapping of his battered sneakers on the grass. "Well I was born in a town called Bethlehem Michael, and I have been travelling far and wide to get here."

"I've heard of Bethlehem Jay," said a joyous Michael.

"You have?"

"Yes Jay, I have. It's in the Bible. I think it's in the West Bank, in the war torn Palestine area?"

"Very good Michael, you do know your geography."

"Whatever, Jay. Anyway, I have news for you my friend, and you may not like it. Not one bit."

"And what is that, Michael?"

"It's that although you have now made it to the so-civilized West, I can honestly tell you Jay, that Brooklyn is also a war torn area." Michael looked to see if his news had depressed Jay, but did not see any signs of a man that was about to break down and cry. "Sorry to tell you Jay, that you wasted your time and trip to be here."

"I do not believe that I have wasted my time or my trip Michael, after all I have met you."

"Err . . . You're such a flatterer Jay, but it's real like in Israel, out here."

Jay did not respond immediately. "Michael, do you believe in the Bible?"

"Err . . ." *Why has he changed the subject?* "Well . . . Not really Jay."

This seemed to have gotten Jay's attention, "Why?"

"Why. Are you for real, Jay?" Now it was Jay who was waiting impatiently for Michael's straight answer. "Okay, it's because it is so full of contradictions, Jay. Things that cannot possibly be real, or have had happened." Michael saw how Jay was scrutinizing him now, but he was still wearing a smile on his face.

"What's so funny, Jay?"

"Nothing . . ."

"So why do you have that smirk on your face then?"

"Just listening to you, I like listen to you Michael."

"And what have I said that is so funny to you, Jay?"

"Mmm . . . Nothing in particular. I just want to hear more."

"You want to hear more about what, Jay? Look my man, I'm trying to tell ya that I'm not a religious freak or person, and my opinion doesn't amount to a hill of beans around here anyway. It's just my opinion, Jay. Okay?"

"Your opinion matters to me, Michael."

"Jay, what is it with you?"

"What do you mean, Michael?"

Michael didn't know how to answer that one. This strange man sitting in the middle of the park, eating seeds off plants, had him on the back foot and speechless. "Look Jay, I really think that the elders of this earth created religion to pacify the uneducated, malleable, and gullible people of the world. And as you get to see this place while your here, I'm sure you will see what I see, that the elders great grandson's and daughters are still inculcating the fatuous peon with that drivel, and are doing a sterling job, if I must say, on the masses."

Jay was just staring at him, unflinchingly, not saying a word. Not wanting to interrupt. He let Michael flow, "All religion has done Jay," continued Michael, "is divide people and create war. We have different religions popping up on a daily basis around here my friend. Do you know Jay, that I can start a new religion of my own, right now if I wanted?"

*Was the man even listening to him?* Now Michael wondered if Jay had shut him, and his bullsh*t opinions completely out of his head. "Jay," continued Michael, because it was Jay who had asked him in the first place. "I'm talking to you."

"And I'm listening, Michael, intently."

"Are you sure you want to hear me go on and on, because I can you know." This brought a smile to Jay's face, "I'm sure you have more important things to do today."

"There is nothing more important than listen and spending time with you, Michael." The furrowed eyebrows on Michael's face, told Jay that he was confusing Michael.

"What do you mean by that Jay," asked a very anguished Michael.

"I mean that I am doing what I came to do, and you are not wasting my time. I came to listen and spend time with you and all my brothers and sisters."

"Err . . . Anyway, the majority of people that you will meet while you're here Jay will let you know that they are very proud atheist, and that they only believe in what they can get from you. I'm telling you my naïve friend, if you speak like this when you get out of here . . ." Michael left the sentence unfinished.

"What Michael. Please say it . . ."

"They'll not only ridicule you my friend, they'll take your robe, sandal, and the seeds in your hand, even if it isn't worth anything to them. They are just takers, blood sucking leeches. But don't let me deter you from helping your lovely brothers and sister, Jay."

"Are you trying to be facetious, Michael?"

"Err . . . Jay, I'm trying to tell ya good buddy, if you go out there speaking like that, you'll see if I'm trying to be facetious, or trying to protect your innocent ass from them sharks in wolves clothing." Once again, Jay was holding his sides, laughing so harshly, that Michael thought the man may be having one of them hysterical trips. "You okay there, Jay?"

"Please pass the beer," snickered Jay, now rolling around in the field.

*You do know how to pick em, Majestic!*

*Yeah, Brainz. We have met some colourful characters along the way.*

Michael passed Jay the 40o/z, watched and waited for Jay to control himself, so he could take a swig from the rattling bottle in his shaky hands. Once this historic job was done, Jay thanked and asked Michael to continue with his humble opinions.

"I really think that atheism is the biggest religion going now, Jay."

"Mmm . . ."

"Mmm . . . Is that it? Jay, are you listening to me?" Michael continued to watch Jay as he started to wash down his picked seeds with the beer. "Are you hungry or something Jay," asked Michael a bit too forcibly. "I can get us something to eat you know?"

"Thank you Michael."

"Well . . ."

"Why are you giving me your drink, and are willing to feed me, a perfect stranger, Michael?"

"Err . . . Because . . . Well because it's the right and moral thing to do. I think."

"I thought you were not a religious person, Michael."

"I don't think I am."

"So, you're not sure?"

Michael sighed, and commenced to sit down on the grass, across from Jay. He did not think that he would have been here this long, away from the ducks. For the past hour he has been standing up and looking down at Jay low figure, and it was getting rather tiring. It was obvious to him now that he was not going anywhere, not anytime soon. He took back the offered 40o/z from Jay's hand, and took a lavish swig of his own. "The few Christians that are left around here Jay," he continued, "are old black biddies, who think they can call on the Lord, after they've been mugged, robbed and raped."

"I'm so sorry that you feel that way about Christianity, and the Bible Michael."

"Oh, you are, are you?" Michael could not hide *his* despicable sarcasm. "So let me hear your *precise* version on religion, Jay."

"There is no reason to be facetious, Michael."

Michael did not know that he was letting his anger and irritation show so lucidly. "Sorry Jay. I'm not a very good actor."

"And for this Michael, I am glad. I am glad that you cannot help but let your true feelings show."

"Well I'm not, Jay. When I'm sad, or I see something unfair, I start to cry, in public. This is not a good thing, Jay."

"Yes, I can see your dilemma Michael. You can get beaten, stoned to death, and robbed for your bottle of beer."

"Err . . . Ya trying to be funny, Jay?"

"No. I just do not want your loving and caring heart to be crust by the blood sucking leeches out there in this despicable world."

"Ha-ha, Jay. Touché . . ." Michael offered Jay the 40o/z, but Jay told him to drink up. *Was the man going somewhere?* "Anyway, I'm more worried about you Jay, because at least I kind of know the abhorrent and maleficent creatures I have to deal with every day. I'm still here, yo."

"And of this I am glad, Michael. Just like you Michael, I am a grown man, and I to have survived." This had Michael smiling, and shaking his head. "Now, can you please pass the beer?"

"Err . . . I don't have any more, Jay. I finished it, after you told me that you didn't want anymore."

"I do not recall telling you that I did not want anymore, Michael."

"Damn, Jay. Why are you so confusing?"

"Sorry, but you are just a confusing, Michael."

"Me. I'm speaking fluent English my friend."

"No Michael, you're slurring."

"Err . . ."

"Err . . . What part of the English language is that, Michael?" Now they were both rolling and holding their sides in the middle of the park. They both looked maniacal, laughing and snivelling in the grass, and all creatures great and small made their pleasant way to safety.

It was a while before they both were able to ebb their hysterics. "Don't you have some more beers in your Jansport," asked Jay, wiping the tears of laughter from his eyes?"

"Usually I would have my friend, but I didn't have enough money this morning." The sadness could be heard in Michael's now quivering voice.

"I'm sure you have one or two more bottle of your beer in your backpack, Michael."

"What part of the English language do you not understand, Jay. I said that I only had enough money to buy one, and a pack of cigarettes."

"Now, now Michael. There is no need to get upset."

"I'm not upset," shouted Michael. "And if I am, you're the one upsetting me."

"Well I did not come here, to upset you Michael."

*I did not come here to upset you?* Jay spoke as if he were from a further place than Bethlehem. "Where did you say you came from again, Jay?"

"I told you Michael, and it's neither here nor there."

"Okay. Okay." Just to appease Jay, Michael did not know why, he went into his Jansport sitting next to him. This was just to prove to the insistent Jay that no matter how he wished or believed was true did not make it so. *Anyway, how the hell did Jay know that I kept my 40o/z in my Jansport?*

Michael unzipped his Jansport, to show Jay that he had nothing inside his bag but his overdue Donald Goines novel from the Eastern Parkway Library, his keys, and his stale pack of Newport cigarettes.

"Do you believe me now, Jay" asked Michael showing Jay the innards of his backpack?" *Wait a damn minute. Cobwebs and dust weren't this heavy.* As soon as he thought it, a couple of 40o/z bottles of Private Stock beer fell out, hitting the grass with a thud in front of them both. With mouth agape, ready to catch any flying insect, Michael sat there, dazed and confused. And he really did not like the smirk that this character Jay was wearing on his bearded countenance.

Jay picked both the unbroken bottles up, and offered one to the far away Michael sitting in front of him. "Thank you Michael," said a Cheshire cat grinning Jay, "but all I wanted was one."

Now Michael was looking at Jay in astonishment. His open mouth was still catching everything that floated through the air. *Am I going mad?*

Michael was questioning his sanity again. *I sure I didn't have any beer in my bag. Sh\*t, if anybody would have known, it would have been me.* "Nice meeting you Jay. Be safe my man." Michael was already on his feet, the Jansport back on his back, ready to take off as if he were Usain Bolt on steroids.

"Are you leaving so soon, Michael?"

"I feel a bit faint," lied Michael, or was it a lie. He didn't know what was going on. "Jay, my man. Truly sorry, didn't mean to intrude."

"It's okay Michael. I liked meeting, and listening to you."

"Nice to meet you to, Jay." Michael was already ascending the big slab steps of Lincoln Terrace, making a hasty get away.

"Maybe I'll see you around," shouted Jay while he watched Michael fly up the giant steps of the park. He cracked open his 40o/z, and drank lavishly, wiping his mouth with the sleeve of his sordid white toga.

"Yeah Jay," replied a now distant Michael, "maybe."

On his way up the hill, Michael looked back at Jay, who was now on his hands and knees . . . Praying.

# SERENDIPITY COMES TO MICHAEL

As he made his way out of Lincoln Terrace Park and back to the noisy and boisterous civilization above, Michael checked once again inside his Jansport. He still could not believe that he had two 40o/z bottles of beer inside it, when he definitely knew that it was devoid of the good stuff when he had left home.

*May be your eyes are playing tricks on you, Michael. You cannot believe everything you see. This is how magicians are able to trick you.*

The guy was weird, but a magician? Pulling out the two big bottles of beer was tantamount to Jay pulling out a live rabbit out of his sandals. *Incredible!* Anyway, at least he gave one to Jay, and had one for himself. *Don't look a gift horse in the mouth, Michael.*

*What the f\*ck is that supposed to mean, Brainz?*

*I don't know, but it sounds appropriate.*

He was about to crack open his 40o/z when he heard his name, "What's up, Majestic?"

"Oh, hi Joe."

"You don't look as if you've been jogging Majestic. You don't look like the jogging type."

"Ha-ha, Joe. Ya so funny."

His oldest friend was smiling. Joe looked at Michael and his 40o/z, "Are ya going to crack that open, and hold onto it like an Oscar?"

The fresh crackling of the top being twisted had them both thirsty, and Michael too a swig before passing the 40o/z over to Joe.

"Got any loot for a bag of weed, Majestic?"

"No Joe. I don't even have any loot to chip in for another beer," and to prove the fact he reached into his Levi's and felt for some coins. Instead he felt a stack of . . .

*What the f\*ck?*

Next to his three day old half eaten packet of Polo mints, he fingered the wedge of . . . *Maybe ma put a stack of Kleenex in my jeans,* thought Michael. His mother

36

was always looked out for him. Even if they had words, she would sneak some fruits, chips, or tissue into his pockets or Jansport backpack. Now he was afraid to pull out whatever the stack was in front of Joe, just in case it would be embarrassing.

Joe attention, thank God, was not on Michael, but on Michael's 40o/z bottle of beer, that he held in his hand.

Michael quickly pulled his hand out of his pocket, "Well," asked Joe? "Like I said Joe," lied Michael, showing Joe his empty hands, "I've got nothing but some rancid Polo's."

That said, Joe tool another lavish swig of Michael's beer, and passed it back. "I'll catch ya later then."

"Yeah Joe, see ya."

Now all alone again, *naturally,* Michael found himself an apartment building stoop to sit on, and cautiously pulled out the mysterious stack in his jeans. Once he pulled out the stack of . . . Paper, he noticed that the top one had a Presidents face on it . . . No, it was not a President, but the one and only Benjamin Franklin. Michael was drooling, raining his spit all over Ben's crisp face, and he could not stop it.

He looked and stared, studied, and scrutinized, and still the eyes of Benjamin Franklin stared back at him, smiling. Ben's smile was not as gleeful as Michael's though. Michael's smile made old Ben's look like the Mona Lisa's.

He quickly looked up and down the street, and then into the empty lobby behind him. *Sh\*t, I'm shaking like a damn leaf in a Chicago winter.* This time around he was not nervous of being seen slinking through the dark gutters of Brooklyn, but of being seen by people he knew. His crack head and thieving friends like Patrice, who would surely rob him. Dirty Debbie would not only rob him, but stab the sh\*t out of him.

*Something weird was going on around here.* His eyes rolled around vigilantly, making him look like a lizard.

The thought of him losing his mind entered his head, and not for the first time this morning. *This can't be some small parlour trick,* he told himself. *Jay isn't even here this time.* He quickly stashed the money inside the Jansport, too afraid to count it out in public, and zipped it up. *I'll count it when I reach home,* he told himself.

As soon as he got up, brush off his bottom, his legs gave way on him. This time Michael doubted that it was because he was drunk, because he hasn't even started drinking yet. Strange things were happening this morning, and all Michael could think about right now was that they were all positive. *Hallelujah!!!*

*It looks as if I'm finally going to have a good day,* and with that thought in mind, Michael now had a bounce, a buoyant spring in his step, as he speedily headed home.

Once he got back to his bedroom, Michael quickly closed the door and dived onto his bed. With the alacrity of a child with an unopened candy bar in his hand, Michael unzipped and spilled all the contents out of his Jansport.

As he was about to separate the stack of money from the dingy Polo mints, and keys, Michael stood there staring at his bed with mouth agape. Now there was more than the one stack he had threw in his Jansport. There were stacks, several of them. He picked one of them up, and turned it over in his hand in amazement. *Is this sh\*t real?*

At least ten minutes had passed before he decided to take off the elastic bands off of each of the bundles. He cleared off his bed in an attempt to put the money in numerical stacks, but there were only three denominations: twenties, fifties, and hundred dollar bills. Before he count his riches, he heard his mother's voice, "Michael, is that you back so soon?"

"Yes ma," he replied laconically.

"Why," she asked from out in the hallway. "What happened?"

Instead of shouting, Michael reluctantly left his bedroom to head his mother off from coming into his bedroom. He surely did not want her noisy ass in his room, especially at a momentous moment like this.

With a coke and a smile he said, "Nothing has happened, ma."

"So why are you back from those grimy friends of yours so soon?"

"Because ma, I didn't get to see any of my grimy friends this morning." He wasn't lying, because Jay was not grimy, though he could use a new wardrobe.

"Well you went out quite early this morning, as a matter of fact, as soon as you got in," said his agitated mother. "They are most probably still all sleeping, like you should be." His mother just looked at him suspiciously, because she noticed that he wasn't high, drunk, or unkempt as usual. As a matter of fact, her son was being rather too polite. *Something is up,* thought his suspicious mother, but she left it at that, because this was a good thing.

Mrs Parkinson was rather glad that her runaway, off key, son was in the house for once, and not roaming the dangerous streets of Brooklyn, doing things that would further embarrass her.

"You okay, ma?"

"Yes, Michael," she sighed. "Just let me and your father know when you're going back out, because we need some things from the store.

"Who said I'm going back out, ma?"

"I did!" They both smile, for the first time, in a long time, together.

Once back in his bedroom, Michael started separating, and counting all the money. Once it registered that the money was real, and was all his, his brain automatically told him to run to the nearest place that sold crack cocaine. *I have enough to have a major session!*

These thoughts inevitably invaded all drug addicts, which had more than two coins to rub together.

When he saw the first Ben Franklin, it took every particle of will power and physical strength not to run to the nearest drug spot and spend the money. Even the money he held had been vibrating, as if trying to tell him; *I was made to be spent, fella!*

It was not easy passing all the familiar buildings and street dealers that he knew sold some good crack cocaine. Even the surprised drug dealers had to call him over, shocked that the fat grimy b*astard had the nerve and audacity to pass them by without buying anything. *The boy ain't even asked me for credit. How dare he!?*

"Yo Majestic, aren't ya gonna cop from me, today?"

"I ain't made any loot yet, Digit. Maybe later."

"Remember Majestic, come to me, and I'll look out for ya."

*Yeah right,* thought Michael. *You sold me Ivory soap last time, ya b*stard.*

A bit further up the street, the massive Trillo jumped out of nowhere, showing that his obesity and good living hadn't slowed him down one bit. "Yo Majestic, ya want me to give ya a little something, until ya can pay me back latter?"

Though it was becoming a platitude this morning, all Michael could think of to say to these shifty characters was, "I don't have any money yet, Trillo. I'm on my way to make some right now."

"How about ya come work for me, Majestic. You know I'll look out for ya."

"Err . . . I don't think so Trillo; I'm not the drug dealing type of guy."

Trillo looked as if he had taken offence to this, so Michael had to quickly get himself out of the hole he was digging. "I can't stand in one place all day, Trillo. I have happy feet, and I need to move around."

"Well, let me know when your fat ass is tired of moving around, and I'll give you a job, Majestic. You'll make a great drug dealer, because you know every f*cking body."

"That's my point, Trillo. I know everybody, and I need to go see them instead of staying on the block 24/7."

"I hear ya Majestic. Laters."

Michael was well glad that he got out of that situation, but only to face his next obstacle. "Yo Majestic, don't just walk past me like that. Word up cousin. Ya want me to bust a cap in your fat crack head ass!"

*Sh*t!* "No, Plush. I didn't see ya. Sorry."

"You will be nigger. Now how much do ya want?"

"I don't have any money, Plush." Michael patted his pockets to show the snarling Mike Tyson lookalike that he was telling the truth, and hoped to God that "Plush" wasn't able to see his heart beating inside his sordid Encye snorkel.

It had been hard work, but he had done it; he had survived the minefield of temptation, and made it home. For just this act, he was well proud of himself. When something went right, he was the first to admit it, but always the last one to know. *Amazing!*

Over three thousand dollars, over . . . *How did that all just happen to be in my jeans?* His body visible trembled, and he was now sweating profusely. He ran to his bedroom window and opened it.

*What's going on around here?*

Even the questions he asked himself scared the sh*t out of him. He then wondered if his parents may have snuck the money into his jeans. *Sh*t, I would have notice a bundle of loot in my pocket, just as would have notice the two heavy bottles of beer in my Jansport. Anyway, why would they do something stupid like that? Three grand, yeah right!*

*They know that the first thing I would do is buy drugs with it. But still . . . They could be feeling sorry for their pathetic son. Hell no. No way, Jose! It would be cheaper to throw me out into the streets.*

He had over three thousand dollars in his hands, and all it was causing was confusion. Three thousand thoughts were flying through Michael's head, as he sat in his bedroom shaking and trembling, and not from the cool breeze coming in from the open window.

The thought that his mother would give his this amount of money, had Michael past hysterical. He knew that she'd rather kill him, and set him on fire.

It was from that morning that Michael had decided that his war against his crack addiction had to begin. No more just talking about it, saying the old platitudes, "After this hit, I won't do it anymore!"

*How many times has he said those words?*

*How many times have you given up,* added Brainz?

Now words were just as empty as when he promised them, with all his heart. He cringed when he thought about all the times he swore on God's life, that he wouldn't do anymore crack. "After this hit Father, I promise."

This time he had to enter the ring and fight his formidable opponent with a different strategy. He didn't have one. *I just have to be strong, and take it a day at a time!*

*With all that money Majestic,* reminded a helpful Brainz, *as a lovely temptation, this is going to be a hard time to consider giving up.*

*Brainz, my precious friend, if I can resist spending the money on drugs, just for today . . . Sh\*t Brainz, you're most probably right, I'll do well today, and f\*ck it all up tomorrow, or the next day.*

Michael's shoulders slumped perceptively, and for the first time in a long while, Brainz felt sorry for his host.

*A good buddy, we'll take it a day at a time, and see how it goes. Okay? Sh\*t, even if we fail like all the other times, we'll get in the ring and try again and again, until we finally beat this sh\*t!*

*Yeah Brainz,* answered an already defeated Michael, *we'll try, and try.* Before getting ready for the streets again, Michael decided to be smart for once in his life, and hide the money so he didn't have it all with him when he went outside. *Sh\*t, with my luck, I'll get mugged for the first time, or get hit by a train on the sidewalk.*

He looked around his small bedroom, trying to find the perfect place to hide the majority of money, knowing that his nosey mother was a better detective than Miss Marple. He decided that by moving his bed, and pulling back the threadbare carpet, he could line the money in quarter inch thick bundles underneath.

After putting the carpet and bed back into place, Michael stood back at his door, and looked to see if anything looked different in his room. Satisfied, that the stacks were slim enough, and far enough out of his mother's roving eyes, Michael left his bedroom feeling rest assured.

# PATRICE – ON A

## PERNICIOUS MISSION

Since sharing all his drugs last night with all his so-called crack head associates, Patrice woke up in "Randy's Pit" the worse for wear, as he usually did after a session. Now that the session was over, and everybody was gone, except for Randy, who was trying to get him out of his apartment, Patrice was feeling down and out: *The big come down!* "Wake up, Pee. You have to leave, now. I have social service coming, and I've got to clean all this sh*t up."

Patrice rolled around in Randy's battered sofa, still trying to get his bearings. He needed a beer, but he had no more money as well as crack. No one needed him anymore. He was spent, used, and now discarded.

"Pee, get the f*ck up, and out!"

Patrice did not like the way was Randy was talking to him right now, but he felt as if he deserved it. After all, without the crack and the money he was just another common homeless crack head, opposed to being "The king of the hill" last night.

"Damn!"

"Damn is right Pee. Look at the state of ya."

"Yo Randy, can you lend me a few buck till later?"

Randy hesitated, and that's all Patrice needed. "You know I'm good for it good buddy. When I come back later, not only will I pay you back, but give you a nickel for self."

At the word "Nickel – For self" Randy reached into his pocket and gave Patrice $5.00. "You better come back, later."

"I will. Don't I always, Randy my son." Patrice had jumped up off the sofa and snatched the $5.00 out of Randy's hand with alacrity. "See ya later, kid."

Randy was just glad to get the last remaining crack head from last night's session was out of his apartment. Sh*t he's been up for the past four days smoking with various people in his apartment, and he was now wired for sound. He needed to get some sleep time, badly.

After Patrice left, Randy locked all the locks on the front door, and put the mostly unused police bar behind it, to make sure no one enter, and he didn't care if they were friend or foe. *Good night, world!*

Like the others that were partying with him last night, Patrice knew that he had to start this morning off by getting some more loot for tonight's session. The thought of going back to one of the supermarkets and stealing whatever he could sell today, just didn't appeal to him. He was just too tired, and it was an all day job just to end up with pittance. Once he managed to steal some items, he then had to go out and try and sell them, at cut price. *No, not today. Too much damn work, Sir!*

After seeing an old black lady getting mugged by "Lowlife Larry," Patrice had a bright idea, but did not know if he'd go through with it.

*F\*ck it! I'll try anything, once.*

He took a long walk to the infamous the Brevouy Projects in Bedfordstyvescent, where everyone seemed to be hustling outside the plethora of tower blocks.

"What's up Pee," asked a notorious drug dealer who was sitting at the curb, inside his spanking new black on black Grand Cherokee.

"Err . . . Nothing, Rock Man.

"What ya trying to tell me young blood," asked a bemused Rock Man, "that you don't want any of my crills this morning, not even a wake up?" They both knew that he wanted, no needed a wake up; just to get him back to the living.

"I do Rock Man, but I don't have any loot this morning, and it's too early to go stealing from any of the supermarkets."

"Yeah I bet, Pee. All the stores around here know you already. You'd have to go as far as Williamsburg, and those Jews will hang your thieving punk ass." This set The Rock Man into fits of laughter mode, and it seemed to be contagious, because the rest of his pathetic crew, standing on the curb beside the Grand Cherokee, started laughing as if The Rock Man was Richard Pryor. Patrice forced a crocodile smile, and this let The Rock Man know that the boy was here for some other type of business.

Oh well . . ." Was all the Rock Man said, and turned back to fiddling with his new car stereo system. Through his peripheral vision he could still see Patrice standing there. "Well young blood, can I help you?"

"Maybe you can, Rock Man."

"Come on Patrice, talk to me." Patrice looked around them, at the guys and gals standing in hearing distance, "Okay guys, take a little walk. Me and the Pee are going to talk a little business, right Pee?"

"Yeah, Rock Man."

The Rock Man's crew moved away as commanded, but made sure that they kept a vigilant eye on Patrice, because they didn't want their Sugar Daddy dead, and that's what they got paid for, to keep him alive.

"Well speak to me, Pee. How can I help ya?"

Though Patrice wasn't known to be shy, he didn't know how to ask, so he just went for it, "I need a gun."

The Rock Man didn't even flinch. "To do what, Pee?"

"To make some loot, some real loot Rock Man. Quick and easy loot."

The Rock Man looked Patrice up and down, but not at his sordid and dishevelled clothing, but to see if he had the heart to do what he was thinking of doing. Becoming a "Stick up kid" was a big leap from being a petty thief. "I'll sell you a pistol for a buck fifty."

"But I don't have that type of loot Rock Man," said a disconsolate Patrice. "I'll pay you after I get the loot with the gun," he pleaded.

"You'll get the loot Pee, but only if you have the heart to go through with it." Still scrutinizing Patrice, The Rock Man asked, "Do you have the heart?" Patrice was taking too long to answer. "Ya think long, ya think wrong, kid."

"I have the heart," mumbled Patrice.

"I can't hear ya, kid."

"I said I have the heart, Rock Man."

"When will I get my money then," asked the smirking drug dealer?

"I don't know, yet."

"Well I know Pee, tonight. Right before you put a stem in between your dry lips. I'm not trying to hear that you spent the money you earned with my gun on one of your session, because if I do . . ." The Rock Man let Patrice fill in the blanks.

# THEY CALL IT: DELANCY STREET

The number two train was rumbling from Utica Avenue to Atlantic Avenue, where he would change to the "F" train. Meanwhile Michael looked around the car, and read the back of newspapers, and stared into phlegmatic faces. His eyes caught a pretty young girl smiling at him lasciviously, but Michael reluctantly looked away from the precocious pre-teen.

Deep down inside, Michael knew that he was a half decent, caring, sharing, and loving person. He knew this, because everyone that counted told him so. Has he changed that much since he's been on drugs? Maybe, but it was his appearance on the outside, but inside . . . He was still the same old Michael, he hoped.

Yet, there was hardly anyone he knew right now, that he could say loved him. No one wanted him around; he was an embarrassment. He was just a visual aid to let them all know how far it was possible to fall from the land of grace. Michael could feel it, see it in their eyes. Even worse, he could see it in his families' eyes.

The person that he has displayed to others, for the past two long years, just wasn't him. It was a person that he did not know. Michael didn't like the person either. This time he had to try harder to stay away from the drug that he loved, but changed him into a troll every night. He had to try his very best, if he wanted to get back to the old Michael, and shine, just like he was supposed to.

Walking up the subway steps of Delancy Street was an exhilarating experience. It has been quite a while since he had come here to buy clothes and CD's. Even the air around here made him feel a bit dizzy, and his knees buckled a moment to concur that fact.

The clothes he saw hanging outside the stores, with their merchants yelling for everyone to come inside and see more of their hidden treasures, had Michael mouth salivating. He had brought along the extra $600.00, leaving the nice round figure of $3,000.00 underneath his bed, hoping it will be more than enough to get through the day. It will be all gone though, he knew if he spent it on the wrong thing. The crack cocaine was already calling him; it started as soon as he had opened his eyes this morning. Now it was eating into his brain, but he knew how to defeat it, momentarily. He had to try is best to distract it, for as long as possible. This was a fine start, going to Delancy Street, and getting away from Crown Heights for a while.

Michael hasn't been down here in years, and the beautiful memories came flooding back to him. Though Delancy Street may have changed a bit, just a little bit, since the days of him buying his suede Pumas and mock neck sweaters, it still smelt and looked the same. It had the same store owners, though aged over time, calling out to him to come across the street. Someone snatched him by the arm and startled him, but only for a second, because Michael was already into his Bruce Lee stance. "No-no kid," exclaimed an old grey haired Hasidic Jew. "You come have a look in my store while you're here. Leave my customers alone, Bernstein." Michael watched as the two Hasidic Jews threw insults at each other from across the street, before Mr Goldberg ushered him inside the small store of his. Inside the store may not have been that small, it only looked so because of all the clothes scattered around the place, to the extent where there was hardly anywhere to walk. "Look, look my friend. We have everything in here that you want." Mr Goldberg was practically pushing Michael deeper and deeper into his stores innards. *Hope this mother f\*cker ain't planning on locking me in here,* thought a suspicious Michael.

Just the window shopping alone was making him high, and for the first time, in a very long time, Michael felt that he didn't need drugs in his system to be elated. That old feeling of having money in his pocket, and being able to treat himself to anything he wanted was overwhelming him.

After looking around Mr Goldberg's store, Michael left without buying anything, to Mr Goldberg's dismay. "If you see anything you like out there, come back and I'll make you a better offer, kid."

He just wanted to walk around and window shop for a while. Michael was in no hurry to spend his money, and he sure was not in any hurry to go back to where all the crack dens were.

*Maybe you should think about staying around here, and avoid the temptation at home,* said Brainz.

*There is only one thing wrong with that Brainz, if I really want to do drugs, I'll find go and find a drug dealer around here.*

*True, true, conceded Brainz.*

What the old belligerent proprietors did not know was that they did not have to call him over to see what they had in their stores to sell him. Michael knew from past experience that they all sold the same things, and it was the garments and items they had on their shelves and racks that did all the talking. *You'll looked divine my son, if you buy me!*

In the end, Michael had shopped and bought clothes, whether he needed them or not, like a woman who saw a "For Sale" sign.

He ran in and out of stores, zigzagging across the street, until he couldn't carry any more shopping bags.

Still feeling very proud of himself for not spending all his money, any of it so far, on crack cocaine, Michael walked back to the Delancy subway station with a smug smile on his face. *Thank you, Jesus!!!*

As he waited for the "F" train to take him toward home, Michael looked at all the treasure in his hands and told himself, *I deserve all this. I do!*

*I concur,* said Brainz.

Michael did not know if Brainz was being sarcastic, but ignored it anyway.

*At least if I fail tonight or tomorrow,* replied Michael, *I'll have all these items to show for it.*

*Oh yeah,* said an acidic Brainz. *When you started sweating and shaking for your crack, you'll sell them all for a lousy $20.00, Timberland boots included.*

*I hate you,* replied Michael.

*I'm only here to help, kid.*

As the "F" Train rocked back and forth down the dark tunnels of New York City's subterranean, Michael's mind was consumed on what an amazing morning it has been.

*So far,* added Brainz.

First there was all the money, quite a lot of it by his standards. *Where the hell did it all come from? Where?*

Then there was the incident in Lincoln Terrace, where he knew that there were no bottles of beer in his Jansport, but "Poof" there they were. There was also the incident where he saw Jay empty his 40o/z, but when the man returned it to him, it was over flowing with barley water?

Unconsciously Michael was shaking his head and smiling to himself, which did not go unnoticed by a few of the other passengers sitting across from him. One of them, an old grey-haired man, who was doing some fake coughing in his direction, was scrutinizing him. The old man's fake coughing was efficacious, because it had gotten Michael's attention. He instantly snapped out of his reverie, and quickly looked around the semi-crowded car. As soon as he spotted some of the passengers eyeing him up, he expected them to look away, but they didn't. Others pretended that they were just too busy to even waste their precious time thinking about his crazy ass. *Just another Looney Tune on our New York subway, ya'll!*

Ignoring their scowls, *what pretty creatures they were,* Michael went back to his thoughts, because they seemed more important to him right now. Something inexplicable had obviously happened this morning; he knew this because he had bags full of fresh gear sitting between his feet. Unconsciously his hand went to his pocket to feel the rest of the money.

Yes, after every drug session he had promised himself that he would never touch the stuff ever again, but this time he had to not only try, he had to succeed. The inevitable will soon arrive once he reached Crown Height, and there was no getting around it. He just had to face it full frontal. Get back in the ring with Iron Mike Tyson, and hope that he could do a Buster Douglas. Still . . . That did not explain the magic, the miracles that were happening around.

When Michael quickly looked up again, he could see the eyes around the subway car were stabbing him in the face. He gave his fellow passengers the daggers right back. "Well," he asked?"

They all immediately averted their eyes, because no one wanted to end up in the obituaries of tomorrow's New York Post.

Quite content that he now had the other passengers afraid of him, because of their stereotype of a young black man, Michael went back to replaying all the events that had happened to him this morning.

*I bought a 40o/z, and that was it,* he told himself. *Then I made my way down to the duck pond as usual. I didn't have any more 40o/z's in my backpack, and I sure didn't have thirty six hundred dollars. What else happened that was out of the ordinary?*

Then he remembered the small descending cloud behind the bushes. The memory had Michael asking himself if he was going crazy, and not for the first time. The memory of the descending cloud had him thinking that he had been seeing something amazing and beautiful at the time, *and now . . . .?*

Then the singing began. Jay had been sitting in the middle of the park, never turning around to see who was approaching. You didn't have to be from Brooklyn to be vigilant, that was just human nature. Instead the man just sat there, eating the top of flowers. *Jay, bottles of beers multiplying and replenishing themselves, and over three thousand dollars?*

"Damn!" His outburst made everyone jump out of their now sordid G-Strings, and they all got up and started to move to other available cars on the train, leaving the mad man by himself.

It all went unnoticed though by Michael, who was scratching his head vigorously in confusion. *No . . . This doesn't make sense.*

He immediately looked around to find that he was all alone again, naturally.

The icing on the cake was that once he found that he had all this money, he did not run to the first crack dealer to have a session. I should be slumped somewhere, with a crack pipe in my mouth, but I'm not.

*No Majestic,* said Brainz, *you're not. And you're not going to either!*

He cuddled his shopping bags, lovingly.

*What was the common denominator?*

"Jay," he squealed out of the blue.

# PATRICE — GONE TO THE HEAD

With the heavy used Beretta 9mm Pistol in his hand, Patrice felt epic. He was now walking with a new found spring in his step, as he searched for his first victim. He just knew that he was going to make some money, and more than he's made by stealing food items from a super market. *Yes Rock Man, I do have the heart!*

He did not know who to rob first, because the choices were abundant. *Taking from and old man or lady will only get me pittance,* he told himself *and a very long stretch in a prison cell. Should I rob a bank? Hell no, too much risk. They're prepared for mother f\*ckers like me. I need to take someone by surprise, someone that smelt of money.*

As he walked around saliently, devious ideas came popping in and out of his now head. Then he saw a lonely store on the corner of Gates and Nostrand Avenue that he knew was run by two old Puerto Rican's, and husband and wife team. *They may not make much as the big stores,* he told himself, *but I know that they sure make enough for me to take from them.* The maleficent thought had Patrice walking much faster toward them, with a despicable smile on his face.

It was good to see that there were several customers in the Bodega *(who also had money)* shopping. It was also goo to see that most of them were from the grey haired posse. *This should be easy – peasy.* Patrice leisurely walked around the small store, up and down its claustrophobic aisles, not looking for anything to buy, but for the opportunity to pull out his Beretta 9mm Pistol. He was waiting for the customers to leave, *giving the old farts a chance,* but they were taking too damn long. *F\*ck it, I'll rob them all. The more the merrier.*

After checking that there was no one else in the back of the store, Patrice made his way back to the front door, blocking the exit with his frail frame.

"Excuse me young man," said an old black lady, who pulled her spectacles down the bridge of her bulbous nose when the young man did not move. She backed up a step, now afraid of the blood shot eyes looking back at her.

The Gonzalez's, along with their other customers, immediately felt the tension cut through the air. Mr Gonzalez stopped packing Mrs Groaniski's shopping bags, "Ay young man, are you going to buy anything, or what?"

This was when Patrice thought it was a very good time to pull out his Beretta 9mm Pistol. "Everyone just hand over your riches!" As he said this, he had pushed Mrs Browne out of his way, knocking her to the floor, and stepped up to the Gonzalez's. "Hand over all the money, or you'll never see each other again.

Mrs Gonzalez went into instant tears, while her husband was snorting like a raging bull. He did not want to hand over any of the little cash that they made this morning, especially to some smoked out drug addict. But still . . . The scumbag had a pistol pointing at him, and his death was not on his "To Do" list this morning.

Reading her husband's thoughts, Maria Gonzalez punched him in the arm, "Hector, please do as he says."

"You better listen to your wife, Hector. As you can plainly see, I didn't come here to play." With that Patrice pulled the trigger, and the bullet just missed Hectors head, shattering the bottles of expensive liquor on the shelves above. Everyone in the store instantly started screaming, crying, and thinking of their own mortality.

"Well," asked a maleficent sneering Patrice. It was obvious to everyone that there will be no more chit-chatting. Hector reluctantly opened both cash registers, and handed over the cash to the c*ck sucking thief. "Hope you go to hell kid," seethed Hector, "where you belong."

"I go there every day," smiled Patrice. "Thank you!"

Instead of leaving with his ill-gotten money, which is what everyone in the store had hoped he had done, the vile miscreant told everyone to throw their wallets and purses on the ground. Mr Succotash threw some coins on the floor, as if Patrice was a street beggar. "Ya think you're funny old man?"

"That's all I've got," said a venomous Mr Succotash.

The bullet had Mr Succotash on the sordid bodega floor within seconds, his blood spewing up into the air like a geyser. This was when all the real money came out of everyone in the store, including food stamps. Even Maria threw *their* secret stash over the counter and onto the floor, in front of the maleficent hoodlum. She instantly knew that this was a very big mistake, by the murderous look in her husband's eyes.

Fumbling through the riches on the floor, Patrice could not believe his luck. "Hector, how could you? You've been holding out on me."

Hector said nothing, and all Patrice got in return of a reply was a stare full of hate. Ignoring it, Patrice continued to collate everything of value on the floor. "You people have been really naughty."

His eyes were directed at Mrs Browne when he said this, whose hand bag he found was filled with cash. He shook his head at her, and at Hector, and kissed his teeth at the both of them. "Very naughty indeed, ya'll."

"Hate to love you and leave you, but . . ." He knew that he had to make his escape now, he's watched enough cop shows to know that the most important part of a crime is getting away, quick fast and in a hurry.

He was gone to the relief of all in the little Bodega, except Hector, who looked like he was going to take his loss out on his lovely wife Maria.

# BROOKLYN CRUISING

Instead of getting the number two train after he had reached Fulton Street, Michael decided to take a long walk, with no particular destination in mind. He needed time and space to think.

With money and bags in hand, Michael decided to amble around the Flatbush area of Brooklyn, while swilling on a 40o/z.

Walking around Brooklyn has made him lose a lot of weight since he had arrived as a fat young boy from England. Now he was practically skinny, because of the crack cocaine, except for the omnipresent beer belly he's worn all his life. *A lot of money went into this stomach,* he often told his size zero, and condescending critics.

Ever since he touched that crack cocaine, Michael knew that he had become such a damn fool, such a low life. None of these characteristic he liked about himself, but the drug was much stronger than him. Anyway, he knew that he had no excuses, as well as will power. It was the "Will Power" that he had to have and the smarts to stay away from his weakness, no matter how loud it called him.

Before the drugs he has read, heard, and saw what drugs have done and could do to people, he knew, and yet . . .

*Today's a new day,* he had constantly told himself, until it became an annoying platitude in his head. *I have been such an idiot to think that there will be a different outcome, after doing the same thing, time after time!*

He looked up, and saw that he was now on Church and East 94th Street. *Shit I may as well go and see my aunt May,* he told himself, *and say hello.*

"Hi ya, Majestic."

"Oh, hi ya Althea." Althea, who he had known as an ugly duckling in Abraham Lincoln high school, had now turned into a beautiful swan. *Damn, the girl looks drop dead gorgeous.* Now Michael was sputtering and fidgeting in front of her.

His uneasiness did not go unnoticed, and she smiled. "What have you been up to Michael?"

"Err . . ." How could he tell this beautiful creature that he had become a professional crack head? "Nothing much, Althea. And you?"

Because he knew that people loved talking about themselves, it was rather easy to change to subject. "Me, well I now go to NYU School of Medicine."

"Damn girl," Michael's uneasiness dissipated. "Congratulations Althea. You doing, and looking well."

She could see the sincere happiness for her in his lovely brown eye, and the memories of why she used to like the naïve British boy in high school came flooding back. "It looks as if you're doing rather well yourself, Majestic?" Michael followed her gazed to all his shopping bags, "I hope you ain't one of them drug dealers," she now said with sadness in her quivering voice. At first Michael found himself getting angry at her negative comment, *the negative profiling of a black man with a shopping bag*. Shit, he should be happy that she hadn't accused him of shoplifting. "No Althea, I'm not one of them drug dealers," he said casually, "or I would be driving up to you in a Bentley, with the top down."

This obviously broke the ice, and the continued to chat for a while, before Althea gave him her cell phone number and left. Pleased like a shining star in the sky, Michael visited his aunt May, who was very glad to see him. "Bwhy, yu luk clean man. Awa happen tu yu?"

"I'm trying," was all Michael replied to the lady that loved him with all her heart.

After leaving his aunt May with a big smile on her face, he decided to walk over to the Ebbets Field projects. Along the way all the other pedestrians could see his torment. His face was riddled with twists and screws, sometimes distorted beyond recognition. As usual, he ambled along degrading and vilifying himself.

*Yeah,* said an aggrieved Brainz, *why leave it to other people to do?*

He was scared. He knew what will happen throughout the rest of the day. He's been here a million times before. The next inevitable drug session will be calling him, and all his lovely words and will power will evaporate into thin air with the crack smoke. *Today Majestic,* said Brainz, *is a new day!*

*How can you say that Brainz, when you know what will happen? I'm just too weak!*

*Look Buddy,* responded a compassionate Brainz, *we'll take it a minute at a time. Okay?*

After a while Michael said, "Okay!"

What more was there for him to say? It was his only hope, to come out of each new day drug free.

*Just keep drinking your beer, until you pass out,* said Brainz. *At least drink until you're too drunk to hold a crack pipe.*

Michael hated being degraded and humiliated, especially in public, but he did it to himself. When, and if he finally got tired of it, that would be when he broke the crack pipe, and not go out and buy another one.

*Only a stone cold junkie would expect a different outcome from doing the same damn thing every day,* he told himself.

First he knew that he had to admit that he could not defeat the powerful drug (the opponent in the ring), and once he could do that, then he knew that all he had to do was stay clear away from it (out of the ring). It was his first step to recovery. *I'll stick with drinking my beer. I promise!!!*

He knew that he was being too hard on himself again, already forgetting that he has had a very good start for the day, they were in his hands, mouth, and pockets. It was something that he needed to keep on going if he wanted to actually achieve something today.

# PATRICE — LIFE IS LOOKING ROSY

He had collected over a thousand dollars, in less than ten minutes from the Gonzalez's Bodega. "This has to be the way, forward!"

For once instead of heading to get high right away, Patrice made his way back to the Brevouy Projects, with a spring in his step. He knew that he had to pay "The Rock Man" first, albeit reluctantly, or his and its new fortune will end in the next ten minutes. After he has paid the Rock Man for the gun, well . . . Ideas were flying around in Patrice's head, and he was already thinking of his next robbery. *This is too damn easy, Sir!*

When the Rock Man saw Patrice heading toward him, he told his crew to watch him, closely. The Rock Man not only knew Patrice had a gun, but had used it by the smirk on his ugly mug. "What up Pee," asked the phlegmatic Rock Man?

Patrice looked at all the fellas that had once put the fear of God into him, all standing guard, scrutinizing him. He wasn't scared of them any longer, and this made him feel good inside. There were quite a few of these guys that he would like to rob and shoot, right now, in broad daylight, but he thought better of it. They have mistreated and disrespected him over the years, and had constantly taken his money, sold him bad drugs. *Now I've got a gun you punks, and I'll be back for your pretty asses,* he promised. *Chill . . . Baby!*

"Hi, Rock Man. As you can plainly see, I had the heart after all, and now I've got your money." Patrice handed over the $150.00 to Rock Man, who flicked his fingers through the bills.

"Where's the rest," asked a serious looking Rock Man?

The shock on Patrice's face had everyone standing outside the Brevouy Projects, reaching for their guns. This did not go unnoticed by Patrice, who took a deep breath to control his volcanic temper. He knew that this was going to be another robbery, this time he would be playing the victim.

"You haven't even counted it yet, Rock Man. I'm telling you, everything is right there as we agreed. A buck fifty."

"Did I say I wanted a buck fifty?"

Since he knew that this was going to be a rip off, Patrice knew that he had to think fast. These young punks were so dumb, they wouldn't think twice of going to prison for his dead body. "Oh come on, Rock Man. Why ya playing with me, yo. You know that I'm going to spend the rest of the money I have left on buying drugs from you. Either way, you'll get it all."

This seemed to have appeased The Rock Man, and he shovelled the lump of money that Patrice had given him into his rabbit fur coat.

"Okay, Pee. I guess you did have the heart after all, and you did come to pay me, before you ran and bought yourself a hit. Well, how much do ya want?"

Patrice was feeling ambiguous, shocked and amazed that he had not asked for a kilo of crack, he even surprised himself by not wanting any right now. He was on another high, making easy money with the Beretta.

*Sh\*t,* he thought, *I better buy something anyway, or they'll all get suspicious.* "Yeah Rock Man, let me get eight nickels for now."

He surreptitiously peeled off $40.00, turning his back toward the Rock Man, who was trying his best to peak over Patrice's shoulders. When Patrice attempted to hand the money over to the Rock Man, the Rock Man turned his back, and walked away, instantly. This act left Patrice with his hands held out, with the $40.00 still fluttering in his frigid fingers. "What ya think ya doing Pee," asked a young fifteen year old, who came running up to him with the speed of Usain Bolt. "Ya trying to get the Rock Man busted?"

"What," asked a shocked Patrice? "What are you on about, Killer?"

"You must know the cops are watching, and yet you try to hand the Rock Man loot in the streets. Are you wired up, or something?"

"What. No killer. I ain't working for the cops. Ya wanna search me?"

"I believe ya Patrice, but "The Rock Man" doesn't do any hand to hand combat, yo!"

"My mistake, Killer. My bad. Sorry, Rock Man," said a sincere Patrice. "Well make sure you don't make that mistake again, fella."

"Killer" was wearing an icy grille now on his face, trying his best to impress his boss, "The Rock Man." Now the little punk was breathing bubble gum fumes into Patrice's face. Patrice couldn't wait to wipe that look off his acne riddled countenance, and bury the young punk in a ton of Bazooka chewing gum.

# UTICA AVENUE – MCDONALDS

After a very pleasant, but exhausting morning, Michael finally found himself back on Eastern Parkway and Utica.

Meeting the Alluring Althea, who he remembers didn't have much time for him in high school, but like him, made him feel as if he was getting back to the Romeo status that he knew was in him. *I'm not ugly,* he told himself. *I am kind, caring and such a loving person.*

*Oh, can't you shut up, big head.* It seemed that Brainz was also happy for his host.

His stomach was also talking to him, trying to cut Brainz off at the pas. *Sh\*t, I'm past being very hungry and starving, I'm f\*cking famished!*

Michael also found that he desperately needed to take a leak, after drinking three 40o/z bottles of Private Stock by himself on his travels. He was not drunk, but he sure found himself on the borderline.

As he continued to amble along on uncontrollable legs, the answer to all his problems was staring him right in the face. The neon lights of the famous "Golden Arches" that was calling him like crack cocaine.

*Michael come talk to me, and I will satisfy all your needs.*

He headed straight for the most famous establishment known to man, woman, and child. "Mickey D's" was the only place to be, when the hunger, and small intestine, started to revolt. Once inside the Eastern Parkway franchise, Michael ran straight to their pristine bathroom, in which a young pubescent girl was presently mopping out. After almost slipping on the wet floor, the young girl just glared at him. *I wished you had busted your punk ass, asshole!*

After relieving himself for the next six minutes, he put cold water on his face, and fixed himself up. Now he was ready to face the world, and his "Big Mac Meal." Michael found himself at the end of a very long queue of teenagers, who obviously had nothing else better to do, than hang out in their "Mecca." The young gang of boys and girls seemed to be doing more playing than ordering of food, and Michael was getting more agitated and famished by the minute.

After the young girl, her badge read: Rachel, had gotten rid of the queue of teenagers fifteen minutes later, she asked Michael if she could take his order. He ordered what he always ordered, refusing to try any of McDonald's new weekly concoctions, "I'll have a Big Mac Meal, please."

As he paid Rachel, and waited for her to finish his order, he wondered how old she was. She looked as if she was ten at most, and Michael wondered if the Child Labour Law was now defunct. *I have been out of the loop for quite a while,* admitted Michael.

Michael took his tray from the Rachel, and thanked her for her excellent service. Rachel winked at him lasciviously, and it took Michael some of his weak will power to leave the queue. He then did what seemed to be a two hour tour of the franchise, looking for a seat that was devoid of any teenagers or homeless people. *Kids. Why the f\*ck aren't they all in school?*

It did not go unnoticed by Michael that McDonalds, all over the world, has become the main hang-out for all teenagers. It was their home away from home. There were now more kids in any given McDonald franchise, than you would find in school during the week. This was "The Mecca," their new version of a tree house. *F\*ck school, lying teachers, and the Perverted Principle!*

After doing another lap, Michael decided that he would just have to share a table with someone, preferably with a pretty young lass like Rachel. *Behave yourself,* said Brainz. *Pervert!*

Michael was wearing a lurid smirk on his countenance when he finally found a seat and settled himself in. Before his ass hit the hard plastic chair, Michael found himself facing a very familiar face, "Nice seeing you again, so soon, Michael."

"Err . . . Jay." Michael was angry because he didn't even get a chance to take his first bite of his much anticipated "Big Mac."

"What the hell are you doing here?"

"Err . . ." Imitated Jay, "Eating, just like you, Michael."

"Okay. That was a stupid question. Only I didn't expect to see you in here."

"And why not, Michael?"

"Err . . ." Michael did not want to be rude and say, *because they didn't sell flower seeds.* Instead he changed tact, "Anyway, Jay. Good to see ya, good Buddy."

"Good to see you also, Michael." After watching Michael clumsily get himself situated and comfortable in the small plastic chair, Jay asked "What do you have in the shopping bags Michael, 4oz/z's?"

Michael almost spat out his first scrumptious bite of his hamburger, "Ha-ha. You're so very funny, Jay. For your information I went out and bought some clothes for myself."

"Clothes, Michael?"

"Yes clothes Jay," said a smiling and proud Michael. "It's been a very long time since I bought myself something other than . . ." Michael found that he couldn't finish the sentence.

"Other than what, Michael?"

"Nothing, Jay."

"Why?"

"Why what, Jay?"

"Why did you go out and buy yourself new clothes. You look fine to me."

"Thanks Jay, but I may look fine, on the outside . . ." Michael found he couldn't finish that sentence either.

"Is there a problem Michael?"

"Err . . . No, Jay. I'm fine."

"Well you do look much happier than when I saw you this morning."

Michael's mouth was snapped shut, audibly. The shame of his addiction, and not being able to tell this caring person sitting in front of him, caused him more pain, mentally as well as physically, than he thought it would. *How could he tell Jay what he had become in the past couple of years? How could he tell Jay why he hadn't bought himself clothes, went unwashed and lived on the streets for longer than a human wished to?* Shame washed over him now, and he wanted to leave the presence of the lovely and innocent man sitting in front of him, immediately.

He did not want to share is downfall as a human being with this stranger. The silence between them lasted for quite a while, and Jay let it hang there, because he already knew. They both ate in silence, until Michael looked at the drool of tartar sauce running down the corners of Jay's mouth. "Guess you got the munchies after drinking all that beer this morning, Jay?"

"Munchies," asked a confused Jay?"

Michael's eyes instantly went into the ceiling of his head, and he ignored his foreign friend's ignorance. *Where the hell did Jay say he was from again?* Michael continued to destroy his Big Mac Meal, and after masticating two giant bites of his burger, he looked over at Jay. "I see you like the fish burger."

"Yes Michael. Fish is my favourite dish."

"Are you trying to rhyme, Jay?"

"No, Michael. It comes naturally." They both laughed, and continued to eat their food in peace. They both jumped when Michael's cell-phone rang, and he told Jay to excuse him while he answered it. Jay watched Michael laugh, turn sad immediately afterward, and then switch off the phone. "Are you okay, Michael?"

"Yeah Jay, I'm fine."

"Something you want to talk about?"

"No Jay, it's nothing."

After they both finished their meals, they sat their drinking their Orange Fanta's. "Can I have a look at your cell-phone?"

Michael looked up at Jay, confused. Then he hesitated, because cell-phone theft was rampant around these parts, and all of a sudden he didn't know how innocent and loving Jay was.

Since Michael prided himself on knowing people, as soon as he met them, he passed *his* cell-phone over to Jay, "It's an old Samsung," he said apologetically. "I don't have the type of money like these pubescent teens you see around here Jay." Jay looked around McDonald's to see all the teens talking on their cell-phones, instead of talking to each other. *So very rude,* he thought. Michael watched Jay's roving eyes, "Their cell-phones have surround sound, and a duplex movie theatre on it."

Jay laughed as he took the offered Samsung Galaxy S II, and turned it over in his hand. Michael watched as Jay studied and securitized *his* cell-phone, as if he has never seen one before. *Sh\*t, even in Zimbabwe they have cell-phones. Where the hell was this place called Bethlehem, anyway?*

"Michael," the suddenness of Jay speaking to him, made him jump. "Did I scare you?"

"Err . . . No," lied Michael. "I was just thinking about something, that's all."

"Anyway Michael," continued a smiling Jay, "I was saying that I wonder what would happen if we all treated *Our Bibles* like we treated our modern day cell-phones . . ."

Michael almost spat out his Fanta, and instantly looked around "The Mecca." "Keep your voice down Jay," he whispered. "Are you trying to get us killed?"

"No, why would I do that, Michael." Just watch what ya saying, because these kids will set you on fire, and film it on their phones. You'll be a celebrity on "You Tube."

"You Tube?"

"Err . . . Forget it, Jay. Anyway, what are you talking about now?" Michael stared at, and wondered about the man sitting in front of him. *Everybody's got game. Everybody has an angle. EVERYBODY!*

Michael has learned that everyone wanted something, even if they didn't know they did. It was called, for political correctness, "Self Preservation."

Whatever you wanted to call it, Michael knew that they were straight up lying to you to get what they wanted, or thought they needed. He liked letting the other person speak, always waiting for them, patiently, to inevitably slip up with the truth. *The truth shall set you free!!!*

It was as if Jay had waited until Michael had finished thinking his thoughts, before he continued with his story about the "Bible." After looking back at Jay, Michael had to ask himself if he had been thinking aloud. *Is that possible, or is this strange man also a mind reader?* Looking into Jay's blue eyes, weren't they green yesterday, it sure looked as if Jay had heard every word he had just thought in the privacy of *his* head. The thought of Jay's inner-sight made Michael more than a little nervous, and scared to be in his presence.

"Sorry I drifted on you Jay," he said apologetically, "I often do that, unfortunately."

"Do what, Michael?"

"Drift off, even when I'm in very good company like yourself."

"Whatever . . . Michael." They were both laughing, until Jay continued with his story of comparing the Bible with the Cell Phone.

"What if we carried our Bible around in our purses or pockets, like we do our cell-phones? What if we turned back to go get it, every time we forgot it at home. What if we flipped through the Bibles pages, several times a day, as we do with our cell-phones?"

"Slow down my religious friend." Michael has heard enough, and was looking around to see if the crowd in McDonalds were watching them.

"What the hell are you talking about Jay," Michael said, lowering his voice. "And why?" Michael was studying Jay the best he could, his eyes divagating from Jay's face to the audience that were watching them, captivated. *This man is amazing,* thought Michael, *and I've met some amazing people in my life.* Michael started to feel sorry for his innocent, but ignorant new friend. "Jay, let me tell you something right now. This country, this world of ours, is run and is full of evil people that don't give a f*ck about religion, yours or anybody else's!"

"But . . ."

"But nothing, Jay." The earlier fear of being in front of Jay had now dissipated, and was now taken over with some paternal instinct. All Michael felt right now was to protect Jay, bring him to reality, no matter how dismal it was. He knew what these selfish and heartless people around here could, and would do to an innocent person like Jay. He just hated to see good and innocent people like Jay get hurt, eaten by the predators of society. *Tough love* is what they all needed, and not any of this *"I'll tell ya what ya wanna hear"* crapola. Jay was about to say something, but his air was cut off quickly, "I'm not finished, Jay."

Jay thought that his new friend Michael was about to burst a blood vessel, the way he was seething right now. Michael was doing all he could to control himself in the public arena, and this made Jay want to laugh, but he controlled it. He sat back and listened, with a Fanta and a smile. "And the rest of the heathens," continued the ranting Michael, "are very proud Atheists that would be quite glad to ridicule you in public about your beliefs."

Michael finally fell silent, *maybe trying to catch his breath* thought Jay. Jay hesitated before he asked Michael, "Are you finished, now?"

"Yeah," said an exasperated Michael.

"Michael," Jay continued as if he had not been rudely interrupted by Michael's outburst. "What if we treated our Bibles as if we could not live without it, just as we do with our cell-phones?"

The loud smacking sound that was heard reverberating throughout the densely packed McDonalds was that of Michael slapping himself on the forehead in resignation. "You are amazing, Jay!"

As they made their way out of McDonalds, they walked in silence, until Michael told Jay that he was heading home to put away his new clothes.

"Okay Michael. I guess I'll see ya around then." Michael tried to give Jay "A Five," but Jay held on to his hand, shaking it thunderously. *Damn this man has a lot to learn,* thought Michael.

After finally freeing his aching hand, Michael asked, "Where you heading off to, Jay?"

"I don't know," was Jay's succinct answer.

This concerned Michael, "Do you have a place to stay, Jay?"

Jay laughed, "Well of course I do Michael." For the first time Michael thought that Jay was lying to him. He did not know why, because he usually did not give a sh*t if a person had anywhere to stay or not. Well not anymore. Why was this stranger getting to him?

Michael has always been a soft touch, but has tried very hard to be as cold hearted as the people in his new world. *It looks as if I still need to do a lot of work,* said the boy that still cried at Disney movies. "I can ask my mum and dad if you could stay for the night if you like."

Tears were appearing in Jay's eyes; Michael was tugging at his heart strings. Jay looked up into the bruised sky, *this is why I came down here again Father, for people like Michael.*

"Thank you Michael, but that will not be necessary." With that said, they parted company, both of them constantly looking back at one another. When Michael finally disappeared from his view, Jay could only think of how people like Michael were confused, and did not know which way to turn or go with their lives. Confusion was the disease that was killing all the good people.

From what he has gathered from Michael, Jay knew that the boy has been fighting with himself, on a daily basis, to try and stay a half decent person in this world of iniquity. All the decent people like Michael now all thought that they were fighting a losing battle, and were out-numbered by the despicable and maleficent people. *Everyone was lying, everyone had game, and everyone would cut your throat to get what they thought they needed, or wanted. W*as Michael so right?

Jay knew that all the good people, *the few that still were left, according to his new friend Michael,* will all inevitably change and become like the rest of the field of bad weeds that surrounded, or be strangled and choked by them. *If Michael is right about his outlook on life, then that just makes my job just a little bit harder.* "Father, help me!"

# MICHAEL — TAKING INVENTORY

As he walked the short distance home, Michael's mind was consumed of thoughts regarding his new friend, Jay. He was still wondering if Jay really had somewhere to stay, and where? Now he was really feeling quite guilty that he never had any intention of asking his parents if Jay could stay the night. That would have had his mother packing his clothes in plastic garbage bags, feverishly.

This was Brooklyn after all, and not some down home State like Virginia or the Carolina's, where you were always welcomed in the house if you were a stranger. Anyway, his mother would have spat in his face.

Michael tried to drink Jay and his outlandish thoughts out of his head. The things that come out of the man's mouth, was just . . . Stupefying.

This time the beer was not helping, because Jay stayed on his mind, and this confused Michael. *I should be thinking about all the money I now have, and all the new gear I just bought.*

First thing first, and that was to take his newly acquired clothes home. *I may even stay in tonight.* Michael laughed at the thought that his mother would have a heart attack and call the ambulance on speed dial. He could hear her now, "You . . . Staying in tonight, Michael?"

"Are you okay, boy?"

"Ken there's something wrong with *your* son!"

As soon as he turned the key in the lock, he saw his mother standing behind the front door looking like a female mass murderer. "Yo ma, chill. It's me!"

"Boy, what ya doing here?"

"I live here ma. Remember me?"

Scrutinizing him to see if it was really her child standing in front of her, "What are you doing here, Michael. Do you realize that it is only 1:30PM?"

"I didn't know that I had to be here at a certain time, ma."

"Don't get snotty with me boy, you know damn well what I mean."

"No ma, I don't."

"Well, let me tell ya then Michael. You're usually out, until the crack of dawn."

"Ma, are you going to let me in, or what?"

Once he made his way to his bedroom, he opened the shopping bags, and set all the goodies free. A wave of vertigo swayed him as he looked down at all his brand new clothes, as if for the first time. The feeling was overpowering. It was as if he was looking at a kilo of cocaine, and didn't know what to do with it. He couldn't wait to wash up, put on some of his new gear, and step out into the world. "Ma . . . Dad," he called as he attempted to make his way to the bathroom. There was no reply, from either one of them. This could only mean that they went out already, and that he had the house to himself. "Hoo-rah!"

Or so he thought, because as soon as he opened his bedroom door, there stood his younger brother Floyd, with his half-naked new girlfriend of the week. His younger brother's eyes were looking past and through him though, and Michael turned his head to where his brother was looking. "Where'd you get the money for all those goodies, Mike?"

"Oh Floyd, don't asked stupid questions. What's up, yo?"

"You're what's up," said a terse Floyd, who stood there like a razor wired fence. He was determined to find out where his big brother got the loot to buy what he recognized as Delancy Street garments.

Michael saw the look on his brothers – *I'm waiting for an answer* – countenance. "Floyd, don't ask. I'll explain, later."

"I want to see what you bought."

"Okay," said a reluctant Michael. "Damn kid."

"Wow, can I wear that," asked Floyd's new young wench?

"Floyd. Who the hell is this?"

"Oh, this is my girlfriend Nakisha, from school."

*The boy was amazing,* thought Michael. It seemed that his younger brother brought home a different girl every week, and he couldn't even get one. *Shame,* said Brainz. *I rather be with your brother!*

"No Nokia, you can't wear any of my new gear."

"It's Nakisha, thank you very much."

"Whatever . . . Anyway, they're all too big for you."

"I know I can rock that New York Jets hoody, with my green stilettoes."

"No I said," screamed Michael. "Stop f*cking begging, will ya!"

Both Floyd and Nakisha moon walked away from Michael's bedroom door, giving him space to manoeuvre. He brushed past them, and all Floyd got was a look that said, *don't you teach your b*tches not to ask me for anything?*

Floyd knew and hated his new maniacal brother, and was scared of him. "Come on Nakisha; let's go get something to eat. See ya later . . . Mike."

"Yeah, yeah, Floyd. Later."

He heard them both mumbling about him, as they made their way out the front door. "What's wrong with your brother, Floyd?"

"I don't really know girl," replied a confused, and saddened Floyd.

Once Michael heard the front door close, he ran back into his bedroom to look out his window. They were in his vision; he could see them walking down the street, hand in hand. *"And they call it, Puppy love . . ."*

*Any love is a good thing,* added Brainz.

Deciding on what he was going to wear first, was an arduous job. *Sh\*t, I'm sweating!* Michael laid out all his cloths, matching them up to make a sparkling outfit, one where the ladies would gush all over him, instantly. *What a difficult, but pleasant problem I have,* thought a now smiling Michael. He quickly stripped naked, and got ready to take a nice warm bath.

As Michael soaked himself in his bubble, Dettol, and Epsom salt filled bath tub, he thought about his life, and how it turned out be like a sailboat in the vast volatile ocean. He has been blown this and that way, with no direction or goal. He knew that it was entire his fault, because he couldn't keep blaming all his misfortunes on happenstance. *Sh\*t,* said Brainz. *Sh\*t happens kid, but still . . . you could have done better, and made better choices in your life.*

Once again Michael wanted to kick himself, in the head preferably. Then he thought that it wasn't absolutely all his fault. It wasn't his fault that he was uprooted from one country to another, when he was only fourteen. What an age to try and adapt to a new world. At least his brother Floyd had been younger, and it had been much easier for him to adapt.

*Timing and luck,* thought Michael, *I don't have any of them!*

It was not his fault that his new environment consisted of impecunious black people that lived their lives in crime, grim, drugs, and alcohol. But you can only play the hand that you are dealt, that was life. Yet, Michael knew that there were people who had it worse off than he, and they have succeeded in their life, against all odds.

All he had for himself were very poor excuses of why he had failed, why he had not gone to college to become a Doctor, Lawyer, or a Sanitation Analyst.

It was a long time ago when he had given up on making plans, because every time he had, it took less than a day to explode into smithereens. There was always something that he had not planned on, a small thing, something that just came out of the blue that made his *perfect plan* null-in-void.

*Hanging out with Patrice, Avarice Angela, Salacious Susan, and Dirty Debbie,* said Brainz, *is not an ideal formula for a successful life.*

He did not want to go back out into the streets, looking like a professional derelict, not today, not anymore. *I'll take it one day at a time,* he told himself, *starting with today.* The tears were now mixing in with the soap on his face, because the fear of the inevitable failure was too overpowering. *I don't want to fail, again!*

There were no drugs today, so far, and he needed it to continue. It was the amount of money that he had, that was bringing the fears, because as long as he had it, the drugs will be calling him.

*Credit to you Majestic,* said a proud Brainz, *at least you still have the money, you bought cloths instead of drugs, and that can only be classed as f\*cking amazing!*

Michael was wearing that maniacal grin on his face as he soaped up. In the silence of the bathroom, he heard himself say, "Thank you, Jesus!"

When his parents returned, they found Michael in the living room, watching the New York Knicks game on television. His mother dropped the shopping bags full of food, her mouth agape.

"You okay boy," asked his concerned father?

"Yeah dad, never better."

"Well take your feet off of the damn coffee table."

"Sir, yes sir!" They all laughed, nervously, together. His parents told him that it was good to see him in the house, and that he smelt good.

Together his parents made their way to the kitchen to put away the groceries, confused, but very happy to see that their eldest son had decided to stay in for the day.

"It's still early, Ken."

"Yeah, I know Mavis, but the kid is trying!"

# LADY DONNA

"Who are you," said a truculent Michael, wiping away the beer that missed his mouth, and was now traveling down his chin. "Where is my friend, Jay?" Michael did not mince his words with this new stranger.

*What the f\*ck was this, a place for new arrivals?*

"Excuse me," said the agitated young lady. "Do you have a problem, mister?"

He had expected to see Jay again this morning, sitting in the same spot in Lincoln Terrace Park, eating some form of plant life. Now he felt cheated and frustration. He had woken up this morning feeling vibrant, and wanted to show Jay the fresh outfit he was wearing. Michael even had with him a *La Mesa* brown sweater, with hoody, in his Jansport back pack. He had bought for Jay on Delancy, so the man could wear it underneath his beloved brown and diaphanous robe. *The man has to be cold!* Michael reminded himself that he would ask Jay if he needed a pair of warm shoes, because them worn out hand-made sandals he wore weren't what was required in a Brooklyn winter.

*Plans, ha! I told you Brainz, this one didn't even get a chance to get started.*

In Jay's place, was another stranger? *Where the f\*ck are these people coming from anyway,* he asked himself?

It was not that he knew every person in Brooklyn, or Crown Heights for that matter, but he's been coming down here to Lincoln Terrace for . . . Eons. Anyway, there stood a beautiful young wench in Jay's place this morning, and he shouldn't be angry or have any complaints.

"Sorry pretty lady," Michael said apologetically, "I just expected to see someone else here this morning."

She stared into his eyes, to see if his apology was veritable, "Well you met me this morning, instead." The stranger turned her back to him, and continued with what she was doing. Without stopping her from doing her work, picking flowers, Michael asked, "Can I give you a hand?" All he got was a grunt, and he didn't like the sound. "Well?"

The young lady turned around, "Do you really want to pick flowers this morning?"

"Err . . ."

"I thought so."

Michael said nothing more. He just watched as she continued to pick the pretty flowers in the field, and put them into a large straw basket. *What was going on around here?*

*What is she doing here and who the hell is she?*

It was funny that he had never asked the same question to Jay, yesterday. *Woe fella*, warned Brainz. *Something is not kosher in Crown Heights.* "Sorry that I sounded so anti-social to you this morning," said Michael, trying his best to make peace.

Since the young man did sound contrite, the young lady turned to him and said, "I accept your apology." Donna had her hand held out to be shaken, and Michael took it, and shook it with alacrity.

"Thank you," said a perceptively relieved Michael. "Have you seen anyone else around here this morning?"

"No," was her terse answer. Michael started following her slowly around the field, as she continued to fill her basket with flowers. The young lady finally stopped what she was doing, and turned around to face her stalker. "Excuse me . . . Can I help you?"

"Err . . . Sorry. I didn't realize that I was sweating you so bad. I just came here, because I thought my friend would be down here again."

"Well sorry, he's not here."

"Yeah, I know that now, but . . ." Donna looked at the handsome young man who couldn't finish his sentence.

"But what," she asked pleasantly?

"Well, I met him here yesterday to be honest, as I've met you this morning." *Her face, such a pretty thing*, thought Michael, was waiting for more. "I saw him again later on in the day, at McDonald's, and I'm a little concerned for him."

"Concerned. Why," asked a now interested Donna.

"Well, the things he was saying. It is obvious that he's not from around here, and I don't want to see him get hurt."

"Why would he get hurt, from the things he was saying?"

"Err . . ." Michael didn't know how to explain it, and really didn't have the time right now. "I need to find him, before he gets himself in trouble, but I don't know where he lives, and that's if he lives anywhere."

"You are worried about him, aren't you?" Donna could see the anxiety in Michael's face. "Do you always care about strangers this compassionately?"

"Err . . . Well . . . No." Michael could read everything that the young lady was thinking right now, *so why do you care what happens to this stranger, so much?*

Michael thought about this, and answered her un-asked question. "I don't know why. Anyway, never mind. Sorry again for bothering you."

"No bother at all. I hope you find him."

"I hope so to," said a defeated Michael. "Anyway, he always seems able to find me," added Michael.

This brought a smile to the young ladies face, "Then maybe you should wait here until he shows up?" Donna did not know why she had basically invited this stranger to stick around with her, but she was happy that she had. The boy just did not know how to hide his feelings, and he wore the fact that Jay did not show up blatantly on his handsome face. *Now that there, will get ya killed,* thought Donna. She thought it a very good time to change the subject. "It's a nice and peaceful park, isn't it?"

"Yeah," was all a deflated Michael could mutter, as if he was talking to himself?

"A lovely place," continued Donna, "to meet people."

"I always come down here when I want a little peace, get away from the rest of the world." At least she had got him to travel back to the present, and he was talking to her, now.

After another long period of silence, Michael realized that he had drifted again. When he snapped out of it, he saw that the young lady had already gone back to her chores. He followed her, again. "Why are you picking flowers?"

"Because I think they are so beautiful," answered an effulgent Donna. "They make the world more kaleidoscopic, and I like to share them with the children in my class."

"Oh, you're a teacher."

"Yes, I am."

"And you're a very beautiful one at that!" This declaration made Donna stop what she had been doing, and she turned to him, with an effervescent smile on her pretty face. "What did you say?"

"Sorry," Michael pinched his lips together with his fingers, so nothing else stupid could escape them. Now Donna's smile turned to laughter. "Did I just say that out loud?"

"Yeah, you did."

Since he did not know what else to do, Michael decided to intervene by introducing himself. "My name is Michael." There was a long pause in her expectant response, because she could not stop laughing. It was a while before she could keep a straight face. Donna eventually told him her name, through tears and snot.

Michael hesitated to go near her, and shake her hand, again. "Nice to meet you, Donna."

"Nice meeting you also, Michael." They both stood there staring at each other, neither moving a muscle, not even a twinge between them. They looked like statues as the flies, bees, and birds buzzed around them.

"Well . . . I better be off then Donna," was all that came out of his mouth. As he started to walk away, Donna told him that she would tell his friend, if she saw him, that he had been looking for him.

"Thanks, said Michael, who was already half way up the hill.

# A GOOD DAY ON STERLING PLACE

There were quite a few people on the block he used to call home at one time, and when he arrived, sparkling like the star Sirius, Michael thought that the "Open Mouth" look must be the new fad of the day.

As he strolled like a peacock down Sterling Place, Michael was beginning to like the shocked and lascivious looks on old familiar faces, especially when he saw that the girls had drool running down their shapely and succulent chins.

*I'm back,* he told himself. *I can stay on top of the world, just as long as I can stay away from drugs.* The pride he walked with was perceptible to all that was out and about. The people that knew him for what he had become, stood frozen and shocked at his immaculate appearance.

"Yo, Mike. Is that really you, boy?" They were all unable to believe that this clean and handsome dude, who was dressed to the nines, was the same person that they were used to seeing scurrying through the night like some vermin. The people all had their eye brows raised to their hairline, and the look delighted Michael ego.

"Michael, is that you?"

"Yeah Belinda," he said with pride. "Of course it's me. Who do you think it is?"

"Err . . . You just look so different from when I saw you last week. That's all."

"Different?" Before Belinda could answer, Michael left her standing alone in front of her apartment building, dribbling down her voluptuous cleavage. He continued to meander further down the block, until he met up with his old friends Joel and Ivan.

"What up my brother," asked Ivan, a burly short young man who looked like an over-fed bulldog? Joel resembled Ivan, also short and burly, but he had long dreads to differentiate them from each other.

Both Ivan and Joel had their obligatory 40o/z in their hands; *nothing's changed,* thought Michael. *This has to be a good thing.*

Michael joined them showing the both of them his own 40o/z. Joel and Ivan smiled, and all three of them clinked their bottles together.

"Good to see ya, Majestic." Joel could not hide his glee in seeing his old friend looking clean, and drug free. "I told you that you can do it, Majestic."

"That you did Joel, that you did my friend. But remember, it's still early days," said a forlorn Michael. They gave each other hugs and high fives, and Michael noticed that both Joel and Ivan were looking him up and down, scrutinizing him, just as Belinda had done. He suddenly felt self-conscious, *is my fly open or something? Do I have booger dangling from my nose, the size of a serpent?*

"What's wrong with you two," he asked, now a bit agitated with their unwarranted examination?"

"What's wrong with you," asked a tooth-filled Ivan?

"Nothing's wrong with me, punk. Why ya looking at me like that for?" This sent Joel into fits of laughter, and this only piqued the curiosity of the rest of the gang, who were having their own street party across the street. Fano, Patrick, Leroy, and Alvin all came over to join the trio. *Something is wrong. Someone is missing,* thought Michael"

Damn Majestic," said the tall Guyanese Fano, "you look like you've scrubbed up?" Before Michael could say anything in response, he was cut off, "Do you have a date or something," asked Leroy, sniffing Michael up and down as if he were a blood hound.

"No, I don't have a date for your information, Lee. Ya gonna fix me up with your mama?" Everyone burst into laughter, except for Leroy of course.

"Michael, I'll fix you up with my mama, if you can stay like that for the rest of the day."

"Stay like what," asked an affronted Michael?"

"Stay looking clean, and looking like a damn human once again."

"Yeah Majestic," quickly added Joel, because he saw Michael's face change into something he didn't like, "It would be good to see if you could stay this way, not only for today, but also tomorrow, and longer."

"When's the last time you smoked that sh*t, Majestic?"

"Err . . . Yesterday, Leroy." This statement only made the whole block fall in the different levels of hysteria. "Yesterday," repeated Leroy to anyone that was in listening distance?"

"Ah come on Leroy," pleaded an exasperated Michael, "can't ya give a brother a damn break for once?"

"Ya looking good to me, kid!"

Before he could get angry and argue with Leroy, Michael turned to face Danique, "Thanks girl."

"It would be grand to have you back around here," said a proud Ivan. Michael's head was spinning from person to person, and he was getting dizzy watching their faces. Some were glad to see him doing well, others . . . *Well, ya can't please everybody.* He concentrated on the ones that he knew wanted the best for him, the ones that wanted their old friend back. There was no valid reason to argue with Leroy, his old friend was right. Michael decided to capitulate, "Well guys, I know it's not going to be easy, but I'm gonna try."

"Just stick to the beers, Majestic." Fano's words had Michael choking up, and he wanted to leave the block, before he started embarrassing himself. Ivan and Joel jumped all over him, because that was how all three of them rolled a couple of years ago. They used to be known as the "Treacherous Three" by everyone that knew and saw them, always together, inseparable until . . . Michael had gone missing. Instead of seeing the Bee-Gees around town, the citizens of Crown Heights now had to get used to "Hall and Oates."

When the 40o/z Busters had all found out that their main man, their "Nutty Professor," had become a victim to the omnipresent crack cocaine, they were crushed, but it had hit Ivan and Joel the hardest.

All up and down the block, the majority of the residents on Sterling Place were already taking bets, the majority against Michael making it out of this very day without drugs in his system. *Shame,* said Brainz.

The odds were now eight to one, that Michael would not make it through the night. *Was not this the same idiot that was already on one of the most notorious drug selling blocks in the entire country?*

"The boy's a complete and utter buffoon," said a toothless Becky to her drug supplier down the street.

Michael heard her nasty comment, and instantly drifted into himself again. Though there was still a large crowd of people around him, Ivan knew that Michael was no longer with them. "He's gone again, ya'll"

"Nothing has changed, but the date on the calendar," announced Joel.

During the day, the people of Sterling Place treated Michael as if he were the Prodigal Son who had just come home. Everyone come out of their apartments, and visited off other neighbouring blocks to celebrate Michael's return. *Or are they just using you to have a drink up,* asked a very sceptical Brainz.

Anyway, Michael was way past understanding what Brainz was telling him right now, because "You're drunk," squawked the dark and lovely Shanice. Though Shanice had also been drinking with the other girls on the block, she now felt very erotic and she wanted to be the new Michael's first.

*It must be a hard life living as a prostitute,* thought Michael, as his senses were awakened by Shanice's aroma of semen mixed with alcohol. Already, the rest of the girls on the block could see Michael's face changing, trying his best to reject

Shanice's advances, but not embarrass her in front of everyone. Her friend Petal saw what was happening, and ran over and tugged at Shanice's arm.

"Come on girl, leave the boy alone." Petal flashed her own lascivious smile in Michael's direction, as she attempted to lead Shanice away.

Michael thanked her, but this did not go down well between the other ladies watching the drama. They could all blatantly see what Michael could not, and that was that Shanice and Petal was all over him like a bad rash. Though it seemed that Petal was not succeeding in getting her friend Shanice away from Michael, the other girls watching knew that it was all a ploy. Shanice and Petal were basically playing, "Good whore, bad whore," on the naïve Michael was falling for their bullsh*t game to the annoyance of a fuming Danique. *Drunken idiot!*

"Let the boy breath Shanice," commanded the Apache complexioned Danique. Though she had her fist in a tight ball, ready to swing and unhinge Shanice's jaw, Danique really wanted to plunge a knife right into the slut's forehead. Both Michael and Shanice snapped their heads around at the intrusion.

An unbelieving Shanice let go of Michael's hand, and was immediately in a defensive stance. "Go f*ck ya self Danique, and mind ya damn business." Danique stepped closer to confront Shanice, but made sure that she kept a watchful eye on Petal, who was already sneaking over to her left side. It was going to be two against one, tag team style, and she had to be on point.

All Michael saw was that both girls had their claws flicked out, and was ready to rip each other's beautiful eyes out. *Why?*

*What the f*ck was happening?*

Though he did not know what was going on between the ladies, their screeching was just too much for him. "Both of you just stop it," he belched.

"F*ck that, Majestic. Let the show begin," cheered an already inebriated Patrick, "that's what I say." Someone in the crowd of 40o/z Busters punched Patrick in the arm.

"Well, well. If it isn't our new boy Michael stirring up trouble already." "But . . . Fano, I haven't done anything."

Fano looked at the truculent felines, "If ya'll know what's good for ya, you'd be leaving right now."

Reluctantly, the three ladies left Michael's presence, but waked down the street vigilance alert.

"Look what ya done di, Majestic."

A sobering Michael asked, "What, Fano?"

"Ya come around here looking all spiffy and dapper, and now these girls can't keep their hands off of ya."

Everybody was laughing, and Michael gladly joined in. "Thanks, Fano. I don't know what the f*ck is going on, but it's a good thing." Though Michael liked the compliment, he did not like the way Fano was circling him as if he were an exhibit to be studied.

After showing the Sterling Posse that the old lovable Michael they all loved was back, they drank, smoked weed, and chatted about the missing years. They told him stories of who had gone to prison, and was now dead. Some of the names they uttered shocked Michael, especially when they told him that their little cousin "Tony" was dead, murdered by some crack addict.

This terrible news brought tears to Michael's eyes, and it wasn't because he was drunk. The 40o/z' Busters slinked away, unbeknoweth to Michael, who had drifted on them, again. They were used to him, and let him be, so the news of Tony's death could sink in. They all knew that "Little Tony" and Michael were close, like butter on toast, and he needed to have his time to grieve.

Tony was one of his one of his best friends, and Michael knew that the ladies loved Tony, because of his renowned massive c*ck. Though Tony was only five-five in height, his languid c*ck almost reached his knee caps. The girls called him "Donkey" or the "Three legged man," and the memories of Tony put a smile on Michael's face as he sat on the wall by himself. Tony was the only one of the 40o/z Busters that actually had a job, a legal one, opposed to just selling drugs. *Damn!* The tears were flowing freely, now.

Tony had gotten up every morning, like the majority of the world that existed outside Sterling Place, and went to work. By doing his nine to five, Tony showed the rest of his cousins and peers, on this drug infested block, that they did not have to sell drugs for the rest of their lives.

*Tony's dead!?* It was a hard pill to swallow, and Michael tasted to salt of his tears.

"We've missed you Majestic," said a tearful Leroy, now crying because Michael was crying over his older brother. "I miss my brother also, Majestic." They fell into each other's arms, and cried like two little girls who had just run out of credits on their cell phones.

Seeing Michael's return brought back a lot of memories for on the block. He was a reminder of better days, better times, for all of them. The world has grown darker since he had disappeared. It was as if Michael had returned from prison, and the memories of the past two years came flooding back to all of them. There were a lot of people missing on Sterling Place noticed Michel, very good people.

Joel and Ivan decided to join Michael and Leroy, and the circle of big crying men was getting rather pathetic. "Okay guys," said a struggling Fano. "Stop ya bullsh*tting, and let's celebrate."

After having a swell day with his peeps of drinking, playing street football, and getting chatted up by the young Phillies on the block, Michael commenced with his goodbyes.

"Going so soon, Michael?"

"Yeah Zaphire," said a smiling Michael. "I'll see ya tomorrow, God willing." This brought a very big salacious smile to Zaphire's already pretty face.

"Why, don't you trust yourself around me, Michael?"

"All I know right now Zaphire is that I need to get out of here. Please don't take it personal."

"I hear ya," commented the omnipresent Belinda. "It must be hard for you staying around here Michael, but *I do* understand."

Both Michael and Zaphire looked at Belinda quizzically. "Err . . . Thanks Belinda," was all Michael said, and Zaphire didn't like the lascivious smile he was wearing.

"Excuse me, Belinda. Michael and I were talking."

"Oh, I'm so . . . sorry, Zaphire." Zaphire did not like the smirk that Belinda and Michael were both wearing right now.

"F*ck ya'll!" With that said, Zaphire was gone like the wind.

"Bye, Michael." He looked into Belinda's pretty brown eyes. Though she was old enough to be his mother, she was still a very pretty and elegant elder lady.

"Good night Belinda," was all he could say.

"Will you be back soon," she asked seductively, "Michael?"

"Err . . . Well, hopefully tomorrow, Belinda."

"It could be just like old times, Michael." Michael gulped audibly, and had to loosen the collar of his brand new white and green leather New York Jets jacket so the steam inside could be released.

After being re-united with his old friends, and having one of the best days of his life, in a very long time, Michael decided that the wanted it to end on a good note. He managed to reluctantly leave Sterling, and made it to the corner of Utica Avenue. As he turned the corner, the relief could be felt perceptively.

He had to start his life all over again, and build back the bridges he had burnt, torn down. *Damn, this is hard work!*

*Who said life was going to be easy?* Once again Michael ignored Brainz, and thought of more positive things. He thought that "Today was a good day," and then he thought of the rapper "Ice Cube."

*It has been a very good day indeed!*

*Well good buddy, guess what?*

Michael really did not want to get into any negative dialogue with Brainz, but he had to ask, *what?*

*The night is not over yet,* teased Brainz, *and you still have a million dollars, and time to spend on a grand crack session.*

*I thought you were supposed to be helping me . . . . ?* Michael wanted to scream, but he knew that this was the inevitable hard part of the day. *Think man, think. You can't fail now,* said a helpful Brainz, who was now confusing the sh*t out of Michael, *because you're practically at the finishing line.*

# MICHAEL — A BRAND NEW WORLD

Michael's dreams merged smoothly into the inevitable nightmare. All the bad thoughts started to slither their way into his fragile mind. He tried his best to will the macabre thoughts to leave him alone, but instead they had him twisting and turning in his single bed as if he were on a rotisserie. The torment had him in pain, both mentally as well as physically. Tangled in his sheet and blanket, Michael had banged his delicate head and elbows on the bedrooms wall on several occasions. It was only when he saved himself from falling between the bed and the wall that he saw the bulge of his hidden money he had, still hidden. *I don't want to spend the money,* he screamed and pleaded! *I don't want any crack . . .*

The fight between him and himself was not a pretty picture; it was arduous and tiring, but familiar to those who were fighting an addiction, any addition. *I'll get some tomorrow, I promise, if you just leave me alone tonight!*

"No, no, no. Leave me alone!"

When Michael snapped out of his nightmare, he found that he had been sleeping in a river of pungent sweat, and his bedroom looked as if it had been nuked. *Ma's gonna kill me for this.*

As she heard the shower running, Mrs Patkinson knocked and shouted through the bathroom door, "Michael, you in there?" There wasn't any reply. Mrs Patkinson almost ran down the diaphanous corridor with her aging bones to Michael's bedroom, and smiled instantly when she saw that his bed has been slept in. *He actually came home last night,* she thought amazingly. The wide smile was glued to her face when she leisurely walked back to her own bedroom, "Ken. You won't believe it."

Mr Patkinson grunted, rolled over, and put the goose down pillow over his head. "Ken. Guess who came home last night, and the television set is still in the living room."

Mr Patkinson jerked up quickly, the pillow almost hitting his wife in her face. "Michael?"

"Yes, *our son.*"

"Be careful Mavis," warned her husband of twenty five years, "don't get your hopes up too high woman, because we've been down this road before."

"It means that at least he's trying, again Ken."

"Yeah, or he's ran out of money, again Mavis."

"Why do you have to be so damn negative, anyway?" There was silence between them as they both listened to the running shower. "Anyway Ken, he would have sold his radio again, or the television set if he had run out of money."

They shushed each other as they heard the door to the bathroom open in the corridor. "I'm going to see what's going on, Ken." Her husband just shook his head in resignation, wishing that his wife would leave it alone, and pulled the covers over it.

As per-usual, Mrs Patkinson ignored her husband and ran out to see if it was really her son in the house. "Morning Michael," she said to her half naked son, who only had a towel wrapped around his waist.

"Hi ya, ma," said a now placid Michael, refreshed and knowing that he had made it through the night without the drugs. "Good morning, daddy," he then shouted in his parents direction.

"Hi son," replied the surprised voice of his father.

"Everything okay," asked his mother, still watching him walking toward his bedroom?

"Yeah ma, I'm fine." Mrs Patkinson was so glad to see her son, *her son and not the other person,* that she offered him breakfast. "Yes please, ma."

His dad was up, already getting dressed. They haven't seen Michael eat breakfast in *this* house for the past two years. His parents looked at each other, "He's getting his appetite back," squealed his pleased as punch mother. "Hallelujah!"

Once they were all at the kitchen table, which Michael has not eaten at in years, his parents only watched as *their* son studiously devoured a very large breakfast. They weren't even touching their own, which already had ice globules forming around the edges of each morsel. Michael hadn't noticed their angelic faces beaming at him, because his nose was so deep into his plate of food, that it had egg yolk on its tip.

His parents have never seen him eat so ravenously, but they both acknowledged that this was a very good sign.

Drug addicts did not find time to eat, and it was not one of their priorities. Michael's mother knew that *her* son had been drinking though, because of the stench of alcohol in the sweaty white sheets of his bed. While Michael was eating his home cooked breakfast, Mrs Patkinson had decided to grab the soiled sheets off his bed, and throw into the washing machine. The stench of alcohol almost knocked her backwards when she had entered his bedroom, but still . . . It was a step in the right direction. *My son the Alcoholic! God help me!*

Now they both watched as Michael finally came up for breath, still masticating a bulging mouthful of food. *What a savage,* thought is father with a wry smile. *The boy takes after me. A*s soon at the thought came to Mr Patkinson, he could feel his wife glaring at him. *You taught him how to eat like this, Ken. No etiquette at all!*

After cleaning his plate clean with the remainder of his toast, Michael looked into both his parents' eyes, "Did you guys give me any money the other day?"

"Did we what? Give you money," his father almost spat his coffee across the room? "You owe us money, boy."

"Ken please, calm down dear. Remember your poor heart."

"Damn dad, it was only a question."

"Michael," asked his placid mother, "why the hell would we do something as give you any money?"

"Because you're my loving and caring parents, that's why."

"I told you the boy was still on drugs," said his now belligerent father.

"Ken. Now dear, you're being very silly. Isn't he Michael?"

His mother was giving him such a stare, that it made Michael want to leave the house, immediately. At least the crack heads in Castle Grey Skull didn't judge him, berate him, or belittle him. At least the guys at Castle Grey Skull all had something in common. *Patrice, Debbie, Randy, Susan, and the rest of the gang must be wondering where the hell I am, or what has happened to me.*

"Thanks for the breakfast guys, I've gotta go."

"Go where, Michael," asked his mother, shocked at the abrupt change in Michael's attitude?

As per-usual she got the same answer she's been getting for many years, "Outside."

His head was still banging as he made his way back to his bedroom, which he still couldn't remember entering last night. He does not recall making his way home, and he surely did not remember crawling into his lovely warm bed, but all in all, this was all looking like a very good thing.

*One day at a time,* he kept repeating to himself!

The children were running around gaily, with not a care in the world, some playing tag, and others hiding seek. Donna watched them play with such happiness as she prepared their lunches. Today she had volunteered to drive a mini-bus filled with the noisy and boisterous boys and girls, and had regretted it at first, but now they were behaving like the lovely they really were. They were enjoying themselves away from the camp that they lived and learned, and this pleased her.

Lincoln Terrace seemed like the ideal place to bring them, after enjoying herself here the day before. Donna knew that she had an ulterior motive, and hoped that he showed up.

She was serving up each dish when one of her pupils interrupted her. "Miss Moore," asked Trudy, running up to her? Before Trudy finished the question, her big eyes were on riveted on all the dishes that Donna was preparing.

"What is it, Trudy?" Donna had no time for this, and was working to a schedule.

"Is lunch ready yet, I'm starving?"

Donna knew that this was not what Trudy had run over to ask, but she let it go. "Almost Trudy," answered Donna, looking into Trudy's bright face. Trudy was one of her favourite ten year olds. "Go and tell everyone to get ready, and remember to tell them that they must wash their hands, or else . . ." Trudy ran off toward her companions with a spring in her step.

*I thought that she was weak with starvation.* Donna quickly finished getting the kids lunches ready, and organized the paper plates around the picnic table. After checking all their sparkling little hands and fingers, Donna allowed them to take their seats around the three picnic tables, and they all said the "Lord's Prayer" together.

Afterward taking a few bites of her own meal, she walked around each table to make sure that everyone was behaving themselves, because she knew them that well. Everything appeared to be going well, but she knew better. She went back to her seat, so that she could finish her own meal, before they inconspicuously slipped some acidic into her Kool-Aid.

It did not take too long before the inevitable bedlam started.

"Miss Moore," called out an infuriated Trevor, with his hand raised on picnic table number three.

"Yes Trevor," said a phlegmatic Donna who reluctantly got up again and made her way to table number three. "What is it now, Trevor?" Trevor always had a complaint, and loved tattling on his peers, which made them all hate him. So it did not surprise her in the least that he was the first one of her pupils to break the peace.

"Barry has stolen my fruits, and he's hidden my "Twinkies."

All Barry saw on his teachers face was a look that always had him wetting his pants. Now he was trying his best to control his small intestine. "Barry," bellowed Donna, because she was in no mood to play around this morning, and wanted all the children to know this, especially with the notorious Barry. Barry put all of Trevor's goodies back where they belonged, on the picnic table, without any further castigation.

"I'm gonna get ya, ya little snitch," whispered Barry. This had Trevor trembling, and wished that he had kept his mouth closed in the first place.

"Barry, get over here now," commanded a now angry Donna. Barry got up from his wooden seat, and excused himself from the others.

*Good boy,* thought Donna. *Teaching them is not all a waste of time.* They walked over to the duck pond, where Barry stood, shivering in front of Miss Moore. He was afraid because he knew that this lovely and caring lady could change like the British weather. Though she was an Angel, there was a wrath behind those eyes that he did not want unleashed. He had his head bowed, eyes looking deep into the graminoids, hoping that he could see a crawling worm or a snail.

"Look at me, Barry." Reluctantly he picked up his head, and looked into her fiery brown eyes. The piercing stare that he received had him losing the war with his small intestines. He started to pee on himself, and now the tears were also flowing. *Everyone must be staring at me,* he told himself, but he could not stop the shaking, peeing, and tears. Now he wished that he hadn't played around with punk ass Trevor's food, because this mortification was not worth it.

"Why are you stealing Trevor's food, Barry? Don't you have enough of your own?"

All he could utter, incoherently was, "Yes ma'am. I was only playing around."

"You do not play around with people's food, Barry."

"Yes, ma'am."

"Would you want someone to take your food away from you?"

Now the tears were brimming over his eyes, "No ma'am."

"Well go back and finish your food, and don't even look at anyone else's plate."

"Yes, ma'am." As he took his seat next to Trevor again, Barry gave him a look that could have got him hung in some parts of *this* planet.

Good morning, pretty lady." Donna almost spat out her own sandwich at the sound of his deep and now familiar voice. She quickly looked up at the tall and immaculate boy, and the smile that grew on her pretty face was obvious to all. Donna then looked at her young charges, hoping that they hadn't noticed the change in her attitude. Michael, as yesterday, was standing in the middle of all three picnic tables, with his omnipresent 40o/z. Everyone was so consumed with their food and hungry stomachs that not even the children noticed Michael's stealth approach.

*Amazing,* thought Donna.

"Is this where you work," he asked giggling like one of her devious little pupils?

Before she could answer Michael, the kids jumped in quickly, "Is that man your boyfriend, Miss Moore?"

"No, he is not my boyfriend," said Donna succinctly. The giggling ran throughout the class, because they could all see that she was fibbing to them. The angelic smile on her face told them different. Michael had his bottom lip out, feigning sadness at her instant declaration.

*Pouting is not going to get you anywhere brother,* thought Donna, *and stop being a damn drama queen.*

The children now had something new to play with instead of their food, so they all pushed their lunches into the center of the picnic tables, and ran over to play with their new toy, Michael. The children circled him as if they were Apache Warriors, and Michael was hoping that they didn't scalp his fat ass.

It was Trudy, *the traitor* thought Donna, that started the verbal attack on her. "You hurt his feelings Miss Moore."

"I . . . I . . ." stuttered Donna, "did not mean to do that, Trudy." Donna was angry at herself, because she did not know why she had to answer to Trudy. Now she could see the glum faces on all the children, all of them now silent and pouting just like Michael's grown ass, and all telling her mentally to apologize to him. *Now would be a good time, Miss Moore! Unbelievable,* fumed Donna.

"He seems nice, Miss Moore," said the little punk, Trevor." It was obvious that she was in the wrong to the children, and that Michael had not done anything to deserve her frosty treatment.

"I really cannot believe what is happening around here." She gave Michael *"The Look,"* but it did not work on him like it did on the kids.

Now Donna had to put up with a tearful Rebecca, who was now holding Michael's hand to comfort him. Rebecca's peers were all sniffling and sobbing theatrically. When Donna looked into the center of the ring, she saw a very smug looking Michael, trying his very best to stifle a laugh. *Now see what you've gone and done,* Donna told him with her fiery eyes.

It was obvious that Michael understood what he had done, the smug b*stard was revelling in it. Donna could not take the stares and the children's silent treatment anymore, so she capitulated. "Okay, okay," she said begrudgingly, "I'm sorry Michael. I apologize for the way I treated you." The children looked up into the big boy's face, to see if Miss Moore's words had appeased him.

To their delight the big boy started to smile, "I accept your heartfelt apology, Ms . . . Moore."

"It's Miss, thank you very much." Though she knew that he was playing around, with her and the children, she let him know with her eyes that she was going to get him back. Revenge was not only inevitable, but impending.

"I was only playing around, Donna." As he started to walk off, Donna excused herself from the children, and followed him.

"Michael," she called after him, and he instantly spun around, thank God. Donna and the children were also glad that his bluff had worked on her. Donna really did not know what to say to him, once she had caught up. It's me that should be apologizing," she uttered. "Thanks for passing by."

"I always come here, as I told you before, Donna."

"So why are you leaving so soon?"

"Err . . . .?"

"Okay, Michael. I said I was sorry. Okay?"

"Anyway, Dee, I can see that you're occupied, and I don't want to intervene while you're working." Donna felt a shiver go through her body. She was beginning to more than like this young man, whom she only met yesterday. *What's wrong with me, God?* "Did you get any chance to pick any flowers today?"

"No Michael." It felt swell to call him by his name, as if they have known each other for . . . Eternity. "The flowers you saw me picking yesterday were for the school." She looked turned her head to keep an eye on the children. "I like to freshen up the place I work, because it's new and quite dull at the moment.

There was a very long hesitation before Michael asked, "Can I take you out for dinner later, Dee?" The hesitation had him in fear. "I mean after you've finished work," he bravely continued."

"Err . . ." Donna did not know why she was hesitating.

"We can go out for a bite to eat, unwind a little."

"Yeah, okay Michael." Donna knew that she was scared; it's been a very long time since she's been out with a guy. Well . . . It seemed like forever. Scared off by tales of horror from her friends, most of whom either already had babies or were presently pregnant, she had decided in her young life not to be like them. Now she was like the only virgin on the planet, and she felt as if she had made the wrong decision.

"Ya think long, ya think wrong," said a beer swilling Michael.

"Where? Where will we meet, Michael," asked a stuttering Donna, wanting to kick herself for not handling this epic situation as cool as she thought she should be doing? "And what time?"

"Do you know where Sterling Place is? It's just two blocks from here."

"Yeah, Michael. I know where Sterling Place is," she lied. *I'll find it, no matter what,* she told herself. "Yeah I know it, but between where?"

"Err . . . Meet me on Sterling Place between Utica, and Rochester Avenue." And as if getting a little nudge from Brainz, "At around six o'clock." With that said, Michael did an about face, and Donna watched him walk up the hill of Lincoln Terrace Park, tripping over every blade of grass and pebble in his nervousness. She was able to laugh now; *At least I'm not alone.*

When she turned around, she found that half her class were standing right behind here, with smiles on their angelic faces. The other unromantic half, were missing. As she glances around, Donna could see them running around the park, but at least they were still in the vicinity. "Can you please go get the others, Trudy? It's time to leave."

Donna now faced with a bunch of smiling and giggling pubescent class, as they all gathered around her. As she looked into each face, Donna realized that she did not like the looks on their mischievous countenances. Not one bit.

"Pick up your cloths," was all she could say to the smug faces in front of her. As the children all made their way back onto the school mini-bus that Donna drove, she was thinking about Michael, and what a beautiful morning this has turned out to be. *Thank you, Jesus.*

Michael headed straight to Sterling Place, with a lavish smile engraved on his face. The beautiful creature he had met had actually accepted his invitation for a date. A date. With him! *Some amazing sh\*t is happening around here,* thought Michael.

He tried to click his heels together as he walked, bounced up the street, but failed, and almost fell on his face. *Shame,* said Brainz.

*I haven't been out with a girl in a millennium.* Michael cringed at the thought, and he found that it was not only his palms that were sweating profusely, but the volcanic heat was emanating from his every pore.

*What should I do?*

*Where should I take her?*

*How should I act?*

A superfluous amount of questions were flying through his docile brain, and it was overwhelming. Brainz replied by telling him to, *just be himself.* Michael ignored Brainz, because it very rarely helped in important decision making. Instead, Michael chose to torment himself with wondering what he should say and do, when he and Donna met later.

*This is a special occasion,* he told himself, *and I don't even know what to wear? I haven't been myself for the past two years,* he told Brainz. *I forgot who the real Michael is!*

Brainz reminded him that he had a very disastrous excursion into hell, and he was to take it slow, and play it by ear.

*Thanks!*

Positive things have been happening to him, since his last hit of crack, and he really did not want all this period of serendipity to end. Ever! *Don't change anything, Majestic,* screamed Brainz. *If it's not broke, then leave it the f\*ck alone!*

*What's going on? Really?*

Lincoln Terrace was where he had met Jay. Then he had met Donna, in the same damn spot. He's been coming here for over a decade, and he has never seen these people before? He even came out of there with over three thousand dollars to his name. *Did it all really come down to serendipity, or was there some mystical, magical thing going on?*

*Was he going through a beautiful Purple Patch in his life?*

*Has his luck had finally changed for the better?*

All Michael knew was that he did not have a clue what was happening, and it was confusing him. He didn't even know if he should be afraid, or not. At the end of the day, whatever what was happening, or whatever it was called, he knew it was a very good thing.

*At least I have money to buy her a meal,* thought a smiling Michael. *If I can keep away from drugs, I'll be on my way back to the living. The thought of drugs made Michael shout out,* "Sh*t, I don't even want any right now."

The fear of failing, and falling off the wagon now had him shaking, perceptively. "It's all up to me," he told himself, over and over again. "It's up to me. It's up to me!!!"

As he made his salient way to Sterling Place, the citizens that were out on this brisk morning started crossing the street, afraid of the maniacal young man approaching.

Jay was on his mind as he turned the corner of Sterling Place. He liked his new friend Jay. There was something about the man that he just couldn't resist. Even though the man wore funny clothes, and spoke as if he were from another world, Jay dropped a lot of pearls of wisdom on his tender brain.

Since Michael had arrived from England, he found that he had always hung out with the older heads in the Brooklyn area. He was a sponge for all their experience and knowledge, and they in turn like the young naïve boy that listened to their every word. He liked the precious jewels of knowledge that they all had given him, and he knew that if he wanted to survive *this* new world that his parents dragged him to, he had to listen. "You can lead a horse to water, boy, but ya can't make him swim!"

He did listen to them, except for that one time, and he had paid dearly for it. "Boy, don't ya go around f*cking with that bullsh*t crack!"

*Of course I won't.*

*I'm so damn silly!* It amazed him that you can do everything in your life correctly, but if you made a mistake, just one, that was what you'll be remembered for.

Jay had shared his sagacious insight about people with him, as he had shared what knowledge and opinions he had with his new friend.

*Each one, teach one,* added Brainz.

Knowing who you are Michael, and who your true friends are, is very important in this life. And I am not talking about associates. I'm talking about people that will be there for you, when times are hard, and the hurricane comes."

"Well Jay," replied a down hearted Michael, "I don't need an Abacus to count them, because that will be a big fat zero."

"You have more people in *your* corner Michael, than you think. You are just looking in the wrong direction my brother."

"Err . . ."

"Having a purpose to *your* life is a good thing also, Michael. When I say purpose, I do not mean having a job, because you can have a job and still be unfulfilled. Your purpose is not defined by what others think about you Michael, your purpose is having a clear sense of what God has called you to be."

"Err . . . And what would that be Jay, because I sure don't know!"

"Maybe, you are doing what our father wants you to do already, Michael."

"Err . . . Jay, what are you talking about?"

"I have noticed that people love to be around you Michael. You make them feel welcome and comfortable, like me."

They shared a nervous smile, but Jay had continued. "You make them smile, and you do not belittle anyone. It seems that you always try your best to encourage them, instead of being one of the jealous types that put them down to make yourself look bigger."

"You've noticed all that already, Jay?"

"I'm a very observant person." Jay smiled, and that meant Michael had to wear one also. "When God gives you favour Michael, you can tell *your haters,* 'Don't look at me. Look at who is in charge of me."

"Jay, please . . ."

"Do you not believe in God, Michael?"

"I do. You know I do, Jay."

"Then what is the problem, Michael?"

"I told you before, Jay. We're outnumbered by these non-believers, who have no concept of God, Jesus, or morals. These heathens will conspire to kill you, because they've labelled you as different, down to skin colour and clothes that you wear."

"I know this already, Michael." Now it was Jay's turn to look forlorn.

"You okay, Jay?"

It was as if Michael had brought Jay back to sweet reality. "I am fine, Michael. I do understand, and I want you to understand that it is not about telling people what to believe in, but showing them how to love one another, showing them how to live. Maybe it is up to you and me to instil some morals into our uncouth brothers and sisters?"

Michael saw the serious look on Jay's face, "Err . . . Stop playing, Jay." Anyway, now it was he that now thought that he could and should help Jay, because Michael thought that Jay really needed to get wise to this new environment of *his,* immediately.

It has been a very long time since Michael has had fun, especially with his old friends on Sterling Place. He spent the day with them drinking copious amounts of 40o/z, and playing around with the young Phillies. After getting a superfluous amount of phone numbers from the girls, he went with the guys to play some basketball around the corner, at the #210 junior high school.

As the moon was exchanging places with the sun, he found himself playing dice with the guys, against the wall of Ivan's apartment building.

"Head Crack," yelled Michael, "It must be beginners luck," he told the aggrieved sore losers.

"I've gotta make a move ya'll," slurred Michael. He realized that he had over indulged, and needed to get off the block, before the inevitable happened. He was learning, finally. Michael saw the signs. He was intoxicated, and he had money, a very bad combination for a drug addict. That familiar feeling was seeping its way in, "The calling," and he just did not want to fail tonight. *Oh God please help me . . .* He did not want to see the pity in his friend's eyes, or the smug look of the people that had betted that he was going to fail.

*One day at a time,* he kept repeating to himself, as he collected his winnings off the ground, and attempted to say his good-byes. God helps you, if you at least try. This Michael also knew for a fact, but he had to try. Trying is not asking God for his help and then head straight to the nearest drug dealer. The more he thought and tried to resist, was the more he wanted to go into one of the apartment buildings, and buy himself a kilo.

He used to pride himself on knowing when to stop drinking and doing drugs, it was only that he started in the first place was the problem. He saw that a lot of his associates wanted more and more, even after they were paralytic with drink or drugs.

One thing he was not, and that was a gambler. Now that he has already won over two hundred dollars from the snarling fellas around him, *Money gets money,* added Brainz, Michael knew that it was not going to be easy to leave the game just like that. Not without any drama.

"Yo, you crack head," said a burly, but eloquently dressed drug dealer. "You can't just quit like that. You have to give me a chance to win my money back." Michael did not know what to say, he just stood there, trying his best not to show any fear.

"He can quit the game," intervened Ivan, "whenever he feels like quitting."

"Mind ya f*cking business, you drunken f*ck." Everyone that was playing the dice game of "Ceelo" instantly grabbed their money off the ground, and made room for the inevitable nightly shoot out on a Brooklyn Block.

"F*ck you, Rock Man," said the evenly burly Ivan, though shorter than the Rock Man by a foot, Ivan's burliness was from lifting just 40o/z's of beer.

Ivan was now in the Rock Man's face, looking up. "Ya can't come around here, and start telling *my* peeps what the f*ck to do. If ya can't stand losing Rock Man, then don't play."

The Rock Man was not backing down, and kept his snarling face on Ivan's. "He's a crack head Ivan," he seethed. "Is that who you roll with now a days, low life f*cks like him?"

Before they could both reach for their guns, a resonant voice stopped them in their tracks. "Michael, I need you to come with me. Now." Michael was now shaking like a lap dancer. *What the hell was Jay doing around here?*

Everyone else was speechless, and all had their drawn hand guns hanging precariously from their limp fingers, including the women.

*Who the f*ck is this weirdo, wearing a white table cloth?* The Rock Man took his attention off Ivan prudently, and now the both of them were scrutinizing Jay, wondering if he had a pistol underneath his . . . *White dress.* "Who the f*ck are you white boy," asked the even more irate Rock Man?

"I am your brother Rock Man" said a placid Jay. "And if you do not change your ways, I will not be able to help you."

"Help me, mother f*cker?" The Rock Man looked around at the other citizens on Sterling Place, as if it was they that had put this stranger up to this. It had to be some type of joke, because everyone was giggling and laughing.

"Yes Rock Man, you need to change your ways."

"Who the f*ck are you," asked the Rock Man, now finding the strength to pick his gun up, and point it at Jay?"

"I just told you, Rock Man". You have ears, but cannot hear." At this everyone started running around the parked car, dying with hysteria, except for Michael. Michael immediately grabbed Jay's arm, and tried to get him the hell out of there.

"Where ya going, Majestic," slurred Ivan?

"Home, Ivan."

"You two aren't going any mother f*cking way," screamed the Rock Man". He had his Uzi pointed at both Jay and Michael, now.

"Chill," said the young Killer, looking around nervously. He did not like being out side of the Brevouy projects, where everyone knew and respected him. The Rock Man followed his young body guard's eyes, only to see that there were more guns pointed at them than there were people. "I think we should call it a day, Rock Man"."

Begrudgingly the Rock Man capitulated, put his Uzi away, and walked away with a face of an angry gargoyle. No one moved, or put their guns away; until they saw the Rock Man and Killer drive off in Rock Man's black on black Grand Cherokee.

"Come on Jay," said Michael pulling Jay by his arm. Michael was angry at Jay, and scared for him also. The man did not belong in this hell hole, and Michael knew that he was only here because of him. "What is wrong with you, Jay?"

"What do you mean, Michael?"

"Jay, this block is not where you want to be."

"So why are you here?"

A speechless Michael could only look at Jay's innocent face. "I have friends here."

"You almost died tonight, Michael." Jay could feel Michael's hand on his arm, trembling.

"Well . . ." Was all that came out of his mouth. "You almost died to, Jay."

"I want you alive Michael."

"I want you alive to, Jay, and that's why I don't want to see you on this block again."

"Why, Michael?"

"Because they have guns, sell drugs, and are willing to kill to keep their riches by any means necessary."

"I was not here to rob or ask them for anything, Michael."

"I know Jay, but they don't."

"Are you still on drugs, Michael?"

"What," asked a shocked Michael? *How the f*ck does Jay know that I was doing drugs?*

"Well . . ."

"No," was Michael's succinct answer. "Then for some inexplicable reason he decided to tell Jay, "Well I used to, but I'm trying to stop."

"Well you going on a block that sells the thing that you're trying to avoid is not a smart move Michael. It is like an alcoholic owning a bar."

The snot shot out of Michael nose, and Jay could only watch, because he did not know what was so funny. They walked until they reached Eastern Parkway, "Well Jay, I was only there to say "Hi" to my old friends."

"You look good, but drunk, Michael."

Michael really did not know what to say to this, so he mumbled something like, "Thanks."

"Don't go back and do the same things Michael, and then expect a different outcome."

"What's that supposed to mean, Jay?" Michael was confused.

"Stop looking with your eyes, Michael."

"What the . . . Jay, are you speaking that gibberish again?"

"Hopefully Michael, you will see the light."

With no idea what Jay was talking about, Michael just said, "Sir. Yes, Sir." He even threw in a salute.

# PATRICE — MEGALOMANIAC

"Thank you," said the tall slim man to the cashier. He then turned to walk out of the bank as he folded the dense wad of money he had just withdrawn. Patrice watched the slim man vigilantly as he put the wad of money into a brown envelope and then into the inside pocket of his dapper Dannimac overcoat. *Foolish mortal,* thought Patrice.

It was the reason that Patrice had ended up at the local Citibank on this chilly morning. His goal on waking up, with the bounty of money, food stamp, and jewellery surrounding him on his battered and overused bed, was to make and get easy money. It was too easy at the Gonzalez's bodega, and it was too little. He wanted more, because the peanuts he had made off the old people, just was not enough. *Damn I've been a fool,* he castigated himself. *If I knew that owning a gun would make money making so easy, I should have invested in one a long time ago.*

He caressed the new love of his life, the Beretta 9mm Pistol, as he watched the slim man head for the exit of the Citibank.

He has heard repeatedly that if you wanted to make some real money, you didn't go around robbing old men and ladies, because the real money was at banks and printing presses.

Though he was not actually robbing a bank, which was his original intention, he decided to go for the impromptu "B-Plan." Though he knew that the money the tall slim man had in the brown envelope was not going to be in the six digit category, Patrice knew that robbing him would be much safer than going through with his original plan. *The bank could wait, for another day.*

Patrice gave the slim man a five second head start, and it was a good thing he had, because Mr Basketball player was doing his best to be alert as he headed for the parking lot outside. As soon as the slim man started to cross the street, Patrice made his move. Staying far away as possible, without letting the impending "Vic" see him, Patrice saw the slim man heading for a brand new white Chevrolet

Captiva. He waited until the man was reaching for his car keys, before he snuck up on him. "Scuse me fella, do you have a light?"

The tall slim man turned around casually, no fear apparent on his face. "I don't smoke mister, and neither should you. The slim man was smiling at him, condescendingly. "It's a bad habit."

Ignoring the slim man's sensible advice, Patrice asked, "Well do you have the time, then?"

The slim man looked the stranger up and down. "What's up with you, young man? No, I don't have the damn time." Patrice could see that the man was now getting agitated with the young bum standing in front of him, but still . . . There was no fear emanating from him.

"Well can I have the money in the brown envelope then?"

The slim man now knew that this was going to be a robbery, in broad daylight, and couldn't believe it. He still had *that* smile on his face though, when he went for the gun under his left armpit. This of course was not before Patrice put a lovely big bullet in his stomach. They both stood there and watched in surprise as the slim man's intestines sluggishly slid out of the open hole in his stomach and onto the sordid ground of the parking lot.

The slim man fell against his brand new white Captiva, turning the driver's door crimson. "Now can I have the money," asked a stoic Patrice? The tall man managed an angry growl. "Is that a yes?"

Patrice stood over the slumped figure on the ground, and picked up the man's gun. "Nice piece," he said laconically.

"Help me," begged the tall slim man.

"What. I can't hear you?"

"Help me, please. You can have the money."

"I know I can," said a maleficent sounding Patrice, who was already going inside the man's Dannimac overcoat to retrieve the brown envelope. "Betcha wished ya smoked cigarettes now, don't ya, b*tch?" With that said, Patrice did an about face, and walked leisurely out of the parking lot, leaving the man pleading for someone the help him, while trying to push his leaking intestines back into the hole made by the Beretta 9mm Pistol. *Damn,* thought the slim man, *where the f*ck is everybody. Where's the f*cking police, when you need them?*

Patrice was back at his shack, drinking 40o/z of "Colt 45, and pleasantly watching the 10:00PM news on NBC. He had the "Cheshire Cat" grin on his mug, because he had already counted the stack of money he had gotten off of the slim man, and added it with the rest of his ill-gotten gains. His found that his d*ck was harder than a three inch thick diamond plate.

The pretty NBC news reporter "Salacious Susan" was telling her public how a man had jumped out of nowhere, *Jumped,* thought Patrice, and slapped one of the security guards on his head with his hand gun. "Hell no," shouted Patrice at the television, amazed that Salacious Susan was embellishing the story, yeasting sh*t up. *B*tches can never tell the truth, even with a mouth full of deposited babies.*

Patrice listened intently as Salacious Susan went on to tell her riveted audience the part that actually happened. "The perpetrator then shot the security courier heartlessly in the stomach, and sped off with the money and the security courier's gun." She continued to say that the thief got away with over $50,000.00 and receipts, which the security courier had been collecting from various banks in the area."

Patrice had counted every dollar with alacrity as he listened to Salacious Susan, just to make sure that the b*tch wasn't lying again. To his delight and erection, she wasn't.

# JAY — CREATION

After a disturbed night of sleep, Jay reluctantly got out of his bed of hay, and stretched his arms to the roof of the stable. In doing so, he could hear all his bones popping and crackling inside him like Rice Krispy's.

*What kind of hay is that,* he asked himself as he looked at the offending bale? *I might as well have slept on the ground.*

After stretching the cold chill out of his bones, Jay looked around, as if he had forgotten where he was, and then decided to go outside to face his new world.

After looking at what lay before him, Jay shook his head in resignation, and took a deep breath. He was already feeling tired, before he even got started. He decided that his first task of this beautiful morning should be fixing up this place. "Good morning father," he said to the nebulous sky.

The Farm house, and all its appendages on the land, looked totally unfixable to the naked eye, but this did not faze Jay, who did not even thing about it. There were many things that needed to be fixed, he could already see, and he hasn't even taken his first step out of the stable yet. There were a plethora of holes in the roofs of the farm house, garage, stable, the abattoirs and pens. The orchard and vineyard could use some help, also. The shattered windows out-numbered the unbroken ones. Even the doors of each building in his view, were swinging off their diaphanous hinges. But still . . . The land for the farm was vast, and Jay knew that he could do some very good work with it.

Jay assumed that he was looking at twenty five square miles, around 6474.970275 hectares of land. "Oh, well."

Mingling in the midst of the brisk air was the acrid stench of petrified animal dung, and their desecrated hosts. The combination of all the smells was making him nauseous and dizzy. *The predators and leeches must have had a feast,* thought Jay has he pinched his nostrils.

He decided to take a long walk around *his* new home, and see what really had to be done, if he was going to have this farm up and running. As he walked the lands circumference, his thoughts drifted to Michael. From what he has seen so far, his new friend Michael seemed to be right. *The situation down here seemed quite bleak.* As soon as he thought these words, Jay could hear his father saying, "I . . . told you so!"

Jay finally made his way back to the dilapidated six bedroom house, and it disgusted him once he went inside. *How long has this place been deserted. Eons?*

The rats the size of dogs, and cock roaches the size of rats were playing so freely, as if it was they that paid rent. With an instant wave of his hand, the horrid creatures scattered to their escape routes, and sordid hiding places. Gone were the rats and roaches, the rotted furniture, dust bunnies and dense cobwebs.

"Now this looks much better!" Vigilantly Jay walked deeper into the farm house, every step of the way waving his hand to get rid of dead carcasses, and clean the place up. He made it into all the rooms, and was now fixing the roof, which had looked like a giant thimble. The old farm house was now looking at least liveable, Jay even thought of sleeping in here tonight. Right now he was pleased with leaving the house devoid of any purveyance, for now. All he wanted was to make sure that it was clean and warm. He would do more decorating, later. Pleased with the job he had done with the farm house, Jay then commenced to go back outside to attack all the other war torn buildings, and terrain. As he walked along, Jay kept waving his hand, and in front of him the overgrown grass and weeds on the land had disappeared. He had the farm land now looking more like a well groomed football field. *Maybe I should add some lines, and a field goal,* he joked. He then meandered over to the broken down garage, with its broken entrails: Tractor, Plough, Harrow, Combine harvester, Mower, Baler, and Pickup truck. With another wave of his hand, all the vehicles were now fixed, and looking pristine. Jay went on to mend the broken fences around the farms circumference, and all the animal pens. He also got rid of the dead carcasses that lay strewn around the ground. *Looking better already,* he smiled. Jay knew that he had to make this land do the work that it was intended for: Produce grain, and livestock. *I have come to feed the poor, and all my weary children.*

# MICHAEL & DONNA

Glad that school had finished, Donna said good bye to her class with a little too much alacrity, and this did not go unnoticed by a few of her young students. "Where ya going, Miss Moore," asked a suspicious Trudy. Donna wanted to tell her, *none of your business,* but thought better of it.

"I am going home Trudy, just like you."

Trudy and the gang were just looking at her, and Donna unconsciously touched her nose to see if it was growing. "You're not going home," said the precocious Barry, "you're going to see that nice guy we all met this morning. Aren't you?"

She wanted to slap that grimy smile off of Barry's maleficent face, but once again, thought better of it. "It's really none of your business where, or what I do after work, Barry."

"Well, I hope he takes you out to see a good movie," intervened a smiling and mischievous Trevor.

"And don't give it up Miss Moore," said a smirking Trudy. "Not on the first date anyway."

"You kids are so incorrigible," said a resigned Donna. She was smiling now, because she knew that she could not lie to them, she could not lie at all.

After the kids had all left, and she had finished cleaning up the classroom, Donna finally walked out of the *The Village* grounds, and now felt free. It felt funny the way the butterflies were acting in her stomach, they were making her weak in the knees, and also had her floating toward town.

It has been one of the best days of her life, and she knew why, and so did the kids. After driving the kids back to school, after their lovely visit to Lincoln Terrace Park, all she could think of was Michael. "Miss Moore," asked the confused Barry, speaking up for the rest of the class, who were still giggling in the minibus behind her. "What the hell are you blabbering on about?"

Donna did not even know that she was speaking aloud, and smiling maniacally as she drove. "Can ya please stay in the correct lane, Miss Moore?" Trevor was holding his palpitating young little heart, as he thought that Miss Moore was driving with her eyes closed. *Not good. Not good at all!*

Since Michael had left them in the park, they all told her that she had to go on a date with him, even though she was trying her utmost to finish teaching them their lesson. "Look guys, we've had a beautiful lunch, but we did not come here just to have a picnic." When they all finally sat down, like good little children, she found that she was unable to teach her class anything. Not in this state. Teach, she couldn't even spell "TEACH" right about now. Donna at this point knew that she was not with it, all because of that damn boy. Thinking of him since they all saw him walk up the slab steps of Lincoln Terrace, Donna wore a permanent peaceful smile on her face.

Now as she made her was to the Suffolk County Bus Station in town, she thought about what was to come. Now along with the smile, fear had her face twitching, as she waited for the Greyhound Bus to New York. Donna did not want to get her heart stomped on and shattered like most of her friends and peers. She has heard infinite stories of being cheated on, getting impregnated by a guy who left to impregnate another woman. She did not want to be a single parent like the majority of her peers. That was why she withstood all the ridicules and sneers from her loose peers, and lived her life like the Virgin Mary. All she wanted to experience was the falling in love part, like she was now. *Is Michael the right one? Timing is everything,* thought Donna as she crunched on her Cheetos.

After finding and reaching Sterling Place, Donna bought herself a Pepsi cola, and waited on the corner, as inconspicuously as possible. She looked down the block to see if Michael was there, but there was no sign of him. *This is not a good start,* she told herself. Tardiness was one of her pet peeves, and if a child was late for her class, they were turned away for the rest of the day. She was already debating about leaving, especially when all these strange guys kept coming up to her, and asking her if she wanted *something?* Something . . . .?

Then it had hit her like a brick in the noggin, *this is a drug block, and I really don't need to be picked up by the police, by accident.*

She struggled to keep the tears from flowing out of her pretty brown eyes. *The b\*stard,* she wanted to scream. *How could he do this to me?"* Donna had made the decision to leave, but when she turned around, it was into the big chest of a tall man standing over her.

"Ya going somewhere, young lady?" She wanted to slap him in the chops, but just couldn't. The smile Michael was wearing was infectious, and she knew it was because she had showed up.

Still . . . She desperately wanted to give Michael one of *her* stares, let him know that she was not at all pleased with his tardiness, and having him meet her on a drug infested Brooklyn block. It was obvious that *her stare* was involuntary, because it wiped the smile off Michael's face.

"What?" Michael could not believe that his luck had run out, already.

"You're late," was all Donna had to say.

"But I'm here."

"You're late," repeated a pretentious Donna. She was really joyous inside now, and felt the butterflies having their party again inside of her body.

Michael was getting angry, "Even people that go to work get a seven minute grace period." At this response, all Donna could do was break out in volcanic laughter, which was to the relief of Michael. "Look I'm really sorry, Dee."

She looked into his face, into his brown eyes, and could see that he meant it, but she was not going to let him off the hook that quickly, so she put the pout back on her face. "Let me make it up to you Dee, take you out to the movies or something." Donna's face lit up like a star in the night. "Where would you like to go," continued Michael. All Donna was doing was smiling, as if she were a "Special Needs" patient.

"Do you want something to eat first, Dee?"

*I love the way he says, Dee. And I am hungry,* she told herself. "Where," she asked laconically?

"Anywhere you want to go," said Michael quickly, well glad that she was no longer angry with him.

"Michael, I want you to know that this is not about the food or the movies tonight. Tonight is about us getting to know each other better, okay," "Okay," said a now complacent and smug Michael.

"If you ever stand me up again boy," added Donna quickly, because she didn't like the look on his handsome mug, "I'm gonna let you see the other side of me."

"Err . . . That can't be a bad thing." Donna kissed her teeth as if she were a vexed West Indian, and bumped into him on purpose. "Okay," he said again, as he felt her soft hand slide into his. "Let's go!"

*Please God, let me make it up to her,* he prayed.

As they were rumbling through the tunnels of New York City on the number "4" train toward 42$^{nd}$ Street, Michael and Donna sat side by side as if they were newlyweds. "I think that I better tell you a little something about me," proclaimed Michael, and this of course made Donna feel immediately uneasy. *Oh-oh,* thought Donna. *Here it comes. Please God, let me at least get a meal out of this night.*

"I don't want you to believe that I am perfect," continued Michael, "but . . ."

"No one is perfect Michael," interrupted Donna, "except *our* Father."

"There is a lot that I want to tell you Donna," said a pained Michael. "Michael," said Donna, now feeling a bit sad for the boy she was sitting next to. "Slow down. We've only just met, and you don't have to tell me anything that I don't need to know right now." She could see that this was not going to be easy for him, or for her. *Everyone has a past, and everyone has baggage to bring into a new relationship.* Donna could see in Michael's saddened eyes that she was going to be unable to shut him up, before he spoiled everything.

"Please don't be too angry with me Dee, because I don't understand half of what is happening to me, myself."

She stopped him right in his tracks. "Please Michael; let's just have a beautiful evening, first."

Michael looked into her beautiful brown eyes, and could see that she was telling him, quite frankly, that this was not the time or place to share his deep secrets. "Okay, Dee. You're right."

Since Michael has never been a dining out person, he took Donna to the only place he's heard people talk about, "Junior's." After a lavish meal, Michael then ordered "Junior's" famous cheese cake, with a cup of cappuccino each. "I'm stuffed," announced Donna opening up the waist button on her Notre Dame skirt for some much needed room. "Why are you laughing at me?"

"Anyone would think you're a Brooklyn home girl, the way you're all stretched out and sh*t." They were still laughing as they made their exit from "Junior's."

As Donna automatically headed toward the subway home, Michael snatched her hand, and spun her around. "Would you like to catch a movie or something before we head home?" She looked up into his handsome face with a smile, "Thank you Michael, but I think you've spent enough of your money on me, and I'd better get ready for work tomorrow."

"It's still early Dee, and I've got enough money."

She looked at him studiously, and then did the same to her Longines Evidenza. "Well okay Michael, It is still early."

"Good girl."

"But I don't want to get home too late, Michael."

*I promise to bring you home at a respectable time, Dee."

She scrutinized him, "Mmm . . ."

"My word is my bond, Dee." They were both giggling as they made their way to 42nd Street. As the number "4" screeched and rumble down the tracks, they sat cuddled up in a two seater in the corner of the carriage. "I've noticed Dee . . ." He cut his sentence off, or was it Brainz?

*Are you stupid or what, boy? This woman knows nothing about your past, so shut the f*ck up!*

"Yes, Michael. You were saying?" Donna knew what was coming, but she could not let Michael know that she already knows all about him.

"I . . . Forget it Dee. It's nothing."

"No, no, no Michael. You started it, say spit it out."

"I thought you didn't want me to move too fast?"

"I also said that this night is to learn more about each other."

"Women, you're all so confusing."

"Yes we are, now spit it out, boy. What have you noticed?"

"All I was going to say Dee was that for the past few days I've noticed that there are a lot of people who would rather see me on drugs and in the gutter, than succeed in my life." Donna instantly knew that this was what Michael wanted to get off his chest, his proclamation of being an ex-drug addict. *Was he an ex-drug addict? After all, it was too soon to tell.* She let him continue talking, *as if I have a choice.*

"And these are people that I thought were my friends, Dee." First Donna saw the sad eyes, and it pained her heart, then she concluded that this may be the very first time in his lonely life that he has ever opened up to anyone. He had chosen her, which meant that he trust his new and special friend. Donna could not control the smile that was wrapped around her face.

"Err . . . Did I say something amusing, Dee?"

"Err . . . No, Michael."

"Well . . ."

Donna was so glad that he felt so comfortable around her, in this budding relationship. It was quite funny, because she felt that there was something between them also. It was if they had known each other for . . . Eons. She was already falling in love with him for his candidness, trustfulness, and truthfulness. The stories he went on to tell her throughout the evening had given her shivers up and down her spine. Michael talked, and Donna listened intently.

As he told her all he could about himself, Michael watched her face change from one extreme to the next. There was: Sadness, gladness, sorrow, joy, tears, and laughter. He only cared that he had someone now to share his life with. *The truth shall set you free!*

*I had to tell her, Brainz. Didn't I?*

*If you never ever see her again Majestic,* said a betrayed and pained Brainz, *you can blame it all on your big mouth, and for not listening to me, again!*

*I didn't want to lie to her, Brainz.*

*Not volunteering information is not lying, Majestic.*

*Yes it is, Brainz.*

*Whatever . . . Smart ass!*

Michael believed that he had made the right decision, because how could he start a new relationship, with a person he actually liked, by not letting her know everything about him? It was inevitable that she would have found out anyway, by the backstabbing gossipers, and then he would be in even more trouble. *Why didn't you tell me, Michael?*

Well he has told her, and if Brainz was correct and he never sees her Donna again, then . . . *Onwards and forwards, ya'll.*

Whatever happens, it will not negate anything the last precious few days has brought to him, and that included her. He did not want her to think that he was the perfect gentleman, when he knew he was not. He had felt compelled to tell Donna everything, even if he felt he didn't want to. That strange feeling had passed through his body again. It was that same feeling he felt, when he was around Jay.

The canard about him coming from a middle class family, only to fall so far down into societies gutter, had Donna in tears. Donna could not hide or help the tears from flowing from her brown eyes like a geyser. She sat back, and looked at him, scrutinized him. The expression on her face told her that she did not know everything about the boy. *I am going to have a few choice words with Jay,* she told herself.

*Michael is not any worse than any other man I have met,* she thought, *and I think he has done rather well in the short time Jay has been working on him. Now it's my turn!*

The teacher came out in her, "Now look, Michael. You should not be worrying about what people say and think about you. These people only want you to stay down, and stay with them in their pathetic world; only because they themselves know that they are insignificant grains of sand on a beach." Donna looked deeply into Michael's sad eyes, to see if what she was saying was penetrating. "They only try to make you look small," she continued, "so they can look bigger."

Michael's reaction to what she has said was to take a swig of his 40o/z of beer. "Everyone has their own demons, whether it be drugs, gambling, sex, or hiding from something even more devious. They all go around thinking that by attacking someone else, the meek, helps them to avoid facing their own two headed demon."

Now Donna knew Michael was listening, because he was not saying a word, but holding her tighter, closer to him. "The problem I have with haters," continued Donna, "is that they see my glory, but they don't know my story . . ."

"Hush ya mouth, baby." They both laughed, as they made their way up the stairs of the 42nd street subway station.

It was refreshing for both of them to be on 42$^{nd}$ street, almost delirious. Michael has not been here for a few years, and for Donna, she has never seen so many movie theatres on one street.

Walking arm in arm, Donna continued to speak to Michael, because he was too quite. "We've all got some haters among us, Michael. Some people envy you just because you can have a relationship with Jay, I mean Jesus, or because you light up a room when you walk in."

"What did you just say, Dee?" Donna was angry that she had slipped up, but played Michael as smooth as she played her "Lyon & Healy" Harp. "I said that some people will hate you just because you are a kind and loving person, Michael. You are always smiling, and that can get the miserable people very angry."

"Err . . . Thanks for the flattery Dee, but please, you're making my head puff up."

"Haters can't stand to see you happy Michael, and you know that. Haters will never want to see you succeed. Most of *our* haters are people who are supposed to be on *our* side, people that are supposed to be close to us. All I'm trying to say Michael is watch out, boy!"

Amazed at how much Donna knew about the jealous, spiteful, and insidious creatures amongst them, Michael asked, "How do you handle your undercover haters, Dee?"

"You can handle these haters by shining, being yourself old self, Michael."

*Did she just say the old Michael,* asked Brainz? *Is she kidding or what?*

"Oh, why don't you just shut up!?"

"Pardon me," asked a shocked Donna.

"Oh. Oh Dee, I wasn't talking to you."

Donna looked around, "Then who, Michael."

"Err . . ."

"I'll give you "Err . . ."

"Seriously Dee, I just spoke out aloud by mistake."

"I was only trying to help, Michael."

"I know, and I truly appreciate and love you for it, but you've got to believe me Dee, I slipped and spoke aloud." He smiled to reassure her. "It's a bad habit I have to also learn to control"

"Do you still have your invisible friend with you then," asked a smiling Donna?

"Err . . . How did you know . . . .?" Donna was amazing him, as Jay had, and now Michael started to truly wonder where the both of them had come from. "If you can call him that, because sometimes it seems that Brainz is far from a friend." This had Donna in stitches, and while trying his best to stop her from having a fit in public, he was cursing Brainz for embarrassing him, in public.

After they walked up and down both sides of "40 Deuce," they looked to see which had the best combination of movies. "We have to get our monies worth Dee," said an excited Michael. "I always go by the combination of movies the theatres are playing."

"Mmm . . ." Donna was smiling, as she feigned disinterest.

"Word up Dee," he knew that she was playing with him, and loved her even more for it. "Though I may want to see that one particular movie over there, two semi-good movies will always be better than one good one and a bad one."

"Whatever Michael," said the angelic Donna, laughing her pretty ass off inside. They chose a movie theatre and went inside. "Not too close, Dee." They went further back, and sat in the middle aisles.

Donna was falling more in love with Michael the more he called her "Dee." It sounded as if they've been together forever. Jay was right about Michael, as he always was about anything, *you will love him, Donna!* She has always been the shy and timid type growing up, still was, watching from the side lines as her girlfriends went on date after date, changing men like they changed their sordid G-Strings. They had all gotten pregnant at an early age, and had several children, by several different males, but this was not what she wanted for herself. It was not how she envisioned her future, or a relationship between a man and a woman. *This being here with Michael was!*

She was often asked by her friends, "Why don't you try and find a Christian man in church, Donna?"

"Just because these men go to church Salina, does not make them the perfect person to have a loving relationship with."

"Then how the hell will you know if the right man ever came into your lonely life," asked a resigned Salina?

"I won't Salina," said a dispirited Donna. "I just refuse to throw myself about to find out."

"So whatcha trying to say, girl?" Donna did not reply, and Salina did not like what Donna's silence was inferring. With that, Salina was gone, out of her life.

With his loving and warm arm wrapped around her shoulders, Donna snuggled up as close as she could into his big chest. She had no intention of watching any of these movies, no matter how good they were. When he received no reply from Donna, Michael knew that she had either fallen asleep, or was just resting. He softly touched her hair, brushed it behind her left ear, and leaned down and gave her a whispering kiss on the crown of her head. *What is a lovely person like this, doing here with me,* he asked himself?

All he knew was that he met this lovely lady yesterday, and now she was in his life. The thought scared Michael, because he has never had to take care of anyone, but himself, and he hasn't been doing such a splendid job at that. Michael found it hard to concentrate on the movies, all his attention was on the beautiful person laying in his arms. He loved the way that she always looked into his eyes, so lovingly. Donna made it obvious that she loved the way he spoke to her, and that had to be a good thing. He was able to make her laugh at all his silly jokes, and there was already that empathy between them that told him that they belonged together. That thought scared him, because the link went straight to his drug addiction. The innocent little boy from England was no longer pure, because of the drugs, and once again he was afraid that he'll indulge and f*ck everything up, again.

Michael knew that once you were either an alcoholic or a drug addict, you had a fight on your hands, for the rest of your life. *Maybe as time passes*, he mused, *I'll have more confidence. One day at a time,* he told himself. *One step at a time! I don't want to go back to living as a pathetic and penniless crack head.* "I'll stick to my beers!" Michael immediately put his right hand to his mouth to silence himself, but not before the angel Donna quickly snapped her head off his chest to look at him. "What?"

"Err . . . Nothing, Dee. I was just speaking aloud."

"Again?"

"My bad." Michael was still cuddling Donna warmly and gladly in his big arms, as she put her head back down on his chest.

It has only been a few days since he has been clean, and the fear of a relapse was still very prominent in his mind. Thank God he knew himself, and was not one of them pompous and arrogant assholes who thought that there was not a drug ever created that will get the better of them. *That is what every drug addict told themself,* thought Michael, *in the beginning of the end.* The good news was that he felt it in himself, the confidence and the swagger was coming back, slowly. *Lord, help me. I don't want to go back to the way it was a week ago.*

*"I'll help the best I can,* said Jay, who was sitting several rows in the dark behind them.

On the way home, Donna slept on the train all the way to Utica Avenue. *Damn! I forgot to ask her where the she lived,* thought Michael. *I'd better wake her up, or else it could turn out from being a good evening, to a very bad one.* He shook her gently, and whispered, "Wake up Dee. I need to know where you live." She incoherently said something like Beverly Road, and that was good enough for him, because he knew Beverly Road well. His aunt May lived down in the Flatbush area. Once they were out of the subway system, he would put Donna in one of the plethora of cabs that were waiting at the Utica Avenue Subway station. The fresh evening air slapped the drowsiness out of her face, as Michael seemed to be dragging her up the subway steps.

They walked hand in hand for the short trip to her house, because she did not want to go straight home, and Michael had nothing better to do right now with his life. *My protector,* Donna smiled as she slowly placed one foot in front of the other. She wanted this beautiful night to last forever, and was in no type of hurry to end it by going home.

"Goodnight Michael," said a dreamy eyed Donna, once they had arrived at her apartment building.

"Goodnight, Dee. Michael was grinning from ear to ear, and simultaneously trying to hide his erection. "Hope I can see you sometime. Maybe we can meet up tomorrow?"

"I hope so also, Michael." They were both happy that they received the obligatory goodnight kiss, albeit quite nervously. They were both acting as if they were novices at this romance game, and their teeth clattered into each other as they attempted to kiss for their very first time.

Michael thought he tasted blood in his mouth, but washed it down with his Private Stock. *Everything tastes better, when in love.*

When Michael was sure that Donna was safely in her building, he started on his merry way home, singing . . . "Giant steps are what you take, walking on the moon . . . I hope my legs don't break, walking on the moon . . ." He has always been a fan of the band "The Police," and when he finished singing "Walking on the moon," he started singing, "My beds too big without you."

After seeing Michael floating down the street, Donna snuck out of the apartment building, and went in the opposite direction. When it was time for him to know where she lived, she'd show him, but for now . . . She also had secrets that she could not tell him, even though she painfully wanted to, but she knew that Jay would not look upon it favourably. "In time, Donna," he had told her before she had left *The Village.*

# Evening — Sweet & Sour

Skipping down the street like a child with a bag full of candy, Michael was wearing a smile that seemed painted on. The smile quickly started to dissolve once he had to come to an abrupt stop. Suddenly, there was a wall of thugs blocking his way home once he got as far up the hill as Empire Boulevard. "Where ya going, crack head?"

"Oh, hi ya Craig," was all Michael could utter in his fear. He was now urinating in his brand new Rocawear jeans, because of the sudden appearance of Craven Craig, and his gang of low life thugs. Craven Craig was grinning enough to let Michael see the obligatory mouth full of rotten teeth, which Craig seemed to pretend were gold.

Everywhere Michael looked around him, there seemed to be one of Craven Craig's thugs, of both sexes. *They looked as if they were going to kick his ass well and proper tonight, and then put it on the internet. The little f\*cks,* said a well p\*ssed off Brainz.

*There must be at least forty of these cockroaches,* Michael told Brainz. *How the f\*ck am I going to get out of this, Brainz?*

*Oh, now ya want to ask for my help?*

There was no reply from his host, so Brainz continued, *Do some of your Bruce Lee on them.*

*But I don't know any Bruce Lee move, Brainz.*

*See ya, hate to be ya!*

*This is what happened to a person,* mused Michael, *when you weren't vigilant, twenty four-seven around here. Damn!*

Unfortunately, he was right. It seemed that the baby swallowing brats only wanted to have fun with him, and show off in front of their little hood rat girlfriends. They now started to circle him like Apache Indians, and the circle was getting claustrophobic. Craven Craig did not even ask him to hand over any money, letting Michael know that this was going to be purely for fun.

*Shame,* said Brainz.

The pubescent thugs started pushing him around in their circumference, and then started kicking him around, as if he were a soccer ball in the middle of a Chelsea Football Club practice session. After roughing him up a bit, Craven Craig asked, "I asked you where ya going crack head." "Yeah crack head," said a young girl in the back row. "Answer Craig, or we're gonna have to beat the sh*t out of you."

Michael didn't answer, anger growing in his face with every punch and kick to his body now. He was still able to sneer at the little *b\*tch wearing the* Slipknot tee-shirt as he got his ass kicked. *I'll slip a knot around her loquacious throat,* thought Michael, as he lay in his own pool of blood. It seemed that the angrier they saw him get, only gave the young snot nosed miscreants more pleasure as they upped their violent tempo. One of the "Ben Ten" punks hit him in the back of his head with something that felt more solid that a fist, and then he ran quickly behind *his* circle of steel, laughing his pimple head off.

Michael got up off the ground, fuming, as they all backed up to look at the grand work they had done on him. He turned toward the young boy, "Why'd ya do that for, ya b*astard?" He now felt dizzy, as he saw the young boy drop the pipe he had used as a weapon. The only sound Michael could hear now was the macabre giggling from their young throats, and this sent macabre electric sparks down his spine. Then one of them snuck up and kicked him in his back, as he was wobbling on his weak legs, like a boxer who got caught with a sweet upper cut. This blow forced him to stumble toward Craven Craig, who still had that grotesque smile on his ugly and grimy countenance. "Yo Craig man," said a weakened and pleading Michael, "what's up? I haven't done anything to you guys. Why ya f*cking with me, ya'll?"

Craven Craig said nothing; he just stood there, wearing that malicious smile. Now he was past angry, Michael had reached boiling point. He thought that if he could just grab one of the little c*ck suckers, and snap his or her young and succulent neck, preferably creating a very loud crunch in his tight fingers, the rest of the *Virgin Crew* will be in their Beyoncé panamas before their parents read them their bedtime story. That was when one of them knocked his precious bottle of *Private Stock* unceremoniously out of his limp hand, and Michael watched as it all in slow motion as it crashed to pieces on the ground in front of him. This was when Michael, surprisingly to everyone and himself, leapt up at the speed of a young cheetah, and snatched the windpipe of the closest kid next to him. He hung on to the boy's windpipe for dear life. *If I go to hell tonight, you're coming with me, p\*ssy!* He just would not let go, his grip on the young boy's windpipe was locked on as if his fingers were the jaws of a starved pit-bull.

No matter what the now anxious and tear-filled crew did to prized Michael's fingers from their friend's throat, they were unable to. No matter how much they punched and kicked and hit him, even using wooden and steel objects, they were unable to get Michael to let their friend go.

"Let him go," pleaded on of the pre-teen sluts, now crying like the little pubescent b*tches they really were. "He's turning blue for God's sake!" "You cruel b*stard," screamed the tear-filled Slipknot girl.

Michael wasn't trying to hear any of it, because he wanted to turn them all blue, and rigid like the one in his hand. For some reason, the punches and kicking suddenly stopped. *Why,* he asked himself, but was too scared to look up, or let go of *his* victim. *A bird in the hand is better than a bunch of birds in a bush.* It was now Michael who was wearing a malicious grille on his face, and it wasn't a pretty sight. He now looked like the Devil incarnate, and this set the group of teens urinating on themselves, and they disappeared into thin air.

Not being able to see any of them, put fear into Michael's thumping heart. He had to know and see what the hell they were up to, so he slowly and prudently lifted his head up. Without loosening his grip on the meaty windpipe of his young foe, Michael could no longer see any of the "I want to be a thug" crew. They had backed up, and given him enough space not to fear another immediate attack. *Why? Were they still filming on their cell-phones, filming him killing their friend?*

"Let the little one go, Michael." Michael's head whipped around, while subconsciously loosening his grip on the young boy's throat. *Was this some kind of trick?*

"Jay," called out a frightened Michael. Fear seeping deeper into his body and soul. There was no sign of *his* new friend, but he was sure that he had heard Jay's voice. Well it sounded like Jay, and the reality of it all made Michael quickly released his grip on the young boy's throat. The pocked marked face of the boy looked as if all the blood had left it, and this made Michael look at his finger nails. There he saw the boy's skin, and Michael shivered. *I almost killed him! I almost killed somebody today.* The tears were now welling up in his brown eyes. *You being drug free,* said a reprimanding Brainz, *is turning out to be worse than when you were a common drug addict.* The tears now flowed freely, but he did not know if it was because he was still angry at the surprise attack on him, or because he could have found himself in the electric chair tonight. Then he saw him, the hippie looking fellow wearing his omnipresent white gown and brown robe ascend from the dark. "They attacked me Jay," said an apologetic Michael, as if Jay was his father, and he was about to get beaten with a belt.

Once Jay was in front of Michael, he gave him his hand to help him up, "I know, Michael."

"Then why did you tell me to let him go?"

"Because Michael, you are not a murderer. It is a sin!"

"A sin," asked a bewildered Michael?" The young lad took this opportunity to escape the vicinity. He was already running with the speed of a cheetah away from the two maniacs, holding his gouged throat. Michael saw him run pass his associates, gasping for air. "Is that all you have to say, Jay?"

Jay was busy brushing Michael off, "Yes, Michael."

"Will you stop that, please?" Michael pushed Jay's hands away. "Well what they were doing to me," shrieked a raging Michael for everyone to hear "was more than a damn sin, Jay."

Jay said nothing. "Look around you my innocent friend," continued Michael, pointing at Craven Craig's crew as they boldly stood there, watching the two weirdoes'. "People like them are sinning as we speak. Why don't you go over and tell them to stop their evil and wicked ways, Jay!?" The anger was coming off Michael's body as steam. Jay just watched and listened, as his new friend vented his venomous frustration. That was why he was here, to help people like Michael. He really felt sorry for people like Michael, he did not deserve this. It was just another spike in his belief in mankind.

Jay waved his right hand, and all the kids in Craven Craig's crew started clutching at their throats, as if they were being choked, strangled by an invisible hand. Michael watched in amazement. "Let's go, Michael." Now Michael turned his head to stare at Jay, and then back at Craven Craig's ugly and gurgling mug. Craven Craig's once violent crew were now crawling in the middle of the street, gasping for breath, and the wheezing was ear shattering. "You okay, Michael?"

"Yeah Jay," said a still disgruntled Michael, while continuing what Jay had started, and patted the rest of himself off. "I've had worse days." They both smiled, though unperceptively. They walked the rest of the way, heading toward Michael's house, "Do you feel like hanging out. The drinks are on me."

"Thanks for the offer Michael, but I still have a lot of work to do down here."

"Work? Down here, Jay?" Michael looked up at the full moon, wondering if he should blame the bright sickle in the sky for all the weird things that were happening in his life. "One, its night time Jay. What work do you have to do at this time? And two, what do you mean by down here?"

As per-usual, there was no reply from Jay, and this time Michael did not expect one. He was already getting used to this character.

Jay wanted to slap himself for slipping up with his choice of words, "My work does not stop, Michael." Michael stopped walking alongside his new friend, and looked at the figure still walking up ahead, not even realizing that he was now talking to himself. Michael hesitated to ask Jay about his work, and then thought better of it. He ran up to Jay, who was still blabbering on about something, "I guess I'll head home then."

"Are you sure you're okay, Michael."

"I've had worse days unfortunately, Jay." This brought a veritable smile to Jay's face, and this pleased Michael, though he did not know why. "See ya around Jay."

"You take good care of yourself my friend," said Jay without missing a step.

"Jay?"

Jay turned around, "Yes, Michael?"

"Thanks."

"You're welcome, Michael."

Jay was already down the other end of Lincoln Place, "Yo Jay," Michael shouted out, "where are you staying?"

There was no reply, although Michael saw Jay look back at him.

# MICHAEL — LIFE IS RATHER AMAZING

He felt as fresh as the new born day, and Michael was ready to shine. After getting dressed in some of his new gear, he looked in the mirror, and smiled. *I am type handsome!*

*You also look so dapper, Majestic.*

*Why, thank you Brainz.* Before leaving the house, Michael went into the kitchen to tell his parents that he was going out. Their jaws dropped at the sight of their handsome and clean son. "Err . . ." Was all his father could say, as he wiped the spat out coffee off the sleeve of his shirt with his New York Post. After the initial shock, his mother was smiling from ear to ear. *I've got my son back. Thank you, Jesus!*

"Where are you going this morning Michael, looking so refined?"

"Thanks, ma." I'm off to see my friends."

"It would be a very good idea if you were off to get a job," offered his father." It wasn't as if he hasn't heard this speech before, but it had slipped his mind for the past two years, and Michael thought that his dad maybe right. He just couldn't continue like this, hanging out on the streets, and he definitely knew that he would not have the serendipity to find $3,000.00 in his jeans every day. *Damn. I should have bought some dress shirts and trousers for interviews.*

*Not to worry Majestic,* reminded a very helpful Brainz, *you still have enough dough for that, later.* With that said, Michael found himself floating down the street as if he had just won the lottery, or was still on his date with Donna. Michael finally noticed where he was once he stopped his ruminating about last night, the good parts of course, and he entered the Dominicans store. He bought himself his daily supplies, and then headed for the park. Cracking open his fresh 40o/z and Newports, Michael walked peacefully toward Lincoln Terrace, now thinking of how everyone's world around here has been turned upside down since the invention of crack cocaine. The area he has lived in for over a decade now looked like Beirut, on a bad day, instead of the once affluent Crown Heights it used to be. The invention of crack had immediately overwhelmed the citizens around the nation, even more than the invention of the cell phone or laptop.

As he descended the slab steps and went deeper into the entrails of Lincoln Terrace, Michael's thoughts were on how this pernicious drug epidemic had started. "Pellgreave, I want you to round up all of *our* erudite rocket scientist friends, and tell them all to meet us at my lab." "You have a lab, Constable?"

"Yes, and I'll let you know where it is, after you've done as I've told you." "But you're a banker, Constable."

"I know what the f*ck I am. Now, will you shut the f*ck up, and listen to instructions!?" Michael knew that he was letting his vivid imagination go astray, but his theory was that this disaster was caused, on purpose, by some rich racist oppressor. This was just a game to him, or them, down at *their* exclusive and racist old boys club. His face no longer was wearing that joyous smile as he made his way down to the duck pond. Then somewhere deep below the earth's core, *they* had finally hit pay dirt after experimenting on some of their own race who they knew were superior.

"Eureka. You and the boys have done well, Pellgreave!" Then *they* put out their new pernicious product out into the inner-cities of America, with alacrity, and watched the darker part of society fall like dominoes. "This is making my d*ck hard, Pellgreave. You want some?"

"Err . . . No Constable, maybe later." First *their* pernicious white rock was wrapped in generic silver foil, before *they* went up market and put the white rock it into mosaic plastic vials. Now crack cocaine in America was selling better than sex, cars, laptops, iPhones, and the child slavery. *Ingenious,* thought a saddened Michael as he took his seat in front of the duck pond.

Now around here looked more like a *"Road Warrior"* movie, or a *Stephen King* novel. It was the end of the world, or damn near close to it. It was now every man, woman, child, and animal for themselves. Michael has seen sons and daughters rob their mothers and fathers for the rent money, and then kill them for the ivory on their corroding teeth. It all started with "Constable's new and intoxicating crack cocaine. *Amazing! The more we go further into the future,* mused Michael, *is the more we seem to go backwards into the Stone Age. Even the depths of Hell had to be more civilized than this.*

Though he was conscious of listening and doing his best to stay vigilant for any noise around him, like someone singing in the distance, Michael could not hear thing, and this saddened him. This morning his new friend Jay, or the sweet

Donna, the two strangers that have changed his life around, was not anywhere to be seen. "Oh my God . . . Donna."

His pleasant memories of their date yesterday eradicated any more dire thoughts in his head of Constable and Pellgreave.

# THE GATHERING

Michael could hear the commotion, as soon as he exited the park. He usually told himself not to go toward a crowd, and instead head in the opposite direction, but it was early, and he was bored.

There he was standing on the corner of Utica Avenue, just outside the subway station. *Unbelievable,* thought Michael. Jay was standing on a plastic milk crate, surrounded by a boisterous crowd of around fifty. *Oh-oh,* thought Michael. *What has he up to, now?* He remembers telling Jay that this was not the place or time to spew his religious beliefs, but did the man ever listen to him? Michael picked up his pace, because he did not know if the crowd was friend or foe, and he did not want to see get himself in trouble, the violent type.

"Excuse me," he said as he forced his way through the crowd. "Pardon me."

"Aah you," growled an evil looking old black lady, "who ya think ya pushing around, ya young punk."

"Sorry, ma'am."

"I was here first!"

Michael ignored her, trying the best he could to save Jay from these rabid Brooklynites. Once he reached to where Jay stood, he made sure that Jay saw him shake his head in disapproval. "Are you okay, Jay," the concern in his face made Jay smile?

"Well hello my friend." Everyone in the still gathering crowd turned their undivided attention to the new arrival. Someone in the crowd shouted, "You know this crack head, preacher?" Michael whipped his head around to see who was trying to humiliate him in public. He recognized the young punk's voice, and wondered what "Killer" was doing outside the Brevouy Projects by himself. This made him instantly looked around for the Rock Man." Jay looked out over the germinating crowd, and then at the young lad who was causing Michael obvious discomfort. "Can I help you, Killer?"

All eyes in the crowd turned to the young boy, who they all thought could be no older than fifteen years old.

"How do you know my name preacher?" Now it was Killer who felt uncomfortable amongst "The gathering." Some in the crowd now recognized him as the little young beast that hung around with the thieving, drug selling, extortionist "Rock Man."

"It's that little heartless and brainless thug from Brevouy Projects, ya'll." "Let's hang him," shouted an old blue-haired white lady, who already had her can of mace in her liver spotted hand. She wanted him dead, even though she knew it was against the law to kill a fifteen year old punk. The boy has threatened her on several occasions, along with the rest of his gun toting crew.

"Where's your scummy friends now punk," she asked the now nervous young killer?"

"Err . . ."

"Let's lynch the young piece of sh*t," said a holy Muslim man, who threw his Quran quickly into the inside pocket of his coat.

"Not until I get my son's X-Box back," said a teenaged mother, unsheathing a lovely dagger from her fake Burberry handbag. The wry smile on Michael's face told Jay that he was happy that all the unwanted attention was off of him and on the right person.

"My people," said Jay with his hands held up, "please calm down."

*What are those red blotches inside Jay's palms,* asked Brainz. Michael looked closer, *I never notice them before.*

The crowd were no longer listening to Jay, because having the young boy named Killer in their midst, without the rest of *his* crew around, had them all feverishly wanting to have his young blood spewing into the air like the "Fountain of youth." All of a sudden, the thought of getting revenge was more exciting to the crowd than what Jay had to say. Jay looked down at Michael, as if to say that it was his fault that everything has gone pear shaped. That is had been going swimmingly, until he had shown up. Michael read the look on Jay's red eyes. *Weren't they green or blue, the other day?* "Now wait one damn minute, there."

Jay's face instantly corrected itself into a big smiling globe. "Do you think that "Killer" deserves to die, Michael?"

"Err . . ."

"Well, do you Michael?"

"I'm thinking, Jay. Give me a minute."

Think long, you think wrong," said a facetious Jay.

"Err . . . Jay, you're scaring the hell out of me." Michael wondered if Jay has been hanging around him too long, already. He then looked over at the once decent, but now feral crowd of citizens, and knew that he did not want to see Killer's limbs pulled from their joints. Not in public, anyway. "Okay Jay, what are *we* going to do?"

Jay raised his eyebrows, *we?*

"Can all of you please be still?" As he asked this, Jay waved his hand, and all was quiet. Even the traffic on Eastern Parkway seemed to have been muffled. The crowd, Michael noticed, were immediately obedient, docile. "This is my friend," announced a proud Jay, pointing at the man with the open gullet. "His name is Michael." The crowd started to murmur, because they also recognized Michael, and to them he wasn't much better than the young snot nosed punk that they already had in their scrawny little fingers. Everyone around here knew everyone else, and they all knew Michael as a sordid rat looking drug addict, though he didn't look like that right now, which raised a lot of eyebrows in the crowd. *The boys cleaned up himself,* some in the crowd murmured. Regardless, the now snarling crowd looked at Michael, and then at *his* co-defendant, Killer. They had to be here together, because none of them were ever seen in day light, hitherto. They had to be up to something mischievous, because none of them were known Christians, so why were both of them here?

From his peripheral vision, Michael saw Jay wave his hand in the air again, and thought the man must have a major shoulder problem. "Jay, let's get out of here."

Jay looked down from the plastic milk crate, "Why Michael. What's the matter?"

"What's the matter," asked a shocked Michael. "Can't you see that the crowd is turning into a lynch mob?"

"For whom, Michael?"

"Err . . ."

"They came to hear me speak about their future."

"Their future?"

"Yes Michael, their future. And to be honest, I only noticed that they all started getting angry when they saw you."

"Err . . ."

"Is there something that you're not telling me, Michael?"

"Err . . ."

"Maybe it's something about your English?"

"Very funny Jay, snorted Michael. "Now, are you coming with me or not?"

"To where?"

"Away from, here."

"But I like it here. I started this gathering for a reason." Jay waved his hand again, and this time it did not go unnoticed by Michael. All of a sudden there was a slight crescendo of hand clapping, and Michael did not know what that entailed.

"Are you thirsty," Jay asked his followers, after getting all their attention back and focused on him.

"Yes, preacher," came the unified reply.

"Michael," Jay looked to his new assistant with a smile on his face. "Will you please do the honours, and give *our* people something to drink."

"Err . . ."

"They thirst, Michael." Jay opened his arms to encompass the whole world. A confused Michael moved in closer to Jay and put his lips as close to the man's ear as possible without kissing him. "Jay, what the hell are you talking about," he whispered. "We don't have anything to give all these people?"

"Don't you have beers in your Jansport?"

"Err . . . Well yeah," said a now possessive Michael, making sure that his backpack was still on his back. "But I've only got one left."

*Did this man just kiss his teeth at me,* Michael asked himself.

"We have been through this before Michael. Please, don't hide, divide!"

*No he didn't,* said a just as surprised Brainz. Reluctantly Michael took off his Jansport, and started to unzip it. "Jay, you're crazy. Do you know that?"

"I know that already, Michael. Anyway, all I am trying to do is nourish our people.

"Nourish them Jay. With what," asked a shocked Michael, louder than he was supposed to?

"Nourish them with food, drink, knowledge."

"Are ya crazy?"

"You have asked me that, already."

"Look Jay . . ." Michael really did not know what to say or respond, so he changed the subject. "Like I told you before Jay, I've only got a . . . Michael's open mouth was drooling into the dark recesses of his Jansport.

"Do we have a problem, Michael?" Jay was smiling down on him.

"I, I, I . . ."

"You what Michael. I cannot hear you?" Michael looked up into Jay's smiling face, but had no answer for him. "Do you need a hand serving?" Jay was obviously too much fun now, and Michael could see that it was killing him inside trying to restrain his laughter.

There must be at least seven 40o/z bottles of beer in his Jansport, and the bag still felt weightless on his back and in his hands. *Surely I would have remembered buying so many, of which I know I never did.*

"Are you okay Michael, asked a now snickering Jay?"

"Err . . . Yeah Jay, I'm fine. *I'm just losing my mind Jay. There's nothing to worry about, ya'll!* Finding the several 40o/z bottles in his Jansport had him punch drunk, and

Michael knew something was going on that surpassed rhyme or reason, but he had to play this through like a pro. "How are we going to share this small amount of beer that just happened to be in my back pack again, with all these people, Jay? There must be over a hundred of them out there?

"Let me worry about that, Michael" Jay could not keep the Cheshire cat grin off his bearded face. "I ask you Michael if you are willing to share what you have with your fellow brethren's?"

After clearing his throat, Michael gave a sincere, "Well of course I am." "Why are you staring at me like that, Michael?"

"Staring. Am I staring Jay?"

"Yes, you are."

"What are you up to, Jay?" Michael couldn't hold the question in any longer.

"Me. I up to something? What possibly could you mean, Michael?" This obviously confused Jay, and he furrowed his bushy eyebrows.

"Jay, these people are just angry and frustrated."

"Angry and frustrated about what, Michael?"

"About the way this sordid world and society have treated them. They are angry and frustrated with this corrupt and despicable planet they live on, Jay."

"No Michael," corrected Jay. "*Our* people are hungry and thirsty, but it is not for food or your beer thy quench for." Everyone was now silent, watching and listening to the two friends argue in the middle of the busy street. After a moment Michael noticed the silence and tried to keep his voice down. He then slapped his forehead with his palm, so loud that it had some of the people in the crowd ducking for safety.

"Killer, come over here," commanded Michael. Killer did not like to be spoken to like that, especially if that person wasn't the Rock Man, but he was happy to leave the clutches of the lynch mob surrounding him. "What's up, Mike?" Michael reached into his jeans pocket, and pulled out a twenty dollar bill, which he handed to the young boy. "Can you please go to the store, and get some juices and plenty of plastic cups?" Killer practically snatched the twenty dollars out of Michael's hand, and was in mid-spin when he heard Michael say, "Please don't do anything stupid Killer."

"Meaning what Mike," asked the offended young one?"

"Meaning just go to the store, and come straight back or it will be Spofford Juvenile Center for you."

"Okay," answered Killer, as he turned toward the corner store on Utica Avenue.

"Now hurry up, because *our* people are thirsty. You and I are going to do something good for humanity today."

Jay was watching Michael with a smile on his hairy face, and was nodding his head in satisfaction. *You're doing well, Michael.*

Jay commenced to tell the crowd about their thirst and hunger, and of the good things that was waiting for them. "If you can see beyond the obvious *my* people, then you would see that you are loved and blessed by *our* father."

As soon as Killer returned with five stacks of plastic cups, and a bag full of boxed juices, Michael started pouring. With the help of Killer, and "Dirty Debbie," they went through the crowd passing out the cups filled with juices, and beer.

"Damn, what kind of beer is this," asked a young woman in disgust. She wore a face that looked as if she had just swallowed a mouthful of Robitussin?"

"Yeah," said another unsatisfied customer, "this tastes like wine.

"At least it tastes better than "Thunderbird," cheered a toothless old black man.

Tired of hearing their ingratitude, Michael cracked open his last 40o/z. Sh*t, it did taste type tart, and this made Michael instantly look over at Jay, who of course still had that mischievous smile on his countenance. Michael was quite sure that Jay was doing his best to ignore him at this time.

"Many times we wonder why *He* would let us go through such bad and difficult times," Jay was in full flow again, standing prominently on his plastic milk crate. "But *our* father knows that when *He* puts these things all in *His* order, they always work for *our* good! *We* just have to trust in *Him,* and eventually it all will combine to make something wonderful!

*Our* father is crazy about you, I can honestly tell you. He proves it by sending you flowers every spring, and a sunrise every morning. Whenever you want to talk, *He* promises to listen. H*e* can live anywhere in the universe, but instead *He* chose your heart. O*ur* beautiful father works this way.

"What was all that preaching about, Jay?" His friend was in a pensive mood as ·they took a leisurely stroll down toward Lincoln Terrace Park. The park seemed to be a haven for the both of them, and Michael was happy to spend his little corner of the world with Jay. *I'm not alone, anymore!*

After all the commotion that Jay had caused on Eastern Parkway and Utica Avenue, they were both lucky to get away from the now frightened mob. Jay's sermon had ended when the police, in riot gear, came storming into the crowd, separating them, by pushing and shoving them around. Michael saw some of the officers using their truncheons on the elderly to emphasize that they were to leave the vicinity immediately. "What's the problem, Officer?" An irate Michael had asked, because he was tired of the uniformed oppressors constantly invading their little gatherings. Even if he didn't agree with everything that Jay had been saying to the crowd, it was the man's right to be able to speak freely. It was his right.

*When the oppressors had nothing better to do, they always seemed to want to put a pin in another person's bubble. I hate them!* Michael was gritting his teeth as the officer told him the mitigated reason they were dispersing the crowd.

"You and your friend have this crowd blocking the flow of traffic," said the burly and cantankerous black police officer, "and that my friend is against the law." Michael had never heard anything so weak, and held his ground in front of the belligerent officer. "Now get the f*ck out of my way, or I'll take you both in for disturbing the peace."

Michael finally capitulated, and stepped out of the officers way. This was what he had been trying to warn Jay about from the very beginning. Preaching and stirring up the public into a fervour could only mean trouble, and Jay was too innocent to go to jail. Michael did not know where all the people had come from, but when the police raided *Jay's Street Party*, the crowd seemed to have numbers in the thousands. He watched as a young female police officer repeatedly struck an old black man over his snow white head with her 38 special.

"Hey officer, aren't ya going a bit over the top?"

"If you don't shut the f*ck up and move out of my way boy, I'll be all over that fat punk ass of yours!"

"Your mama likes it," retorted an unwise Michael, and before the police officer could point her gun at him, Jay was standing between them. There were no words exchanged; only a staring match. Before he knew it, Michael could hear the pernicious feline apologizing, "Sorry sir," before they both watched her run off to help her fellow officers disperse the crowd.

As they continued their walk, Michael wondered what Jay had done to the bearish feline officer to make her apologize and practically run for her life. *The she/man looked as if he had sh*tted in his G-String.* "What is so funny, Michael."

"Err . . . Nothing, Jay."

After a long day walking around and helping Killer and Dirty Debbie hand out the plastic cups of beer and juices to all the citizens who gathered to hear Jay speak, Michael immediately removed his timberlands boots and rubbed his poor calloused and aching feet as soon as they were sat on the park bench in front of the duck pond.

They both sat quietly where Michael had first heard Jay singing in the fields beyond. He looked over at the reticent Jay, and the man looked far away, too far away. *Sh*t, I'm obviously not the only one that drifts far away.* He needed to bring Jay back to this world, now. "You want some beer, Jay?"

"Do you have some left?"

"I'm sure I do Jay." Michael was looking at Jay's smiling face.

"Thank you Michael. I think that is exactly what is needed right now." "You're not angry, are you Jay?"

"Why would I be angry Michael? I think it went rather well when all is said and done?"

"We almost ended up in jail tonight, Jay."

"Yes we did, but we did not." With that they drank, laughed, and looked up at the stars. They both drifted with their own thoughts consuming them. Michael thought of the young boy, Killer, and how he had to go back to the store on several occasions to buy more cups and juices, while his Jansport was constantly being replenished with more and more 40o/z bottles of beer. Michael was no longer shocked or surprised at what he found in his back pack or pockets anymore. He was not shocked or surprised at anything that happened, not as long as Jay was around.

"This is ridiculous, Majestic." It was obvious that Killer and Dirty Debbie weren't too happy with playing the role of Gopher. There were so many people, and Michael joined them in with their incredulity. Why had all these people shown up to hear Jay speak? He was there, and it seemed as if Jay had them all enthralled with his words, with his commanding voice, but still . . .

It was Jay's turn to watch Michael drift off beside him, both in mind and body. Jay knew that Michael had become a loner, only because he did not understand, or want to accept the way *his* real sordid world worked. The world had turned out diametric to the way it was told, and inculcated to him from birth. *Confusion now ruled the world,* thought Jay. The poor boy had inevitably succumbed to the drugs that infested *his* environment, just so he did not have to face what was apparent around him. Jay watched Michael as he drank unconsciously from the 40o/z, and fiddled with the bottle of beer. *At least the boy had not become a heartless thief or murderer,* thought Jay. *Well, not yet.*

The boy sitting beside him was still a caring, kind, giving, and loving person, Although Michael tried his best to put the tough guy façade on, Jay knew better. *The young man sitting next to me is just a big ole teddy bear at heart.* Jay smiled, and then burped voluminously. "Excuse me, Michael." Michael acted as if he did not hear a thing; he was too far gone. Jay was very proud that Michael had not spent all the money he had given him on drugs. *You have passed your first big test, Michael.* Jay smiled again at the unconscious Michael, knowing that it had also gone unnoticed. *The boy was fighting against all odds, refusing to give in to this new and corrupt world around him. Yet he had the audacity to refuse to stay down, when it would have been easier for him to conform to society.* It was obvious to Jay that Michael's inner battle with himself was killing him. Michael did not know who he was, or what he was supposed to do with his life, he was like a small sail boat in the vast ocean, going anywhere the wind took him. Michael travelled this earth alone, but now he had company. *I'll be your friend, Michael.*

"What, Jay?"

"I did not say anything, Michael." Jay wondered if he had spoken out aloud, but he knew that he had not.

"Oh." With that Michael went back to his drifting. Still scrutinizing him, Jay could see that Michael had a lot of pride, *maybe too much for his own good,* but this was just one of many characteristics that attracted him to Michael. Jay also liked the fact that Michael was not completely vain, he did not want the biggest gold chain around his neck, the flashiest car in the neighbourhood, or to become the most notorious drug dealing thug around the area. *This was a good thing. A very good thing!* All Michael wanted was to get his life back on track, even if he did not know what his life was meant to be about. Jay knew that Michael knew that he was not brought into the world to just hang out on a Brooklyn block and become a professional drug addict. Studying Michael's face, Jay could see lucidly that the boy regretted almost every decision he has made so far in his young life. *You will be okay, Michael. I promise!* "Michael, are you okay in there?" That snapped Michael out of his reverie, "Yeah Jay. Sorry. I'm just thinking about things, that's all."

"Well my friend, thinking is a good thing."

"Oh Jay!?" It sounded if Michael was in pain.

"What is it Michael. Can I help?"

"Oh, forget it Jay. Sorry. It's something I've gotta figure out by myself, anyway."

"Everyone can use some help once in a while. No man is an Island."

"I know Jay, but . . ."

"But nothing," Jay cut Michael off. He had to grow up, sometime, and hopefully soon. "If you need help, call me. Prayer works you know." And with that Jay got up off the park bench, "It's time that I made my way home."

"Where's home, Jay?"

"Suffolk County."

"Damn you live far."

"You just do not know kid."

"What's that supposed to mean?"

"It means that it is close enough that you can come and visit me for once." They hugged and smiled, and then headed in different directions. "Thank you Michael for everything today."

"You're thanking me? Jay I need to thank you for everything you have done."

"And what have I done, Michael."

"Well, I want to thank you for all . . ." The sentence went unfinished. How could he tell Jay that he suspected him of giving him all the money, all the beers, and for saving his life tonight?

"Well Michael?"

"Look Jay, thank you anyway. Have a good night, Buddy."

"You do the same Michael, and I hope you can figure everything out in your mind."

"Err . . . I've been trying for years, Jay."

"Farewell for now my friend." As per-usual, all Michael could see of Jay was the back of the retreating man.

"Can you please stay out of trouble for the rest of the night, Jay?" Jay shouted back, "I will, but only if you will."

"Good night, Jay." "Peace my friend!"

# MICHAEL — I MISSED YOU!

He was up earlier than usual, because he could not sleep, and this has been happening for the past two weeks, the last time he has seen either Jay or Donna. Michael was very conscious that everything was going back to the way it was before he met the two lovely strangers, and he was now thinking about going to one of the drug dealers and getting a lovely hit. He wanted, and felt that he needed to be in that special zone of not being able to think about anything. The bad thoughts were coming back, and with revenge. "No," he screamed, "I have to handle it."

*Maybe just one hit will help, Majestic?*

*Please Brainz, not now!*

Interspersed with the nightmares were dreams of Jay and Donna. Life had been a good thing to live when they were around, but now they weren't. Now he was all alone, again, naturally.

He knew he was stalling. It was as if he were afraid to go out into the murky streets of Brooklyn, without his new friends by his side. *Sh\*t, I got used to them.* Without Jay and Donna in *his* world, life was back to being worthless. Now he had to go back to seeing with his naked eyes, and all he saw with them were people selling their minds, body and soul. It was as if everyone was trying to outdo the next person in the dirty deeds department. "Sh\*t, I'll out do that mother f\*cker that gunned down all those innocent children, and put it on "You Tube!"

"What do you have in mind, Ihateem?"

"I'll strap myself with dynamite, and pull the pin when I'm running across Yankee Stadium."

"That's good, Ihateem. That really sounds like a plan!"

"Why, thank you, Irate. I bet the infidels never thought that *our* people would fly a few of *their* commercial airliners into *their* lovely imperial skyscrapers."

"Yeah Ihateem, that was pure fun to watch on *their* tel-lie-vision"

*Who could have thought that the world that God could have created such hate and fatuousness?* Now the world of the future consisted of a bunch of lunatics who thought that taking innocent lives was like hitting the lottery, and these were the people that didn't take drugs.

*It is quite amazing, Majestic.*

As he walked down to Lincoln Terrace Park, in the hopes of seeing either Jay or Donna again, Michael threw his half smoked cigarette away in frustration. *I am so filled with hate, now. Am I turning into one of them?*

The thought sent shivers up and down his body, and he perceptibly wobbled in his stride. Hate and intolerance was growing inside his heart, and the more it did, was the more he wanted to get a hit of crack. Being drug free only was worth it, if you had something better to do with your pathetic life. But still . . .

Michael was now praying that he did not do anything stupid, and smoking crack again would be very stupid, it would undo everything he had achieved in the last month. The money and clothes will all be gone, and the shame of his parents will be back on their now smiling faces. It was obvious to Jay that the boy had lost his new bounce, and was retreating back into the old and inconsolable Michael. He was really sorry that he couldn't be here for him over the past few weeks, but he had other things on his agenda, and other people to take care of.

"Is everything okay, Michael?" Michael almost dived into the duck pond with fright.

"Don't do that!" Michael was hugging and sobbing all over Jay and Jay found it hard to get out of Michael's bear hug.

"Michael, please. I can't breathe boy." Michael released his grip around Jay, and used his now empty hands to wipe the tears of joy from his eyes.

"Where have you been, Jay?"

"I told you that I have a job to do Michael."

"Is that where you've been, working?"

"Yes, and it's coming along nicely."

"What is your work?"

"You need to come and see it, Michael. You will be proud of me."

"Err . . . What have you done, Jay?"

"It's a good thing, Michael." With that said, Jay handed Michael a scrunched up piece of paper with the address on it. Why don't you come over tonight, I'll be waiting."

"But it's all the way in Suffolk County."

"Do you not have enough money to get there?"

"Err . . ." Jay did know about the money. It was in his face, and in his voice. "I'll be there, Jay." How could he not be there for Jay, when ever since he met the man,

Jay has always been there for him? Michael was happy again, and that was what he had come down here to see, the spiritual glow of his children.

"Have you been spreading the word again about *our* father's love and grace?"

"Yes Michael that is what I have been doing." Jay looked into Michael eyes, "And I have built a little village in Suffolk County for where all our dis-hearted and meek brothers and sisters can come to be fed, and learn more about *our* father."

"Say what . . . .?"

"Yes Michael, this is what I have been doing, and now I would like you to come and see it." Jay looked into Michael's face to see if he was willing to come, "Do you think you can make it, tonight?"

"Jay, I said I'll be there, God willing."

"That is good enough for me, Michael. And what have you been up to since I saw you last?"

"Nothing much, Jay." Michael said it as if he was at the stage of self-harming. "I met a girl, Jay." The glee was all over Michael's face as he started to speak about Donna. "I met her right here, just like I met you. As a matter of fact, I came down here looking for you, but instead of you, she was here."

"You sound like you like her very much, Michael?"

"Yeah, she's quite and angel, Jay." The both sat down on the park bench, and watched the mallards playing around in the pond for a while. Michael cracked open a fresh 40o/z, and didn't even bother to look at Jay as he automatically passed over his 40o/z. The audible guzzling from Jay's dry throat was all that could be heard, along with the singing and happy creatures this morning. Michael watched as Jay's Adam's apple went up and down like a ping pong ball. "I asked Donna, the girl that I met here, if she knew you Jay."

"And . . . What did she say, Michael?"

"Do you know her?"

"I asked you first, Michael."

"She didn't say either yay or nay." Only the natural noises of the park ruled the moment. "All I know is that instead of finding you here the other day, picking flowers and eating their seeds, she was here picking her own flowers."

"Was she eating the seeds?"

"No Jay. She is not as crazy as you." Their laughter reverberated throughout Crown Heights, and Michael was even snorting on himself. "Well, do you two know each other?"

"Why would you think that, Michael?"

"Because I met you here, who I have never seen before, and then I met her here, who I have never ever seen before."

"Mmm . . ."

"I've been coming down here for years," continued Michael, "and I haven't met anyone that wasn't either jogging or walking their dogs. Now all of a sudden I happen to meet two lovely people, and everything in my world has changed for the better."

"Why, thank you Michael." The birds were tweeting and chirping, and Jay watched as the squirrels played "Hide and Seek." Then for their entertainment the mallards started to play basketball, using an unfortunate sunfish as the ball. *Pass the pill, you selfish piece of sh\*t!* "Why do you come down here all the time, Michael?" Michael did not know what to say, so he just left his mouth open. "Don't you know," asked Jay?

"Err . . . Well Jay . . . Of course I know."

"Well?"

"I come down here to get away from everything that is out there Jay." "But I thought you liked hanging out with other people?"

"I do Jay, but still . . . Even though I am a very gregarious person, I find that I really do not have anything in common with a lot of my brothers and sisters."

"What do you mean, Michael?"

"Err . . . Well, let's take for instance priorities. My people's priorities are to look good on the outside, but inside . . ."

"You're saying that your associates are meretricious?"

"Merit . . . What?"

"Meretricious, Michael. Meaning that they look good on the outside, but on the inside, they have no value at all."

"Err . . . Yeah. That's exactly what I'm saying." Michael didn't know what the f\*ck he was talking about. "Some of them seem to have everything they own on their backs. They have all the expensive gear, gold chains, and some have cars that they really can't afford parked at the curb. Then when you get the unfortunate chance to go to their dwellings . . ."

Jay could see Michael visibly cringe and trembled at the thought. "Roaches and rats are running all over the place, over the unwashed cups and plates in the sink, and their baby's faces. It's amazing."

Jay's eye brows were furrowed, feeling the pain of his friend beside him. "I went in one of my associate's apartments Jay, and it was if it was the insects and rodents that paid the rent. I even think that some of them were watching me, and not the television."

Once again the voluminous sound that came out of Jay's chest had the mallards retreating back to the molluscs underneath their home, and the birds fleeing out of the trees. "Jay, stop laughing. I'm serious my friend, it's as if these people display everything that glitters on the outside, but inside it is as rotten as a dark heart."

There was that omnipresent silence between them again, as they shared Michael 40o/z of Private Stock. "Anyway Jay, that's why I come here all the time, to be by myself. I don't want to be a big time drug dealer, thief, thug, or a heartless scum. I just want . . ." The sigh from Michael's mouth was as audible as Jay's boisterous laughter. "I really don't know what I want Jay. Sometimes I wonder why I have nothing, and these same people that I speak, seem to have it all. This is one of the problems I've been trying to tell you Jay, that why in the hell would a person want to be good human, when all they see is the maleficent ones getting everything they desire, and using and killing people to get it?" Jay looked over at his tear-filled friend.

"What makes it worse Jay is that they don't seem to get the punishment they deserve. And when the good people see this, they decided that since there is no punishment, then they may as well do it."

"Do you think that this has a lot to do with the lack of faith in religion, and the churches?"

Michael sniffled up his snot, "Well of course, Jay. Chat, chat, and more chat. That's all we get from our religious leaders, as we continue to watch with the naked eye the evil people of the world get what they want. This is why the new religions of today are being a very proud Agnostic or an outright Heathen."

"It's dangerous to be like somebody else Michael. If *our* father wanted you to be like somebody else, he would have given you what he gave them, their dark and immoral heart." There was no reply from the still sniffling Michael.

"You never know what people have gone through to get what they have . . ." Jay sighed and closed his eyes. "You should listen to Donna."

Michael stopped sniffling, and just stared at Jay's face. Jay had his eyes closed, and head leaned back, as if he were looking into the deepest part of the bright sky. "She's good for you, Michael." Michael continued to say nothing.

After sitting in the silence for a while, Michael drinking and smoking way too much during this time, Jay announced that he had to go. "Go where," asked a surprised Michael.

"Go back to work. Hopefully I will see later, Michael."

"Err . . . Yeah Jay, whatever . . ."

# THE HOLY VILLAGE

Spending the day in the house had Michael's parents in a delightful shock. It did not go unnoticed by them that they have been seeing a lot more of their son in the past few weeks. This either meant that he was getting tired of the drug and violent infested streets, or he was hiding or running from someone. They prayed it wasn't the cops. They were all sitting around the kitchen table this evening, except for Floyd, who was once again out on a date with his new girlfriend of the week, Shambolique.

Michael's parents just watched their sons every move and twitch, wondering what was going on inside the brain of his. They were glad to see him scrubbed up, *wearing new clothes,* and ready to eat. They gave each other a suspicious look: *Where did he get the money for the clothes?*

"What's for dinner, ma?"

"You okay, son?"

"Yeah, I feel great daddy." Both his parents smiled at him, and then watched him devour everything in sight. His dad had half a roast chicken sandwich, custom built, hidden on his lap underneath the dining table.

When his wife shrugged to let him know that they had ran out of food, Ken capitulated and reluctantly threw *his* treasured roast chicken sandwich onto Michael's empty plate.

"Where you off to this evening Michael," asked his curious mother? "Oh, I'm off to see a friend, who lives on Long Island."

"Oh. Is he okay?"

"Yeah ma, he's fine."

Mavis looked over at her husband, who could only shrug his shoulders. "Just be careful, okay dear?"

"Yes ma, I will."

"Long Island is far, and it's getting late."

"I'll be okay ma, I promise."

Michael loved that his mother worried about him, and that they had both stood by him while he was going through his drug addiction, but the questions she asked were incessant. She had become worse than a game show host. After filling his stomach, Michael went back into his bedroom, and collected his keys and a couple of hundred dollars from his stash. He put them both in his Brooklyn Nets black and white leather jacket, and put on his Brooklyn Nets baseball cap. He looked in the mirror, and he wanted to make love to his own arrogant ass. *Life is good.* He paid for his ticket to get on the LIRR, and once he got to Suffolk, he found that he was already lost. One of the good things about Michael was that he was not shy to ask questions, and he proceeding to asked for directions to *The Village.*

"*The Village.* What are you talking about son?" The elderly white man, who had been doing at least 70mph on his Quingo five wheel motor scooter, had stopped to help the pathetic lost child, but was already regretting it. Michael could see in the man's wrinkled and liver spotted face that he wished that he had run him over, instead of stopping to help him. Michael quickly pulled out the piece of paper that Jay had given to him, and showed it to the old man, who was now scratching the few grey hairs that was left on his balding head.

"This place has been left derelict and arid for the past twenty years, kid." The news sent bolt sadness through Michael's body, and he was hoping that he had not travelled all the way here for nothing. Then he remembered who he was dealing with: Jay. It seemed as if nothing was impossible, when this man was around. *You need to come and see it, Michael. You will be proud of me.*

"Please," he begged the old man who was looking at Michael strangely. After looking at the crumpled piece of paper again, with the fictitious address on it, the man told Michael where he had to go, and how to get there. "There'll be a lot of walking involved, kid. Like I said, the place has been desolate for decades." As he turned onto a long and dusty road, Michael could see nothing akin to civilization. The only thing that came to his mind was Elton John's album cover: Tumbleweed Connection.

He went into his omnipresent Jansport and took out a 40o/z of Private Stock. *Looks as if I'll be needing this,* he told himself, and commenced to crack open the large bottle of beer and started guzzling. After wetting his whistle, it seemed as if he had been as walking forever on the dusty path, and he has yet to see anything resembling a home, or village.

*This ain't looking too swell, kid.*

*I know, Brainz. But still . . .*

But still he kept on walking, putting one foot in front of the other. Michael looked back on several occasions, but decided that he had come too far to go back now.

*Sh\*t, I'm gonna die out here!* He looked up to see if there were any smiling buzzards swirling around. *This is getting kind of scary.*
*Yeah, like in those horror movies, Majestic.*
*Oh, shut up, Brainz!*
All he passed on his trek to nowhere, were broken down shacks, that had obviously been abandoned many moons ago. It seemed as if the last people that live around here were the indigenous, who were then run out of their town by General Custer's cavalry. A mischievous smile crept onto his handsome face, as he kept putting one foot in front of the other. There, on the edge of a prairie, Michael could see multitudes of insects moving around in the open fields as he squinted his eyes to focus. Now his pace was now quicker, and as he approached he could now see lights shining in windows. Now he could make out several building that looked quite out of place, incongruous to the scene he had just passed through.
*Where the hell am I, anyway?*
The scene looked like something out of the Twilight Zone, and once again Michael felt the urge to urinate. He kept going, and some children ran past him, laughing and giggling. Michael thought he recognized some of them, but from where?
*That looks like one of them kids that you met in Lincoln Terrace, Majestic.* Brainz was right; he may be bad at remembering names, but faces . . . He had met the kid when Donna was having a picnic with her class in Lincoln Terrace. *Did this mean that Donna was around, also?* Though the thought brought a smile to his face, his feelings right now were mixed. *She said she did not know Jay.*
*I don't recall she did, Majestic. She just did not admit that she knew him. Whatever . . .*
As the children played gleefully, running around him in circles now, Michael jumped in front of them, and they stopped, laughing as well as giggling. He told them not to be afraid, and asked them how far was *The Village?*
"I'm not afraid of you," said a young black girl named Rudy. She stared at Michael as if she had met him before, "Ah, you're our teacher's boyfriend, aren't you?"
"Err . . ."
"Yeah, it's my man Michael." Michael whipped his head around to look at the young boy that he thought he had recognized. Barry was smiling up at him.
"Ya come to see ya girlfriend, cutie?" Michael recognized Trudy right away, and standing behind her was the cowardly Trevor. *She is here!* "Yeah, Trudy. I've come to see Donna, is she around?" With that, instead of telling Michael where to go, they all lead him into *The Village*, with Trudy holding his hand. The kids led Michael through the small village, waving and saying hello to the people they all knew along the way. Michael could see that they were taking him in the general

direction of a big house, one that reminded him of the Texan JR and the show "Dallas."

The whole encampment seemed placid, as everyone went about their chores, smiling and waving at the stranger that had just arrived in their town. *This sure ain't Brooklyn,* mused Michael with a wry smile on his countenance. He started to pass several separate circles of people gathered in their own groups, who seemed to be either praying or worshiping, or both? This scene was new to strangers like Michael, who was only used to a circle of people in a dice game on the sidewalks of Brooklyn.

Trudy was practically pulling him along, as he stood to watch as people in the circles fell to the ground, as if slain. The only reason Michael knew that these people were still alive was because they sometimes were convulsing, and started to speak gibberish. Some of them he saw even jumped up out of their stupor, as if possessed, and started uttering prayers for their lost soul.

Astonished at his new surroundings, Michael could hear men, women, and children declaring the wonderful works of God, and the glorious mysteries of the gospel. Their appeals were solemn, heart-penetrating, bold, and free.

"Yo Dee," screamed Michael as he approached a girl fitting Donna's description over at the big house, the one that JR must live in. She was teaching a multitude of children outside, and stopped when she heard his familiar voice. At first Donna was glad to see Michael, and then her mood changed. *Is she angry with me?* Donna ignored him and went back to teaching her class, but Michael wasn't having any of it.

"Yo Dee, what's up?"

"Excuse me class," she told her pupils. "I'll be right back." She walked toward Michael and the children. "Okay Trudy, you can let go of his hand now." Trudy held on tighter, and Michael perceptively winced as she practically crushed his boney fingers. "I said let him go, that means now, Trudy." The bass in Donna's voice made Trudy not only let go of Michael injured hand, but she poked out her tongue at Donna, and then ran off from whence she came. "Where have you been for the past week," asked an angry Donna?

"Err . . ."

"And what are you doing here?"

"Err . . ."

"Oh, shut up, Michael!" With that said, Donna turned to return to her class, as if she had not been rudely interrupted.

"Err . . . Now wait one damn minute girl. I should be asking you the same question, Missy."

Donna spun around to face him, "And what that," asked a laconic Donna.

"Where the hell have you been?"

"We do not curse around her, Michael!"

"Curse? I didn't curse."

"I hope you haven't come here to argue and cause trouble Michael, because I have a job to do around here."

Now she was getting to him, which if she knew him, was a fatal mistake. "How could I have come here to argue with you Dee," he shouted, "when I didn't even know you were here?"

Donna was not fazed by his anger and loud voice, "Where have you been for the past few weeks, Michael?" Donna said this with a touch of sadness in her voice. "I thought we had a good time together."

"We did, Dee." Now Michael felt bad that he had raised his voice, and now had the whole village watching them. Everyone loved a little drama in their lives, especially if they were not the ones involved. "I just had to sort myself out, if you know what I mean."

"No Michael," she sounded angrier by the second, "I do not know what you mean."

"I told you about my problem, and I had a fight on my hands, Dee." Donna looked into Michael's eyes, and felt so bad for him. Now it was she that felt angry with herself for thinking only of herself, and her broken heart. "Sorry, I apologize for thinking about myself, Michael."

"It's cool, Dee. I missed you too."

"All you had to do was give me a call, to let me know something was wrong. I would have come to help you, hold your hand while you went through it, Michael."

"Thank you Dee, but addiction is something you have to fight by yourself."

"No it's not, Michael."

"Please Dee; I'm not used to sharing my faults and failures with anyone. Please forgive me, okay. And if I get into any more trouble, I promise I'll call you first, before I call my lawyer."

Even the crowd was laughing now, and Donna ran into his big arms, and held on to him for dear life. "Don't you ever leave me again, you hear me? We can go through good and bad times, together. Okay, Michael?" Her tears were already soaking through his new *Mitchell & Ness* Brooklyn Nets leather Jacket. *F*ck it. This is a good thing!*

"Deal, Dee."

After a while Donna stopped sobbing, and realized what Michael had said. "Deal, Michael, but don't let it happen again, or else . . ."

*Damn!* Michael was laughing. *This must be what it's like a in a budding relationship?*

After asking Michael again what he was doing here, Donna took over from the kids, and led him into the *Big House*. She went through the unlocked door and asked, "Have you seen Jay, Sylvia?

Sylvia was at her 1921 Ibach Baby Grand piano, practicing for the big Christian festival tonight. "Yes dear, he's upstairs. Do you want me to go and get him?"

"Yes please, Sylvia. Please tell him that he has a surprise guest."

"It's not a surprise," Michael quickly corrected. "He invited me."

"Yeah, I know Michael, but it will still be a surprise, because everyone betted against you showing up tonight."

"Err . . . Say what . . . .?"

"Joke, Michael. It's a joke. Ha-ha."

"Dee, you're killing me with your sense of humour."

Michael walked around the big palatial house, while he waited for Sylvia to go fetch Jay, and Donna had left him alone to roam around the big palatial house. *I have a class to finished, so make yourself at home Michael. I'll be back soon.*

"Wow," exclaimed Michael as he looked around the large living room, amazed at all the gold and marble artwork around the walls. *Jay has a lot of explaining to do,* Michael told himself. This place was nothing like what he had envisioned when Jay had said that he lived in Suffolk. Sh*t, he really did not believe Jay when he said he had somewhere to live. But this . . . This was truly incongruous to the man's personality. Jay had all this, yet he dressed as if he was impecunious and homeless.

Jay caught Michael looking up at the bejewelled four foot high gold cross on the living room wall. "Do you like it?" Michael swivelled around, once again surprised at the man's stealth.

"Err . . . Yeah, I guess it's alright. I can't wear it as a medallion though." Jay predictably laughed, and threw his arm around Michael's shoulders, once he made it down the baroque staircase. *Did he just float down toward me?* Michael rubbed his eyes, and blinked repeatedly.

Jay led Michael through the vast building he called home, showing him around while telling him all about what he was trying to do for his people. "Look out there Michael." Michael looked out the window of the top floor. "Everyone came here quite inconsolable and some suicidal, but look at them now Michael, they are happy and at peace for once in their lives."

"Not everyone, Jay."

Jay raised his eyebrows, "What do you mean, Michael?"

"Remember what I told you Jay, when I said that when you're doing well, there will be some people that want a piece of you, and if you don't give it to them willingly, well . . ."

Jay mulled over Michael's unfinished sentence, knowing that Michael would only tell him the truth, as he knew it. "I'll try to stay on guard, I mean on point, Michael." With that said, they made it out of the big house, and Jay walked Michael around *The Village,* showing him all the different works that was being done on the land. Michael walked pass teachers, like his dear Donna, in open air classes, adult supervisors who were openly training both children and adults in a craft or trade, and counselors who were heavily in demand for most of the depressed and despondent dwellers of *The Village.*

As they walked even further around the once desolate land of Suffolk County, that Jay now had shining like a star in the sky, Jay proudly showed Michael all the positive things that he and he's new family of *The Village* were doing.

Most of the new buildings were run by a "Cabin Leader," and there were plenty of them, one for each building, all doing different projects. You could tell these *Cabin Leaders* from the rest of the population by their Military styled Stetson hats, and their commanding voices barking out orders. The *Cabin Leaders* were assigned to their specific group of cabin dwellers. They all had their own small groups of campers that belonged to their cabin. The chore of running *The Village* was tantamount to running a residential holiday for children, who were away from their own homes, and needed guidance.

To Michael, this was a holiday camp. It was as if Jay had built it around the theme of Lake George in Warren County, not too far from here. The plethora of cabins could be seen spotted all over the once arid land, in which Michael could see the young and innocent playing, making tree-houses, singing songs, doing modern art, making kites, and playing adventure games together. The traditional summer camp was a woody place, and it included hiking, canoeing, and campfires, and these were the signs that Michael were looking for. It was obvious that Jay's Village offered a wide variety of specialized activities, because Michael could see the classes being held on this lovely and sunny evening in Suffolk. There were performing arts classes, music, magic, information technology, mathematics, and if you wanted to learn a new language, it was all here for you. Jay even had special cabin leaders to help the "Mentally and Physically Disabled in the crowd. And on their way around *The Village,* Michael could see that there was even a cabin leader for the clinically obese, who presently had her pleasantly plumb, but hyperventilating students doing laps running around the camp.

*Amazing,* thought Michael. *Where did he find these people?*

"I thought I already told you Michael, they all came from near and far once they heard the word."

"Did you advertise this place, Jay?"

"Don't be silly Michael. I am not foolish enough to put an ad in the newspaper, I just had a few of my followers had out flyer on street corners."

"Jay, sorry to tell ya this good buddy, but you can get in trouble for all this ya know."

"Why?"

"Why. I'll tell ya why Jay . . ."

"I'm still waiting, Michael."

"Err . . . Well, like I said before, the tax man, the government, somebody is going to want some of *your* good fortune. That's how these people operate Jay; they're like blood sucking leeches."

"I know Michael, said a dis-hearted Jay, who knew that Michael was telling him the raw truth, "But somebody has to try Michael. Don't they?" Michael could see the pain him Jay's face, and he hated when someone was in pain, it made him pain also. "Sorry, Jay. Just don't want to see ya get in trouble, that's all."

"Thank you Michael, but I have to do something for *my* people, and true friends." A tear dropped from Michael's brown eyes, when he saw the way that Jay was looking at him when he said this.

After walking in silence the rest of the way, they found a spot on the edge of *The Village* to sit down and rest. Michael passed over a fresh bottle of Private for Jay to crack open, and they drank lavishly.

"The primary purpose of this Village," Jay continued to tell Michael, "is about educational and cultural development of oneself. This Village environment allows people to take healthy risks Michael, in a safe and nurturing environment.

Being with Jay made Michael feel safe and happy, and he did not know why, and he did not care why either. It felt exhilarated sitting by Jay on an old felled tree trunk. "Jay?"

"Yes, Michael."

"Err . . . Well Jay, I've kind of noticed that in the past few weeks or so that I've known you, I've given up smoking that life depleting drug called crack, and I've even had a little serendipity in the financial and love department."

Jay raised his eyebrows, "Serendipity?"

"Well . . . It's just happening so fast. My life has spun around diametrically, and it's a good thing, Jay."

"I'm glad you are happy, Michael." Jay was wearing that wry smile on his face, the one that Michael got used to when he first met the man in Lincoln Terrace Park.

"I've even noticed that I have become a little kinder to myself, and I've stop treating myself as if I were born to live in the gutters and alleys of Brooklyn."

"Now ya learning, kid!"

"Ha-ha, you're so funny Jay."

"I do practice on my stand up." Michael tutted, and kept telling Jay the *Good News.* "I've become my own friend again, Jay."

"I thought that you were always your own friend, Michael?"

"Sometimes, Jay. Anyway, I'm not so self-deprecating anymore. Jay, I've seen too many dear friends, associates my age leave this world too soon, before they understood the great freedom that I feel right now." The delight inside of Jay was bursting to get out, he was so happy for Michael's new happiness. The boy deserved all of it.

"Seems that you've thought of everything around here," Michael finally said, as they both stood on top of the tree trunk they had previously been sitting on, and looked out at *The Village* that Jay created.

"I do try." Michael gave Jay a high five, and passed his 40o/z back over to Jay.

"You've done well in the short time you've been here Jay, and I'm so proud of you."

"Why, thank you Michael. Like I said before, you do not belittle or degrade anyone, but encourage them, and share in their joy."

"Well . . . That's little ole me Jay, who some would call a fool."

"I call you a wonderful human being, and may God bless you, always." Michael couldn't take any more of the flattery, so he changed the subject. "I surely hope Jay, that you're eating much healthier now."

"I like eating seeds, Michael."

"I'm not referring to the seeds, birdman; I'm talking about the petals." They were both laughing, as they made their way back toward town.

Once back in Jay's lavish home, Michael decided, for once, to call his parents, just to let them know that he was okay. "I may not be coming home tonight, ma."

"And why the hell not this time, Michael. Are you back to hanging out with those toe rags, smoking that evil drug again?"

"No ma. I'm staying over at a friend's house here on Long Island for the night."

"That man Jay you spoke of?"

"Yeah ma, so don't worry. Okay?"

"You wouldn't be lying to me again, would you Michael."

"Oh ma, Please. Trust me, this time."

It sounded as if his mother had started to cry, he could hear her sniffling through cyber space. "Please Michael. You've been doing so well these past few weeks."

"I'm at a place where there are no drugs in sight, ma." With that said, Michael hung up on her, because he couldn't take any more of her pleading for him to come home, safe from the sordid streets of America. Jay had put Michael up in the bedroom next to his upstairs in the palatial palace. The bedroom was so big;

Michael figured that the New York Jets and Giants could have a good game of football inside it.

He commenced to have a pleasant night's sleep, dreaming of all the good and positive things that have been happening to him, since he has met Jay and Donna, and chosen not to smoke anymore crack cocaine.

Even Donna was here in *The Village.*

*What a coincidence? If it doesn't work this way my brother,* said the sagacious Brainz, *then you have to do it that way. Was life was that simple,* Michael asked himself? *Did it come down to just choosing the right path, and staying on it, no matter what obstacles or temptations were inevitably thrown in your way?*

After everyone that lived in the *Big House* got up, and did their morning hygiene, they simultaneously raced downstairs to the large kitchen, where the aromatic smells of Sylvia's cooking was calling them. All their stomachs were ravenous, some screaming, and some even crying audibly. Jay almost pushed both Michael and Donna down the stairs on his was to get to the kitchen before them. Sitting at the head of the large dining table, and already masticating some of his breakfast, Jay asked, "Did you sleep well, Michael?"

"Yeah, thanks Jay." Michael then thanked the lovely Sylvia for putting a full plate of food in front of him.

"Can you please pass me two slices of bread, Michael?" Michael passed the bowl of bread to Donna, who then passed it to Jay. "Thank you." "You're welcome." Jay could feel the tension between the two around the table, but he decided to leave them be.

"Will you stay for a while, Michael?"

"A while Jay. What do you mean by a while, because I'm going home, sometime today?"

"I want you to stay our big gathering this morning, and then I'll have Donna drive you to the train station. Okay?" Michael securitized all the faces around the kitchen table, with suspicion. *What gathering was Jay talking about, and why did he want him to attend? What are these people doing here?*

*Be on point, like a pin,* said a concerned and nervous Brainz.

"Jay," asked worried Michael, because enquiring minds wanted, no needed to know. "What are you up to?"

"Me, Michael. I'm not up to anything, well not anything devious? I just want to show you what we have accomplished so far here."

"I've seen what you've accomplished Jay, and it is a good thing, but still . . ."

"Come on Michael," Jay almost threw his bread on his hefty plate. "You should know me better than that by now."

"Really and truly Jay, I don't know any of you." It was obvious to everyone that Michael was on the defensive, and scared of the new. He looked as if he was ready to strike at the first person that said anything he didn't like, and that included Jay and Donna.

"Michael," commanded the once reticent Donna. "Show some respect here!" Michael's mouth was still wide open; about to say more, then his jaws snapped shut. "After you've finished your breakfast," said a placid Donna, "we'll take a walk, and I'll explain everything to you. Okay." The look that she received told her that Michael didn't trust her, and it was like a knife in the heart.

After a long and tense breakfast, everyone around the twelve seated dining table excused themselves, and Donna asked Michael to come with her. They walked around the grounds at a leisurely pace, "Sorry for barking at you at breakfast Michael, but you have no idea who you're speaking to in there."

"What." Michael stopped dead in his tracks. "Are you referring to Jay?" "Yes, I am Michael. Do you know who he really is?"

"Err . . . He's just some guy I met in Lincoln Terrace, who was eating the heads of flowers."

"Is that all you know about him?"

"What's with all the questions, girl? Yeah, that's all I know about him. Why, is there something else I should know about him?" Michael was getting angry again, and Donna took a step back, out of his reach. "Please Michael, all I am asking is that you show him respect, after all you are in his house."

"Not only do I know more about you than you've told me, Jay knows you more than you know yourself."

This raised Michael's eyebrows into arches, "Pray tell, girl."

"You are an angry young man Michael, but please stop acting like the thug that we all know you are not."

"Look Dee, I don't know what you guys are up to around here, but I want nothing to do with it. Okay?"

"We are not a Cult if that is what you're thinking," answered Donna a bit vociferously." He was trying his hardest not to disrespect her, so Michael snapped his jaws back together. Biting his tongue was not one of his good characteristics. After all, Michael already knew that biting your tongue could be physically painful to oneself, when it could and should be used to blow the enemy away like a scud missile. Instead, he went into his Jansport, and pulled out another 40o/z of Private Stock.

"Can I have some of your Private Stock?" Michael looked at her studiously, and in complete and utter shock. "You aren't going to tell me you drink also?"

"Are you going to share some of the beer with me, or keep asking stupid questions?" It was obvious that Michael was in a much better mood now, after he saw Donna gulped some of *his* Private Stock.

*I've got my Dee back!* "Now Dee, you said that you were going to tell me something."

"I don't know how to say this . . ."

"Just say it for the love of Christ."

"Speaking of Christ . . ."

"Am I interrupting," asked a curious Jay?

"Err . . . No Jay. Dee was telling me, or was about to tell me who you really are, and what your work was really about. Am I correct Dee?"

"I think I better run along and get the children ready."

"Where ya going . . ." Michael and Jay watched as Donna rushed off in the direction of a plethora of cabins that looked like a school. "What a lovely person, Jay."

"That she is," answered Jay.

Michael studied Jays face, and not for the first time he asked, "What's going on, Jay. Speak to me my friend."

"Like I said before Michael, I'm not up to anything."

"What is this place, and how the hell did you get the loot to afford to run it?"

"I do not need loot, Michael. As you can see, the people here plant their own food, and build their own homes. Helping one another is how we've developed this land hitherto."

"That's all good Jay, but for what?" Michael asked, still suspicious.

"We built it for ourselves, and the rest of *our* people."

Michael was shaking his head, "I love your dear heart Jay, but this sh*t ain't gonna work. Do you know how many people died trying to get black people to unite, and have you seen the state of *my* race lately?" Without a word from Jay, Michael answered him, "It's as if *we* are going backwards, and these good people all died in vain."

Jay was still silent, because he liked listening and learning from Michael, even if he was wrong. "Jay, I don't want you to die in vain my brother!"

These words touched Jay's heart, and it took a while before he could speak. "You are partly correct Michael, it seems as if a lot of good people died in vain, but this just proves that we have to go back to basics. Everything has grown, advance, and gone wild to the point that no one cares anymore, except for themselves."

"That's what I've been trying to tell you Jay, since the day I met you in Lincoln Terrace Park that your kind and loving heart is not going to work around here." Once again, Jay was silent.

"What I've learned Jay, and I pass on to you with all my heart, and this is only because I care, is that there are three types of people." This had Jay arching his furry eyebrows. "There will be a group that will love you for being you, and obviously this is the group you need to be around, all the damn time, but these people are in the minority. The next two groups share the other 90% of the equation. This is divided by the ones who only like you for what you can do for them, and the ones that hate the sh*t out of you. Why you ask, because they can?"

"Thank you Michael. I know you would not share this information if you did not care, and I totally agree with you, but this is why we need to get back to helping each other, showing each other love. We need to get back to teaching the little children, the next generation, how to respect human life. That is why there are Angels like Donna, she is only on this earth to spread *her* love, and hopefully *her* love will be all the world needs." All that could be heard as an answer from Michael was the gulping of his throat.

"I'm going to take a bath, and get ready for our big event this evening. Like I said before Michael, you are more than welcome to stay and come along, and I really wish that you would."

Looking into Jay's eyes, all Michael can do is say, "I'll be there Jay, but only because I don't want you to get yourself in any trouble."

"Me in trouble," laughed Jay, "never that my friend."

They went their separate ways, Jay heading in the direction of the *Big House,* and Michael divagating around the grounds of *The Village.*

*There must be thousands of people,* mused a shocked Michael, as he entered the giant sized circus tent that the harmonious community, that Jay had created, had set up. The attendees were mostly strangers to each other, as if they arrived in *The Village* just like him, only yesterday. He walked casually around the back of the big tent, looking at the tense and anxious faces a waiting for the event to start. Michael did see some recognizable faces, and he wondered what the hell Patrice was doing here. He fought through the crowd and tapped Patrice on the shoulder, "What the hell are you doing here, Patrice?"

"I could ask you the same question, my brother."

"You mean you came all the way from Brooklyn to attend this event?" "Yeah Majestic, I was going off the rails. Then some lovely and kind lady stopped me on the corner of Utica Ave, and told me that things could be better, and that I was loved, no matter what I've done in the past."

"It wasn't our fault that we got hooked on drugs, Patrice."

"Yeah, this will be true my friend, but the things I did to get a hit of crack, just wasn't . . . Kosher!" Michael could see the sudden sadness in Patrice's face as he retraced his past endeavors. "Majestic, you don't know the half my friend." With that said, Patrice ignored Michael, and his attention was back to the stage in front of him. When Michael was about to walk away, Patrice grabbed his arm, "Since I saw you last Majestic, in Randy's apartment, I've been doing more than stealing food and clothes."

"Err . . . Like what, Pee?"

"Put it this way Majestic, I surpassed stealing and selling food for half its original price."

"Whatcha talking about, Pee?" Now you could see the fear etched on Michael's face. "Have you killed someone?" Patrice did not reply, instead he went back to ignoring Michael, and looking back at the stage. This time Patrice did not stop Michael from leaving, so Michael went back to the back of the tent, and found a spot where he could chill out and watch the proceedings.

He could see everyone immediately in front of him standing so close together, as if they were a close knit family. They were not only stepping on each other's feet because there was no room, but were close enough to share each other's clothes. It was really crowded in the *Big Tent,* and Michael was hoping that someone like *Earth, Wind, and Fire* were coming on stage. Further up front Michael could see that *The Village* community had done a swell job in setting up the plethora of chairs into columns and sections. It almost looked like Madison Square Garden, except that the chairs were all the same color.

As he swiveled his head from his left to right, he could see a lot of people like himself, standing around the outer circumference. The lights shone on the stage, and the Master of ceremony finally got on the microphone, "Welcome ladies and gentleman, God bless you all on this special occasion." It was Donna's voice, and it snapped him out of his reverie. Donna looked as if she were miles away from him, up front on her own, on that big stage. *The tent looked bigger inside, than it had looked from the outside,* thought Michael.

"This meeting is a chance for us to change," continued Donna. "Change ourselves and our world for the better. Change that person that we have become and do not like inside of us. We have all done bad and regrettable things, but *he* still loves us, and *he* will continue to love and help us, but only if we attempt at least to help ourselves."

There was thunderous appraise inside the tent, and Michael could feel the breeze from the clapping hands. He was so proud of Donna, as she spoke as if she was used to being on stage, and speaking in front of thousands of people. He wondered if she was going to reveal that she was really Diana Ross in disguise.

There was no sign of stage fright or shyness to be seen, as Donna spoke confidently to her audience. *Damn Dee, ya really got it going on.* The old black man standing beside him could obviously see the sordid smirk on his face.

"Thank you, ladies and gentleman, my brothers and sisters. Now I would like to introduce to you *Our Savior.*" Now there was a standing ovation, as Jay made his way majestically to the front of the stage.

"Jay," Michael couldn't believe his own eyes. *Our Savior?*

He felt faint, and was about to hit the ground, but was saved by the old black man standing next to him. The old black man gave him some of his Perrier water, and started to fan Michael's face with his New York Post. "Are you still with us, young man?"

"Err . . . Yeah. Yeah, thanks. I'm okay." Michael straightened up his clothes and got himself together. The old black man was still staring at him. "I'm fine. Word up, yo!"

"Are you sure?"

"Yeah, I'm sure."

The old black man ignored Michael truculence, "What happened there, young man?"

"Err . . . I don't really know. I just felt a bit faint. May be it was the introduction of my friend Jay." Michael pointed up to the stage. "They introduced him as *Our Savior.*"

"Oh, do you know him personally?"

"Yeah, we hang out, all the time." Michael was now getting fed up with the old black man's interrogation, "And who are you again?"

"Oh forgive me young man, my name is *Jacob.* I am also an old friend of *Our Savior.*"

"His name is Jay, and my name is Michael."

"Nice to meet you, Michael."

"Same her Jay, I mean Jacob."

"You called me Jay also, and then you corrected yourself."

"It was a mistake that's why, Jacob."

"Then why don't you correct yourself totally, and call your friend Jay by his rightful name?"

"Which is . . . .?"

"Jesus."

Michael thought his ribs were going to crack open with laughter, and then he began to feel faint again. *I feel higher than when I smoked some good weed.* The humor immediately left him, and now he was back to being an ignorant and belligerent n*gger. He was about to scream on Jacob, who had helped him, when the crowd around them silenced him before he could utter a word.

"Shh . . ." The congregation immediately around him simultaneously had their index fingers to their lips, just in case the savage in their midst did not understand plain English.

Michael commenced to force his way through the dense crowd in front of him, doing is best to get up closer to the stage, but he was not the only one trying. "Excuse me. Pardon me." The people were not happy with him pushing and shoving them about. They gave him a good and nasty glare. *Shit boy, if looks could kill,* said Brainz.

He pushed his way in between a loving couple, who took offense, and pushed him right back. Then they blocked his way as if they were linebackers for the New York Jets. "Excuse me young man," asked the maleficent Toni Braxton lookalike, "you don't mind if I stand next to my husband."

"No," answered Michael, changing places with her willingly. The acid sarcasm from Miss Toni seemed to have flown over his head. All he wanted to do right now was get closer to the stage, and hear what jay had to say. Knowing Jay from his previous exploits, Michael knew that there was going to be trouble, it was inevitable. The memory of the police breaking up Jay's unauthorized meeting on Eastern Parkway was still fresh in Michael's mind. He positioned himself next to the loving couple, knowing this was as far as he was going to get to the stage, and relaxed.

"Pray with us today," commanded Donna, and when she bowed her head, so did the thousands in the *Big Tent.* "Jesus, we thank you that you are Our Savior and King. The one that can calm the wind and the seas, the one that can hold the earth in the palm of his hands, and that you have healed a broken land like this for us to share. We thank you, because we can trust you with everything. Jesus, please give us knowledge, wisdom, and understanding for this day, and the strength to continually pray and praise your holy name. Amen!"

"Amen, said the transfixed congregation.

"Thank you Donna," said a placid Jay, as he moved toward the microphone. "What a lovely prayer and introduction from precious *Angel* Donna." Donna took a bow, and then stealthily left the stage to join the others in the front row. Michael wished that he could get closer to her, but it was an impossible missing right now.

"Glad that you could all find time in your precious lives to come down here to The Village and share the good news. I will not take up too much of your time," Jay looked over the eager crowd, "I just want to let you know about *our* loving father's grace and mercy."

The place erupted, as if Jay had just moon-walked across the stage like Michael Jackson, or did one of MC Hammers shuffle moves. Jay already had the people in the *Big Tent* captivated Michael noticed, as he had the people on Eastern Parkway mesmerized. The man was a veritable speaker, and it was obvious to Michael that the people wanted to hear more of what he had to say.

"Before we can help *our* fellow brothers and sisters, we have to help ourselves first my people. First we have to appreciate ourselves, and cherish ourselves."

"Yes Lord," screamed an elderly white woman, her hand up in the air, like she just didn't care.

"Amen," came a chorus of voices. As the evening progressed, Michael could see that multitudes of the congregation were struck down under awful guilt within themselves. The cries of the distressed filled the whole tent, the tears flowed like a fountain, and Noah's Ark came to Michael's mind. *Shit Majestic,* said a facetious Brainz, *you should a bought you a wet suit on Delancy Street.*

After looking out at the distressed and inconsolable souls surrounding him, Michael could now see people heading for the stage, some of them getting onto it, to confess their sins in front of Jay. He couldn't believe his eyes when he saw *The Rock Man* approach Jay, on his knees, pleading for forgiveness. *Was this the same man that wanted to shoot Jay just a few weeks ago on Sterling Place?*

It was now obvious to Michael that all the poor and the needy had come all the way here to get Jays blessings, even some of the so-called scum of the earth. Together, they all cried out in severe pain that was within their poor souls, and Michael started to cry also.

After watching Jay put his hands on each individual that approached him on stage, that was mostly everyone in attendance, Michael watched as they all kiss Jay's sandaled feet, as if it was obligatory. There were even little children ranging from ages of five to twelve praying and crying for redemption. "In the blood of Jesus," the little ones screamed. Though he thought that he had gone through some tough times in his life, Michael could not believe the agony of the distressed being manifested before him. *There is always someone worse off than you,* said Brainz. When Jay said that they all needed to go forth into *The World,* and spread love and mercy, they all knew that the evenings proceedings were coming to an end, so they all started to dance and prance around the *Big Tent* as if they had finally found Utopia.

"Yes," said Jay, also enjoying the moment. His commanding voice made everyone stop in their dance of redemption. "Every one of you is worth more than you know. You are worth more than you value yourselves, and treat yourselves." The noise in the place went back to the deafening syllable, as the applause rose to thunderous status.

"You have to have mercy on yourselves," continued Jay. You must learn to forgive yourselves." The sweat on his brow was quickly wiped away by young "Killer," who was standing beside him with an Egyptian cotton towel.

After hours of listening to Jay speak, the *Big Tent* started to empty, and once outside, everyone who once had the omnipresent dark cloud over heads, could now only see a blue and clear sky. They all stepped out of the *Big Tent* with a new pep in their step, a new hope in their hearts, and a new smile in their faces. Even the aged seemed to look two decades younger, their once rough and aged faces seemed to have lost all its wrinkles and their hair it's shades of grey. They all felt alive, and were ready to live again. They started to skip down the dusty roads of *The Village,* past the snail paced young.

The next morning Michael woke up in his bed, still in Jay's palatial house. He was having a sweet dream by the smile on his face, when he opened his eyes to see Jay and Donna standing over him. "You okay, Michael." It was the soothing voice of Donna that spoke first, who looked as if she had three heads at the moment. Michael shook his head so that he could focus more lucidly.

"I'm fine, why?" He stared into both their eyes, as if he was expecting them to lie to him.

"You passed out last night," said a grinning Jay.

"I did? You mean I fainted, and you think it's a laughing matter, Jay?" "No Michael. I just thought it was funny when "The Rock Man"" recognized you, and also fainted into the couple standing next to you." "The Rock Man" fainted?"

"Yes," interjected Donna, "And once he knocked over the couple with his weight falling on them, it had a domino effect. People started tumbling back into the people standing behind them, until they almost pulled the whole tent down. If you look out the window, you can still see people crawling out from underneath the giant canvas."

The story of last night had Michael in stitches, and he had to get himself up into a sitting position. After he was able to stop laughing, he then got very serious. "Who are you, Jay. Really?"

"Who do you think I am?"

"I asked you first," said a childish Michael.

Jay repeated his question, "Who do you think I am?"

They were both looking and waiting for him to answer, "Well I thought that you were just some innocent and naïve guy I met in the park."

"And now, Michael?"

"Well . . . Now I don't know what to think, Jay," said Michael honestly. After a moments silence, "I still think that you are that innocent guy I met, but not as naïve as I thought." This made both Jay and Donna smile. "What's your game Jay? What are you telling these people that could have them all so mesmerized and captivated, as if you were Martin Luther King or Malcolm X.?"

"All I'm doing Michael is telling them what *our* fathers has told me to tell them, that he loves them and he cares."

"He loves and cares about you Michael," said a beaming Donna.

Once again Michael scrutinized the both of them, "And you my fair lady, who are you Dee, and what part are you playing in all this?"

"I'm not playing at anything Michael. We have come here to spread the truth of God's love, and to help our fellow human."

"Okay, okay. I believe you. But let me tell you both this," Michael swung his legs off the bed, and was now standing in front of them with his formidable figure. "Just like Martin and Malcolm, who are both dead now, murdered, you can expect the same treatment from these ungrateful people.

"Don't you have faith in your fellow man, Michael?"

"Jay, you're still not listening to me. Hello . . . ."

"Someone's has to try, don't you think, Michael?"

"And you're willing to die for all of us, Jay?"

"I already have." Michael hadn't flinched, and this pleased both Jay and Donna.

"And you still haven't learned anything from that experience?"

"Yes, but I'm willing to do it again."

"Why, for crying out loud Jay!?"

Both Jay and Donna were happy that Michael did not notice what Jay had just said, and now it was Donna who interjected, "Would you prefer that we just leave this hideous and maleficent world as it is, Michael?"

"But you know that you can give us humans anything we desire. You can give us all the money, food, and clothing that a human can wish for, but once you're gone, *dead,* nothing would have changed one iota. We will be at each other's throats, robbing and killing each other, as if you were never present and amongst us." Michael had the both of them silent, but it was not because he had won the argument as he may have thought, it was because they both loved listening to his earthly and sincere opinions. They were here to change Michael's darkening heart, and save him from sliding over to the Devil's side.

They let him continue, "Once again guys, let's look at the example of *our* beloved Malcolm and Martin. These two guys were very good and religious people, who only wanted the best for their people, just like you two, but look where it got them. Look at the behavior of *my* black people of today. If anything, we have gone backward and not forward. I think that there was more unity within *my* race the further you go back into the Stone Age." Michael's shoulders slumped perceptively, "I'm ashamed of *my* race Jay. I'm ashamed of the whole human race!"

"So am I, Michael." It was plain to see that Jay was touched by Michael's compelling words, and the veritable concern of his welfare. "I thank you Michael, but I cannot just stand by and watch mankind deteriorate, just like Malcolm and Martin. If death is the price . . ."

Michael did not let Jay finish the sentence, "Watch what happen, Jay." Michael was practically screaming in Jay's face with frustration, and Donna cringed. Jay did not though.

"I cannot stand by and watch as the Devil tempts, traps, and kill *my* people."

"It's not all the Devil's doing Jay, it's *your* people who are doing it to themselves, and worse, to each other." Michael sighed, as if he was really getting tired of talking to Jay and Donna. It was as if nothing he was telling them was getting through to them.

*Tough love is what was needed, but it isn't working.* All he wanted was for this innocent and naïve man to understand what the hell he was dealing with out there. These people didn't play around, and they don't give a flying f*ck how kind and loving he is. He had to let Jay and Donna know that this sh*t was real, like in Israel. This was not some damn Disney movie, where everything works out fine and dandy in the end for the loving and caring hero. "Look ya'll, the Devil is just like the character "Jigsaw" in the movie "Saw." He puts the choices in front of us, and we have the choice to choose. Unfortunately guys, it is quite obvious that we as humans do not choose very wisely, but selfishly."

"You forgot one thing, Michael," interjected Jay.

"And pray tell Jay," said a facetious Michael, "what would that be?"

"That the character Jigsaw gave you a choice alright, but the only outcome was that you will lose in either one you made."

"Okay Jay," said a frustrated Michael. "You win. I can't argue with you anymore." The silence between the three could be cut with a blunt instrument. "So guys, what are we going to do next?"

"We?" It was Donna that almost fainted this time, but it was Jay that was smiling.

"Come on," announced Jay, "Let's get out of here."

They all left the house, and headed out to meet and greet the new citizens that arrived each day. There was a chain that they had set up to hand out drinks, food, and clothing. Donna was at the end of the chain, handing out pieces of paper with a number on it. The numbered piece of paper told the new arrivals in which dorm they will be staying in. After the morning rush of arrivals, it was break time. All three of them headed back to the house to have some of Sylvia's prepared and healthy meal. Michael demolished what was put in front of him, "That girl can cook," was all he said as he winked at Sylvia. Sitting back in his chair now, capitulating to Sylvia's offer of more food, Michael drank his nice and cold refreshing Kool-Aid. As Jay and Donna at, like civilized people, Michael stared at the over his glass.

"Jay, what did you mean when you said that you had already died for us?"

Jay and the other ten people around the dining table spat out whatever was in their mouths at the moment, in shock at the out of the blue lightning bolt. Michael was smiling inside, because he had waited purposely for to bring this up. This time he wanted a straight answer.

Jay wiped his mouth with his napkin, and smiled. *He had heard me after all.* "*I have been here before Michael . . .*"

Donna did not let him finish, "Can you excuse us please." With that said, Donna got out of her chair, reluctantly, because she had not finished her scrumptious meal, and grabbed Michael by the arm.

"Err . . . I'm not finished yet, Dee."

"Oh yes you are. Now let's go."

Donna took Michael for a nice leisurely walk, "*He* really is an amazing man," announced Michael.

"Yes, he is Michael."

"Do you love him?"

"Well of course I do, Michael." Donna answered him as if it was a very stupid question. Then she saw the look in his face, "Not like that, silly." They found an esoteric place amongst the trees, where they talked, hugged, and kissed. "I thought you brought me out here to tell me what he meant when he said he had died for us before, and has been here before?"

"You don't mince words, do you Michael?"

"Err . . . No."

"Okay, I will not mince my words either. Jay is really Jesus Christ." "Mmm . . . Jesus Christ. The one from the Bible?"

"Yes, Michael. The one and only." Donna could feel Michael's eyes piercing her soul. "It's the truth, Michael."

"You really want me to believe that?"

"Believe what you want Michael."

"I guess it's time I take my leave, Dee."

Donna knew that the inevitable was coming, but was sad anyway. "I understand Michael. We can still see each other, can't we?"

It was Michael's turn to answer her as if the question was a fatuitous one, "Well of course, Dee. You can't get rid of me so easy." They laughed and kissed, and Michael started on the dusty path that brought him here. He never looked back, until he felt a hand on his shoulder. "How the . . ." *I've walked for at least a mile, and haven't heard or seen anything here.* Michael looked at Donna, and only saw a superfluous amount of feathers floating around her. "What's with all the feathers girl?"

Donna gulped perceptively, "You never mind about the feathers, just know that I don't want it to end this way, Michael." She made sure that she stood facing him, until her wings were folded into their compartment on her back.

"Dee, what are you talking about?"

"I'm talking about Jay."

"Dee, you don't have to explain anything to me. It was nice meeting ya'll, but I'm not one for joining brainwashing cults. I have a lot of Muslim, Jewish, and even Five Per-center friends who have tried their very best to get me to join their religion, and what I've told them, I'm telling you. No!"

"Michael," pleaded Donna, "I'm not asking you to join anything, or do anything you do not want to. I am just trying to answer your question Michael. You wanted to know who Jay really was. Did you not?"

"I also watch the World news, Dee, and I've seen what religious people can do to each other, in the name of their favorite God, in the name of their favorite passage or verse from their favorite book."

"Now look, Michael." It was obvious that Donna was getting angry. Michael was hard work.

"Who are you Dee?"

"Little ole me, ya'll? Well I'm just one of Jay's many angels."

This had Michael gulping down his Private Stock with alacrity. He was more confused than ever before in his life, all he could do now was study Donna, as if she were the enemy. "Why, why are you playing with me, Dee?"

"Michael, you have just left a place where you used your own eyes, and you always told me that you would believe in what your eyes see more than believe in what someone was telling you. Fair play to you, but now you have seen what Jay has done with the once desolate land, he built a Village, and you have seen how *The Village* has changed the once maleficent and venal people of the earth."

Michael was silent, and being speechless was not his forte. "Think about it Michael, you had nothing, until you met Jay in Lincoln Terrace Park. When you left him you had money and beers that you knew that you never had that day."

Silence and harsh breathing was all Donna could here emanate from Michael. At least she had his undivided attention now.

"Now look at you Michael, you have a new spring in your step, you look as mint as a gold bar, and you no longer have a care in the world. You have got to trust someone Michael, and I hope it is me."

"Mmm . . ."

"I love you Michael, and the last thing I would do is lie to you."

For the first time, Michael decided to speak. "You may not intend to lie to me Dee, but just because *you* believe something is true, doesn't make it true." Now it was Donna that was getting frustrated with the man she loved.

"Okay wise guy, explain the beers in your Jansport then, and the $3,000.00 hidden under your bed." Michael almost guillotined his tongue, after his teeth snapped shut audible like a bears trap.

*How could she know all this, Brainz?*

*Sh\*t kid,* said a truculent Brainz, *I didn't tell her anything. Why ya trying to blame me for?*

"How could you know that I had the money," asked a stuttering Michael, and where I hid it, Dee?"

"I told you Michael, I'm with Jay, I mean the Lord Jesus Christ, and he knows everything." Donna watched as Michael as he drank copiously from his 40o/z, and then started to cry. She really felt sorry for him, because she knew that when one hears the truth, good or bad, it was always hard to fathom. "Let's go back Michael, and you and Jay can speak to your friend Jay, face to face, Mano el Mano!"

They found Jay in the Carpenter Shop, busying himself sawing a four by four, "Err . . . Jay, there's a new invention called an electric saw."

Jay kissed his bulging biceps, "I know, Michael."

They gave each other a bear hug, but Michael did not release Jay, because he did not want Jay to see that he was still crying. "Everything will be alright my friend. Have no fear, because I am here!" This only made Michael ball and shiver in Jay's arms deeper. Everyone in the carpentry shop knew what was happening, and they started to make themselves scarce.

"Dee has been telling me who you really are, Jay." Jay looked from one to the other. "Is it true, Jay?"

"I'm afraid so my friend." Michael did not know what to do as a person that always wanted to believe, but thought the Atheist, Agnostics, and the Scientist may be correct with their bullsh\*t "Big Bang" theory. Now Jesus was standing in front of him, and he did not know if to bow down, kiss the man's dusty and worn out sandals, or pass him the 40o/z.

"Jay, I'm so-so sorry." Michael wept, "I didn't mean to put you through all the things that I've been through."

"I know Michael that is why I went where ever he went and needed me."

"Oh Jay, why?"

"Why, because I love you, Michael. Always have, and always will my friend!" Now it was Jay that had tears in his eyes, and was choking up.

"You have never lied to me, Jay. Is this all true. Please tell me the truth Jay, because I'm just tired people that I love turning out to be the ones that had their daggers out, and pointed at my spine column."

"It is true my friend Michael, and when you get home, you will find that there is more money that I added underneath your bed. I only wish that you continue to spend it wisely, and think of me."

Michael was balling, shaking, shivering, and screaming, "Will I ever see you again, Jay?"

"In the words of the Jackson Five Michael, "I'll be there.""

This brought a little giggle and a sniffle from Michael, "Ya learning Jay." He looked Jay up and down, with a smile on his face. "Yes my friend, you are learning."

"You're a good person Michael, just hang in there. Everything will be fine. Remember Michael that after each storm, the sun comes out and shines its radiance."

"Err . . ."

"I know you understand what I am saying to you Michael. Just let go and let God, and you will be okay. With those pearls of wisdom said, Jay watched as Donna walked Michael to the periphery of *The Village*. "Farewell my friend," Jay smiled at the person that he first met in Lincoln Terrace Park. The boy still had an open 40o/z of beer in his left hand, while he puffed on his Newport cigarette with his right.

# SKIES TURNING GREY

"I really hate to see you leave Michael," Donna was almost choking on the heartfelt words.

"Ah, come on Dee. Everything will be alright, girl." Michael only half believed the words he spewed, but always said them, hoping and wishing he was right. Being in each other arms felt so good, and they both did not want to let go, but they did immediately, when they both saw a couple of helicopters fly close over their heads. "Wow, they're flying pretty low." Donna just kept watching the two helicopters as they started their descent. Then her attention was taken away from the skies, to behind where Michael was standing. The sound of the sirens, and the sight of the flashing blue and red lights, had her ears and eyes at their peak. Michael watched the contortion of her pretty face in front of him, because at the moment he could not see or hear anything that warranted his attention. He saw them before he could hear them, as they flew by the both of them on the dusty road toward *The Village*.

The both stepped back from the road, for health and safety reasons, as they watched a mass of police cars, fire trucks, and ambulances speed by them, spewing dirt into their horrified faces.

He knew they were here, even before he heard their screaming sirens entering *The Village*. Jay, who was doing his daily chores of praying and healing the sick in the center of town, quickly got a message to Sylvia, who instantly told the surprised Patrice and Killer to go and spread the alarm of the imminent invasion.

"Come on Michael, we have to go back."

"I knew it, Dee. I tried to tell ya'll, but would anyone listen to my dumb ass!?"

"Later for all that Michael, Jay is going to need our help."

"But you told me that Jay is Jesus Christ, so why would he need my help?"

"Because he wants you to help, that's why!" Michael just stood his ground, "Are you refusing to help your friend Jay, after all he's done for you?" Now Donna sounded angry.

"Err . . . No. Let's go, girl."

When they arrived in town, they saw all their fellow brothers and sisters feebly trying to block the officers from desecrating their holy ground. Donna and Michael snuck around the circumference of *The Village,* and made their way to big house, where they both hoped that Jay had sense enough to be hiding in. "Why," was all he could ask, as he startled the both of them as they snuck by his throne in the living room?

Catching her breath, "They are just collecting our brothers and sisters out there," said an inconsolable Donna, "and asking them to either give you up, or they are all going to jail."

Michael and Donna watched as Jay thought deeply, and then he rose out of his throne, and told them that they had to save *our people.*

All three of them quickly rushed out of the *big house,* and ran to where all the commotion was. Once spotted by some of the police officers, they were snatched, pulled and shoved toward the front of the ever growing crowd. Now up front, Jay could see the officer in charge giving out orders, and this was where he untangled himself from the officers manhandling him, and forced his way to the front of the line. Now some of the other police officers saw him and ran toward him, neglecting everyone else in their presence.

"Can you please take your maleficent hands off of me?"

The new commotion now alerted the chief of police to what was going on, and that they now had their man. Chief Fatkinson now put the well-used bullhorn down by his side, now that the mission was now complete, and all he wanted now was to get back to his office, lock the door, and pour himself a half a gallon of Jack Daniels.

Chief Fatkinson now told *his* peons to bring the infidel to him.

"What is the problem chief," asked a dishevelled but still placid Jay? "Are you the leader of these people?"

"Why, and who would like to know, asked a confused and angry Jay?

"I am chief Fatkinson, and my orders are to bring you in for trespassing out here, and for forming a religious cult."

"Trespassing? This land belongs to everyone under the sun, and I have not formed a cult, I am just spreading the word of *our* father."

Chief Fatkinson looked at the drug using hippie with a degrading smirk on his fat chops. "Whatever, kid. All I know is that you and your groupies are on land that does not belong to you, of which you have had the audacity to build homes and houses on, that I might add have not been inspected by our local housing department for safety checks."

Jay stared at the obese man in bewilderment. "And don't you know that it is illegal to gather feral and under age children, old people that don't even know their own names, and a bunch of criminals that should be in prison." Chief Fatkinson thought that he had the pill popping hippie on the ropes, but he was completely and utterly wrong.

"This land was barren when I came here, and these people you call unworthy for society, came by their own freewill chief Fatkinson.

"Yeah you fat mother f*cker, "said an old white man, who resented the fact that the chief believed that he and all his friends were dumb and feeble because of their age. "You better believe I still have my faculties with me, and so does my very old lawyer friend who is going to sue the sh*t outta you!"

The chief was not fazed by the old man's outburst, or the angry mobs disapproval of him. "You're all under arrest, until we can sort all this mess out!"

"Under arrest," screamed a nervous Patrice. "We haven't done anything."

"Shut up," said the rookie officer standing in front of him. "Shut your face, punk." With that said, Patrice received a lovely blow to the stomach with the rookies night stick. With Patrice folded into the foetal position on the ground, the surprised and innocent crowd were now snarling at the officers in front of them, young and old.

"What did you hit him for," asked a bared teeth Donna?"

"You just stay out of it Missy," said the gleeful rookie, "or you'll be next."

"Okay, okay," came the booming and commanding voice of Jay. "Look chief Fatkinson, these people have not done anything wrong, and they are not responsible for taking this land."

"Then who is," asked the smug chief, now pulling out a long Diplomaticos Cigar from his pocket, rolled it around in his chubby fingers, which were the same size of the cigar, and then lit it at a leisurely pace.

"I am responsible for all this."

"I know," said the smiling chief. With an imperceptible nod of his head, several officers gathered around Jay, and threw him to the ground as if he were a common drug dealer on Sterling Place. Once they had him in handcuffs, they picked him up off the sordid ground, and threw him into the back of a squad car. Chief Fatkinson looked out at the belligerent crowd, and told them that they'd better be off the land, soon-ish. "I'm giving ya'll twenty four hours, and when I come back, and I will be back, whoever I find here will be joining your friend in prison."

All the officers started to make their way back to their squad cars, and he inconsolable paramedics and firemen reluctantly got into their vehicles, miffed that they had not participated in saving lives and putting out fires. All the officious intruders left the same way they came to *The Village,* sirens blaring and lights flashing. This had been a very easy pay day for them, and they left grinning.

"They're some noisy mother f*ckers aren't they," a livid Dirty Debbie said to no one in particular.

The now snarling chief Fatkinson turned his fat head to face Jay in the back seat of the squad car. "The problem you're in hippie, if you can't see it through your hazy eyes, is that you illegally amassed a lot of people, who we have no idea what you or they are up to, on land that doesn't belong to you."

"I repeat chief," said a very calm Jay, "the people came of their own accord. If I am guilty of anything, it may be that I was on land that no one was using in the first place."

"Don't play with me hippie, we all know that you're up to something."

"Like what, chief?"

"Well, you may be on some James Warren "Jim" Jones type sh*t."

"Jim Jones. I think I know him."

"Bet ya do, hippie. He was the one that ran the "Peoples Temple," and had all his brainless followers give him everything they owned, and then killed themselves to save him."

"You've got it all wrong, chief."

"Yeah, whatever hippie." After a moments silence the chief had to ask, "Are you trying to copy your hero *Jim Jones,* Hippie?"

"No. No . . ." Jay mulled over everything that the chief had said, and it brought back some terrible memories. James Warren "Jim" Jones was one of too many men that ran what seemed to be veritable groups, parties, gangs, which in the end turned out to be a pernicious cult. The tears were forcing their way out of his eyes at the memories of how these despicable leaders had their innocent but docile followers commit mass suicide.

Along with the "Peoples Temple," Jay could recall groups like "Heaven's Gate" and the "Order of the Solar Temple." How could chief Fatkinson possible compare him to them? This saddened Jay so much that he did not even attempt to plead his case any longer. He just sat back in the back seat of the squad car, knowing that that his veritable words would only fall on deaf and unwilling ears.

He made himself comfortable, as best he could, and fell asleep until he was later awakened harshly by a burly female officer. After being frog marched up the steps to the precinct, the burly female officer then threw him into a sordid cell. *All alone and no one to be with.*

Jay looked around at all the graffiti, and burnt walls and ceiling in the cell, it was obvious to a blind man that it has been over-used. Jay immediately ran over to the bars of the cell, and asked for his one phone call from the pubescent black officer sitting outside reading his "Right On" magazine. "In a minute hippie, can't ya see I'm reading about MC Lyte?"

"I have a right to that phone call, young man." The way Jay was spoke to the young black boy, had the young rookie instantly throwing his magazine on the floor, and running out to get someone with more authority. When the rookie came back to the cell, he had in his hands a key ring the size of a black girl's earring. He put one of the many massive keys into the cells lock, and shoved Jay, with the help of the other two officers that came back with him, toward a well-used phone on the wall in the reception area. All three officers took a step back, but it wasn't of their own free will. Jay instantly dialed the only phone number he knew, and hoped to his Father up above that Michael answered *his* phone for once in his life.

"What the . . ." Michael searched for his old Samsung in the darkness of his bedroom. He usually put on vibration, and then under his pillow, not really expecting anyone to call him. This time he knew that the constant buzzing sound was not just a notification from Facebook. Using only his ears to pinpoint where the sound was coming from, he found his cellphone where he always did in the mornings, under his bed. How it got there, no longer fazed him.

"Hello . . . Who is this?" Michael looked at the time on the display.

*2:30 AM. What the . . . .?*

"Hello Michael . . ."

"Jay? What the . . ."

"You said that already, Michael."

*Sh\*t, I didn't say anything.*

"Jay, do you know what time it is?"

"I need your help, Michael."

"I knew it Jay. I tried to tell you, but would you ever listen to me?"

"Okay Michael, you were right. Please . . ."

The deep sigh from Michael's hefty lungs could be heard down the telephone line. "Okay Jay, where are you?"

"In jail, and I need you to come and bail me out."

"Err . . . Did you say jail?"

"Yes, Michael."

"Did you say bail you out?"

"Yes, Michael."

"You're f\*cking around, aren't ya Jay."

"Please Michael, I need you now: not later."

The voice had a little finality to it, and Michael was getting dressed as he told Jay, "I'm on my way, Jay. What jail do the Jakes have you locked up in?" There was silence for a while, while Jay asked the officer where he was, and in what precinct. "Suffolk County, Michael. I'm in the 1st Precinct in West Babylon."

"How much are they asking for bail, Jay?"

"They are asking for three thousand dollars, Michael." The heavy thud on the other end of the line made Jay think that he had just given Michael a heart attack. "Michael. Michael, are you okay . . ." All Jay could hear was silence, so he repeated, "Michael . . . Michael . . ."

This is when the three offices fought to get the phone out of his hand, and drag him back to his cell. "Your free phone call time has ended, Hippie."

"But I was not finished."

"Ya think?" All three of the rookie officers were laughing their obese asses off when they lead and threw him back in the sordid cell. Now Jay sat on the diaphanous mattress, head in hands, despondent.

"Where is he?" Morning coffee was spat out of mouths, and into their fellow officer's faces. Once the officers got back their composure, they all got up out of their *Lazy Boy* seats, and surrounded the young man that was rude enough to invader their pleasant morning. "What the hell do you want punk," asked the now angry desk sergeant. He was a massive black man, but not the same one that had invaded *The Village* last night. This one had the face of the anti-Christ, and Michael tried all he could not to look as nervous as he felt. The circle of officers were so tight around him now, Michael was getting claustrophobic. They were all staring at him; he could smell their bad breaths, while they waited for an answer.

"I'm here to see my friend, Jay."

"Jay," asked one of the officers breathing bad coffee and doughnuts in his face. "We don't have anyone in here called . . . Jay."

"Can ya'll please back the f*ck up, and let me breathe some fresh air?"

"Yo punk," seethed the aggrieved officer standing behind him, smelling his armpits. "You can't just come up in here, in *our* house, demanding things. We are officers of the law if you hadn't noticed, and we demand respect."

Michael flinched at the man's hot and stench riddled breath. Michael turned to look into all the officer's faces. He knew he had to change his tactics. "Please except my sincere apologies, officers. I am only here to bail out my friend, and take him home."

"Well," intervened the anti-Christ desk sergeant, "like we said before, we don't have anyone going by the name Jay in here."

Before they all turned away dismissively, Michael tried his best to describe his friend. "You must have a man in here that came in wearing a white gown underneath a brown tattered robe?" Michael looked into their phlegmatic faces, "and he has long hair, all the way down his back." Now they all knew who he was talking about. "The Hippie," exclaimed the desk sergeant. "You know the Hippie?" Now they all turned back to face Michael, almost unbelieving. "How the hell are you two friends? Did he brainwash you like all the others in *The Village?*"

The desk sergeant had all his fellow officers laughing at the stupid young man standing in the middle of their precinct, but Michael did not mind, as long as they gave him room to breathe. Michael walked up to the desk sergeant, "Well . . . Is he here?"

"Yeah," said the desk sergeant reluctantly. "His bail he's here. His bail is $3,000.00 punk; do you have that type of money on ya?" Michael could see that the desk sergeant was enjoying himself tremendously now. Enjoying every moment of f*cking with the "Special needs" young man standing stupidly and alone in *his* precinct.

*The fat b*stard,* offered Brainz. The desk sergeant did not like the smirk that this intruder was now wearing on his face. "Can I see him first? Please . . ."

Once again, Michael had the officers on the back foot, because this was not the time to get any more bad publicity for the precinct. The desk sergeant nodded his head at the young black officer that was Michael's age, and the young officer took Michael down to visit Jay, but not before being searched vigorously. "Damn ya'll, I don't have a hacksaw in my ass."

"Jay. Wake up, yo!" Jay stirred, and Michael could even swear that he saw a smile on Jay's face, as the man slowly woke up. "Are you okay, Jay," asked a concerned Michael?

"Good to see you Michael. I knew you would not let me down."

"Jay, forget all that right now. Are you okay? Why do they have you locked up in here? What have you done?"

Jay looked at the young black officer standing behind Michael, and this made Michael look at the young black officer also. "Can you excuse us please," asked a polite Michael? "Just give us a minute. Please?" "Okay," said the young black officer reluctantly. "But I'll be standing right outside the door, so don't try anything stupid."

"Err . . . Where the hell are you expecting us to escape to," asked a facetious Michael? The young black officer ignored Michael, and stepped outside, reluctantly.

Now that they were alone, Michael asked once again, "What are they charging you with, Jay?" Jay did not answer right away, because he was still happy to hear

Michael's familiar voice in his ears. After a while, Jay told Michael what had happened once they had taken him from *The Village*.

"But you didn't do anything?"

"According to them, I am a brainwashing Jimmy Jones, who has built a whole town illegally on their government owned land, without paying rent or taxes. They said that this is a federal crime."

"But . . ." Michael did not get to finished.

"Visiting time is over," said the desk sergeant, as he barged through the door with the rest of his officious gang. With no logical reason at all, both Jay and Michael were wondering what happened to the young black officer.

"I'll see you soon, Jay," was all the desk sergeant allowed Michael to say, before he was carted out of there. Michael was a nervous wreck as he sat across the street drinking a 40o/z of Private Stock and smoking a Newport cigarette. He knew that he had the bail money, but he didn't want to give it all up, just like that. He had just got it, and now he was supposed to just had it over? Hell no! It would have been better if he had bought and smoked an ounce of crack, and let his heart stop beating from the over-dose. Then at least he would have gotten something out of having all that money. He didn't even get time to spend any of it properly. But still . . . *Sh*\*t, I didn't have any money before I met Jay* . . . "Damn!!!" Michael was torn between the harsh decision he had to make, keep the money, or just give it away? *You've never had so much money before in your life, Majestic.*

*I know, Brainz. But we can't just leave him in there.*

*We can't,* asked a dubious Brainz? *Majestic, how often do you get your hands on $3,000.00?* Michael drank from the 40o/z of beer as if he was trying to finish it in one go. "Damn!!!"

"Do you have the bail money," asked the astonished desk sergeant, at Michael's return.

"Err . . . Well of course I do." Michael opened up his Jansport, and reached in and counted out the money, throwing the stacks in front of the desk sergeant. After he counted to $2,500.00, not really remembering how much he had spent out of his windfall. He started to shake with nervousness, but on looking in his Jansport again, there was no need to be nervous. A little scared, yes, but not nervous.

To his surprise, he could still see a superfluous amount of bundles of cash lying at the bottom of the back pack. *The money is having babies,* said a confused Brainz.

Michael kept counting, until he reached the $3,000.00 asking price. *What the hell is going on . . . .?* He was well over the moon to still see multiple Ben Franklin's staring, but quickly zipped up his Jansport, and signed the bail release papers for Jay.

"You do know that if the Hippie jumps bail, you lose all your money, don't ya," asked the venomous desk sergeant, who was looking at Michael suspiciously?

"Yeah, I know," said Michael, who just wanted to get out of there. "Where did you get all that money?"

."Err . . . Sergeant, I do believe that it's none of your damn business," said Michael, quickly folding and pocketing the bail receipt. "Now can you please release my friend?"

Once outside, Jay took a deep lung full of fresh air, and stretched his aching bones. "I hate being caged up."

No reply came forth from Michael, "Are you angry with me Michael," asked Jay as he watched as Michael did his best to give him the "Silent Treatment?"

As they walked away from the 1st Precinct in silence, Michael inevitably pulled out a fresh 40o/z from the Jansport, and took a lavish swig. Jay waited to be offered the bottle, but it was not forth coming.

"Oh, come on Michael." It was Jay that was getting a little peeved now, because Michael was acting too childish. "Michael, you act as if you have never gotten yourself in trouble before."

Michael spun around to face Jay, "But I tried to tell you about these people, but you didn't want to listen to me."

"I did listen to you, Michael." Jay sounded sad and defeated when he said this, "but I had to give it another try."

They both sighed, and Michael passed the 40o/z to Jay who took the offered beer as he had done when they had met for the very first time in Lincoln Terrace. Jay commenced to drink seventy per-cent of the bottles contents.

"Damn . . ."

"Sorry, I'll buy you another one, Michael."

"No, Jay. You don't have to buy me anything. I was only kidding around with you. When ya gonna learn?" They were both laughing as they walked up route 109. They both stopped in their tracks after seeing a crowd of people sitting in the middle of the road.

"What the . . ."

"It's *my* people, Michael."

The crowd was out in numbers, protesting with their "Sit-In," and holding a vigil by candle light. Michael could hear them chanting, "Free Our Lord. Free Our Lord, Free Our Lord . . . Now."

Michael looked over at the smug looking Jay, "Free Our Lord?"

Jay just shrugged his shoulders, and kept marching toward the crowd.

"Hi ya, Michael."

"Patrice," asked a surprised Michael, "what the hell are you and all these people doing here?"

It was Dirty Debbie that answered, "We all came up with the bail money." "You what . . . .?" It was as if they enjoyed the surprise look on Michael's face. It read: *How come you haven't spent all the money on crack yet?* Then he thought that the same question could have been asked of him. "What," interjected a very sarcastic Salacious Susan, "ya think that you're the only one that can change their life, punk?" After looking at the Motley Crew for a while, Michael just burst out laughing, and they all joined in.

The police had the crowd surrounded again, and Michael didn't believe he could take any more of this sh*t. "Jay, let's get out of here." Jay hesitated too long. "Jay, I'm speaking to you."

Jay was obviously moved by the crowd's kindness, "Can I at least tell them that I thank them for coming, Michael." Michael was wondering why Jay was actually waiting for his permission. *The man is amazing. Who is he really?*

*They say he is the Lord Jesus Christ, Majestic.*

*I know what they are saying, and I know that they believe it Brainz, but it doesn't make it so.*

*You're such a pessimist, Majestic.*

*Oh, shut up, will ya!*

*Don't you believe them? Don't you believe him?*

*Brainz, are you serious? You . . . .?*

"Well I agree with Brainz, Michael." It was Donna who intervened into his private thoughts. "What will it take to convince you that you are in the presence of the Saviour?"

"Err . . ."

Michael looked into her beautiful eyes, and then over at Jay's smirking face. "Go ahead Jay, but make it quick," was all that Michael had to say. Taquan, who was an old friend of Michael's, the old Michael, looked at the crowd, "What's going on, Majestic?"

"Well, to tell ya the truth, officer, I don't even know."

Taquan removed his police cap, and brushed back some of the long dreads out of his eyes, "What is your friend up to, Majestic?"

"Nothing," said Michael too defensively. "He hasn't done anything Taquan. All he has done as far as I can see," continued Michael more placidly, "was preach to these people, and "The Filth," I mean the police locked him up yesterday for some of the most pathetic reasons like: Loitering, trespassing, and disturbing the peace. It's all bullsh*t!"

The look that Taquan gave him, told Michael that Taquan has heard it all before. "Let me get this straight Majestic, your friend did nothing, so my fellow police officers locked him up, and now we've been called back here to disperse a riot?"

"What riot, Taquan? Do you see a riot around here?" Michael was getting angry, and was getting rather tired of Taquan's ignorance. "All I see here is a crowd of people sitting here, protesting for his release."

"They are sitting in the middle of the damn road, Majestic."

"It's still not considered a riot, Taquan."

"Well your friend has been released now, and he is free to go. So can you please tell these people to get out of the damn street?"

"I'm telling you Taquan, the man has done nothing."

"Get them out of the road, Majestic, or there will be violence."

Michael went back to joined Jay and Donna, and told them what Taquan has been saying, and wanted them to do. Jay immediately went into the crowd, and waved his hand. Like obedient children, they all started to get up off the ground, grabbing their belongings, and started on their way up route 109. Jay, Donna, and Michael followed, but Michael stopped when he felt a hand on his shoulder.

"Why are all these people willing to go to jail for him, Majestic?"

"Err . . . Maybe it's because he is our Lord and Saviour Jesus Christ. That's why!"

After Taquan looked at Michael as if he were crazy, and then left, Jay and Donna looked at Michael. "I cannot believe you told such a lie to that police officer, Michael."

"I didn't lie, Dee. You told me that Jay was the Lord Jesus Christ, and now you're saying that I lied to Taquan?"

"I know what I told you, but if you don't believe what I have told you, then you must have lied."

Michael stared at Jay studiously, and the tears started to roll down his cheeks, "I didn't lie," he screamed. Jay held Michael's trembling body in his arms, until the trembling subsided. It was a while before the three of them started on their way to catch up with the rest of the crowd.

Once the crowd had hit the center of Suffolk, they started to dwindle, and go their own way. The police had been following them in their cruisers at five miles an hour, to make sure they did not congregate somewhere else in their town. Now the police officers were quite happy to see that the crowd disperse, because they were also tired from the night's ordeal, and wanted to go home to their nice comfortable beds.

There were more important things for them to be doing with their lives other than baby-sitting peaceful protesters, like doing their real job of stopping violent and uncouth criminals. None of the officers appreciated standing in the middle of a road on such a cold night.

"We should be out in the streets," offered a female rookie, "shooting people."

They should have been home a few hours ago, and officer Dingles wanted all his fellow officers to know it. "F*ck the over time, Taquan. I've got some succulent p*ssy waiting for me at home."

"Calm down, Dingles, she'll still be there when you get there."

"Don't tell me to calm down you predator looking savage," snarled the belligerent Dingles. Whether she's there or not, I'm too f*cking tired to do anything with her tonight."

The other officers kind of agreed with officer Dingles, but they had other things on their minds.

It was now three thirty in the morning, and the frost was covering the parked cars and streets. Michael kept cracking open a 40o/z's on the way, and was rather paralytic and blurry eyed when they finally reached Donna's apartment building.

"Do you really live here," asked a slurring Michael?

"Yeah, I do." Donna snuck a quick look at Jay. "Do you want to come up and see?"

"Err . . ."

"I'm taking him home, Donna." Jay snatched Michael by the collar, who was attempting to go into Donna's apartment building, but had trouble negotiating the concrete steps of the stoop. "Let's go, Michael."

"I want a kiss!"

Jay just looked up at the start in the nebulous sky, and then shrugged his shoulders in resignation at Donna. A smiling Donna crawled into Michael's waiting arms, and kissed him passionately. "I'll see you tomorrow, Michael. Go home and get some rest."

Instead of taking Michael home, Jay took him back to Lincoln Terrace Park. Jay poured some of Michael's beer into his hand, and then wiped it around Michael's face as if it were Holy Water. Instantly Michael came alive, but still not completely sober. Shaking the fuzziness out of his head, Michael saw a sordid white gowned Jay sitting next to him near the duck pond. *How the hell did I get back here to Lincoln Terrace?*

Jay still had that sordid little smirk on his countenance, the same one he had when he first met him. Michael shook his head again, to make sure that he has not been asleep for the past few weeks, and what has been happening was real. He quickly went into his Jansport to check if the money was real, and he found out that it was, after he removed several 40o/z of Private Stock. Michael looked over at Jay suspiciously. *Is he also as real as the money and beers?* Michael gulped down a lavish portion of fresh beer, and then he automatically passed it over to Jay, who tried to decimate it. *Damn this boy is always thirsty.*

He intentionally displayed to Jay that his Jansport was still full of money and beers. "I didn't do this, Jay!"

"Do what, Michael."

"Put all this money and bottle of beers in here."

"So?"

"So Jay, I know that you have something to do with it. Before I was just suspicious, but now . . . I've been thinking a lot, and though you may think that I have to be quite a dumb person to become a drug addict, I'm far from completely stupid."

"I did not say you were dumb, and I sure did not say . . ."

"Jay. Stop it. Just stop it. It's that time, Jay."

"Time. What are you talking about, Michael?" It was obvious that Jay was having fun, Michael could tell by the wry smile on his sordid mug. "Time for the truth, Jay. You do know what the truth is, don't cha?"

The thunder of Jay's laughter reverberated throughout the dark park, and Michael swore, after flinching, that the mallards were also laughing. After the thunder from Jay's chest had dissipated, the cloak of silence diametrically enveloped Lincoln Terrace. As cold as it way, Michael could see that Jay was wiping sweat off his forehead.

"Why, Jay. Why did you give me all that money?"

The silence was deafening. Jay could see that Michael had tears welling up in his eyes, again. "I did it, because I love you, Michael."

"But Jay, we only met just the other day. You don't know me that well, and you can't love me that much."

"I've known you all *your* life, Michael." You could now hear the slight sobbing sounds emanating from Michael in the dark silence of the park. He was never shy of showing his feelings, because playing a hard man, with no emotions, was not in his DNA. "I can't pay you back, Jay," was all that come out of him that was coherent to Jay's ears.

"I did not ask for anything in return, Michael." What Jay did not know was that his loving kindness was killing Michael, who was not used to someone caring and looking out for him. He was not used to someone who wanted to do something for him, without asking for something in return.

"I can't pay you back," repeated Michael, "No one can pay you back for all the good things you have done for us." Jay let Michael continue, because words came hard for him now. "I don't understand why you keep helping people who don't even thank you, acknowledge you, and take everything you have given them for granted?"

Jay just drank, only because he had no reply for Michael. "Instead they treat you like sh*t, spit on you, and want to hurt you, even worse, they are willing to kill you for a piece of copper."

"Do you want to spit on me, hurt me, and kill me, Michael?"

"Jay. Now you're being really silly."

"Well . . ."

"Of course not Jay, but still . . ."

"You will understand one day, Michael." Jay passed the 40o/z back over to Michael, it was left over suds. "I just want everyone to live right, Michael. I want them to know that you are all brothers and sisters, and that you should all care for one another."

Jay's words sobered Michael up a notch, because he's never heard so much crap in his life. "Jay. You know I wouldn't lie to you, right?"

"I do believe that, Michael."

"Well I'm telling you Jay, that that sh*t ain't gonna happen. It hasn't happened, and it will never happen. As a matter of fact Jay, things are worse in this world than it has ever been." Frustration was now taking over his inebriation, "Can't ya see that, Jay?"

"Yes Michael, I can see what you're saying. That from the beginning of time, all mankind have been doing was the extreme opposite of what *our* father wanted them to do. Now it was Jay who was getting all melancholy, "But I gotta try, don't I?"

The tears started streaming more profusely from Michael's sensitive brown eyes, because he now knew what he was doing to Jay and his beliefs. He has always been told that he had a tongue that could kill.

*You may not know how to fight Michael,* Ivan once told him, *but you sure know how to get yourself in trouble with your big mouth.*

It was never his job to destroy anyone's dreams or beliefs with his sharp like a Ginsu knife tongue, no matter how far-fetched their dreams and beliefs were.

"I don't want to die again, Michael."

Jay hugged Michael and they both cried freely in each other's arms. Jay's gone . . .

When Michael awoke in the next morning, he found himself lying in the grass, covered with Jay brown tattered robe. After wiping the sleep out of his eyes, Michael looked around vigorously. Jay was gone, like the wind. Sitting up sluggishly, in front of him Michael could now see a line of at least twelve 40o/z bottles of Private Stock, and a second Jansport back pack beside them. He quickly whipped his head around the scene again, but received the same result: No Jay.

Michael's brown eyes came back to rest on the goodies that lay in front of him. It was obvious – to an idiot like him – that Jay had left him a parting gift.

*He's not coming back kid!*

*I know Brainz,* said a forlorn Michael.

The dozen bottles of Private Stock put a smile on Michael's face, and when he nervously went over to the Jansport, he was pleasantly surprised to see it filled to the zipper with more money than he could count. He instantly turned back to open his own Jansport, that Jay had put under his head for a pillow. It was also filled with money.

*Where did Jay get all this money, and why leave it for me? Doesn't he know that I'll only f\*ck it up?*

Before he could analyse his own question, Michael saw a plastic Ziploc bag filled with various items inside, with a note.

Quickly he opened it up, and unfolding the note. It read . . .

Good morning, Michael.

I have to go away for a while, and I just want you to know that you have been a good friend while I was here. I have left you a few things that will help you on your way, until my return. I call it "The Daily Survival Kit." These things should help you each day, so take heed.

I have left you a "Toothpick" to remind you to pick the good qualities in everyone, including yourself:

1.  "A rubber band" to remind you to be flexible, because things might not always go the way you want them to, but it can be worked out.
2.  "A Band-Aid" to remind you to heal hurt feelings, either yours or someone else's.
3.  "An eraser" to remind you that everyone makes mistakes, and that it's okay. We learn by our errors.
4.  "A Hershey's candy Kiss" to remind you everyone needs a hug or a compliment every day.
5.  "A mint" to remind you that you are worth a mint to your family, and especially to *me*.
6.  "A bubble gum" to remind you to stick with it, and you can accomplish anything.
7.  "A pencil" to remind you to list your blessings, every day.
8.  "A tea bag" to remind you to take time to relax daily, and go over the list of all God's blessings.
9.  These are the things that will make life worth living, every minute, every day. God bless you, my friend.
    Ps – 10. "I love you!"

The area around where he sat in front of the duck pond was as wet as the letter he held limply in his shaking hands. "Why, Jay? Why?"

He cried and balled his eyes out, until he started shaking and sniffling uncontrollably. The earthquake in his body only stopped when there were no more tears to be shed.

The angelic voice he heard singing, along to the tweeting birds of the morning, sounded familiar: Donna. Michael quickly tried his best to fix himself up, wipe the tracks of tears off his face, straighten his clothes, and put everything away.

*How the hell am I going to hide twelve 40o/z bottles?*

Instantly Michael looked for a good hiding place for his two back packs and the bottles of beers. After searching for far too long, he quickly put them beside the nearest tree. "Hi ya Dee," he said as cheerfully as he could.

Donna stared at him silently, as if she had been there all along.

*Did she hear me crying, and see me trying to hide everything?*

"What are you doing here, Dee?"

"I remember you asking me that same question when you first saw me here."

"Err . . ."

"You need to get some originality into your vocabulary, Michael."

"Err . . ." They both laughed, and then hugged each other. Michael was holding onto Donna so tight, that she was beginning to feel her bones being crushed.

After feeling her struggling to get out of his "Ivan Rasputin" bear hug, he loosened his iron grip. "Sorry Dee. I'm just so glad to see you."

"Well I'm glad that you're glad, and you better be to." Michael grabbed her again, and this time he held her in his arms, and kissed her softly. This time there was no struggling from Donna.

"What are you going to do with all that money Jay left you, Michael?"

"Err . . ."

"I knew you would say that."

"Err . . . I really don't know Dee, but I'll think on it after I drink all the 40o/z he left me." They both laughed, and after gathering all his gifts from Jay, Michael asked Donna if she wanted to come to his house.

"I am not that kind of girl, Michael."

"Oh shush, girl. I just want to put these things away, and then we can go somewhere. Spend the day together."

"Mmm . . ."

"I can introduce you to my parents," exclaimed a gleeful Michael.

"As what," replied Donna?

"Well, as my girlfriend, of course."

"Mmm . . ."

"Well . . . Are you coming?"

"First I think I am going to need a swig of your 40o/z."

They marched up the hill, giggling, laughing, and holding onto each other quixotically.

# DONNA MEETS THE FAMILY

After being introduced to Michael delirious parents, Mrs Patkinson was over the moon to see her eldest son bring home a half decent female. Sh*t, she would have been well happy to see him bring home anyone of the female persuasion, even if she was the "Happy Hooker."

Mrs Patkinson took Donna to the kitchen, on the pretence of making her husband and son something to eat.

While breaking out some cookies from the cupboard, and putting the kettle on, Mrs Patkinson started the inevitable interrogation. "Where did you meet Michael?" She was not going to mince words, but Donna knew what was coming, because Michael had prepared her on the way home. "I met Michael in the park, right there in Lincoln Terrace."

"Oh yeah, do tell."

"Well then, we got to talking, and he was so sweet."

"Mmm . . . What do you do for a living?"

Donna was laughing inside, this woman was no joke. "I'm a teacher, at a Christian Junior School."

"You're a teacher, at a Christian School?" Donna thought that Mrs Patkinson was going to pass out. "Are you a Christian?"

"Yes ma'am, a devout one."

"You mean that my Michael has finally met a Christian woman. Thank you, Jesus."

Donna did not like how Mrs Patkinson was looking up at the kitchen ceiling, "You okay, Mrs Patkinson?" Donna helped Mrs Patkinson into a seat around the kitchen seat, and then ran over to the sink to get her a glass of water.

After taking a sip of water, Mrs Patkinson seemed to come back to the present. All she did for the next few minutes was stare into Donna's beautiful brown eyes. "Are you sure that my Michael has told you everything, girl?"

"Yes, I am sure he has."

"Are you sure you know what you're doing, child?"

"Yes, I do Mrs Patkinson. Your son has changed a lot since I met him."

"Yes, he has. I've seen the change in him, and it warms my heart to see him getting back on his feet." Mrs Patkinson was now looking through Donna. "Are you the reason for the positive changes in my son?"

"Well I hope so, but I cannot take all the credit."

"Why do you say that, child?"

"Well . . ." Donna hesitated, "Did Michael ever tell you about his friend Jay?"

"Err . . . No, said a now confused, but an even more intrigued Mrs Patkinson. "Why. Who is this character Jay?"

"Jay, you know him also Mrs Patkinson, but not as intimately as your son."

"Talk to me girl!" Donna took a seat at the kitchen table next to Michael's mother, and started telling the unbelievable story.

Michael and his father were watching the "Family Feud" with the very funny Richard Dawson on day time television. They were both laughing their heads off, and enjoying the stupidity of the "Imbecile family," and so were Richard and the live studio audience.

"They had some balls going on that show," said Michael's father.

"They sure did, dad. They should have chosen to go on one of them kiddie shows on Nickelodeon instead." Michael was enjoying this rare quality time with his father. *It's been a very long time.*

They were still laughing when the girls finally arrived with their lunch. "Cookies and tea," Ken was not happy in the least? "You girls had enough time in that kitchen to bring us some real food."

"Yeah," concurred Michael, "where's the oxtail, rice and peas?"

They were all laughing, except Mrs Patkinson, who was just staring at her precious son.

"What's the matter, Mavis?" His wife looked . . . Happy. She was looking at Michael with eyes full of love and bewilderment. *What the hell went on in that kitchen? Regardless of what was said,* Ken was glad to see that look on his wife's face. He has not seen his wife give their eldest son that loving look in such a long time.

Michael and Donna was only ten minutes into the story before Ken asked his wife Mavis to pass the Wray & Nephews, "No ice, please dear."

"They were actually hanging out with *our* Lord Jesus Christ, Ken."

"Mavis, please. Just calm down." Ken emptied his glass of rum quickly, and automatically passed it back to his wife to have it replenished. "The people telling you this far-fetched tale are kids, and one of them happens to be our drug addicted son, Mavis."

"Whatcha ya saying, pops?" Michael could understand why his father wouldn't fall for a story like this, but it was all true. "Daddy, this is not a joke, and I'm not smoking any of that sh*t anymore." He looked over at Donna, "Surely you can't believe that Donna is a drug addict also?"

"I don't know this you brought into my home, Michael. Sh*t, I hardly know you, anymore."

Everyone in the living room was silent, because none of them knew what else to say to convince Michael's father that he was no longer doing drugs, and that his best friend was the one and only "Jesus Christ." Michael got up off the couch next to his father, and went into his bedroom behind them. When he returned, he had both Jansport back packs in his hands. He immediately emptied their contents onto the living room carpet, and watched both his parent's faces turn from one primary colour to the next. He started to get scared when his parent's faces started to turn as white as Casper the friendly ghost.

"Daddy, say something," beseeched Michael.

"Err . . ."

"Err . . . What dad?"

"What have you two done Michael," asked his sputtering father?

"Hope you didn't go there," was all his mother could utter?

Michael looked over at Donna, "Go where, ma?"

"What your mother is trying to say boy, is that she hopes you haven't graduated from doing drugs to robbing banks."

"No, no," quickly intervened Donna. "Michael got all this from Jay, I mean Jesus."

"So let me get this straight ya'll." Now they could all the sarcasm seeping out of Michael's father. "Jesus came down from Heaven right, he then ended up in Lincoln Terrace, where he met my drug addicted son. Then they became the best of friends, and Jesus decided to give him all this loot?"

"Err . . . Well . . . Basically yeah, dad."

"Boy, shut ya mouth!"

"But it's true, Mr Patkinson."

"And who are you again?" Ken was getting angry with the girl that Michael had brought into his house, but he was even angrier with his son for bringing her here. One drug addict was enough to deal with, and he wasn't about to play their low life games either. This bullsh*t game they're playing had to stop, and stop right now. *But where did all the cash come from?*

Money or not, Ken hated when people tried to play him for a sucker, or thought that he was that drunk. It hurt him even more that the people right now were his gullible wife and drug addict son.

"You want to know who I am Mr Patkinson. Well I'll tell you. I am one of God's Angels," answered Donna. This made Michael's parent's look at her as if she was smoking more crack than their son. Michael sat there just as shocked at the news. *An Angel?*

*I knew that there was something up with her*, said Brainz.

*Just shut up Brainz. Please.*

"Ya see Mavis," exclaimed Ken, "these two are smoking something special out there in them streets."

Donna stood up in the middle of the living room, quite tired of this façade now. Michael and his parent's watched her as she commenced to take off her B3 Pilot Bomber Jacket. She threw it into Michael lap, and then set her wings free from her back. Her wings covered the width of the living room, the tips touching both walls. Then she started to ascend toward the ceiling, just in case the wings trick did not convince her open-mouthed audience. When she looked down at them, she could see saliva drooling down their chins. After believing that she had done enough to convince them, especially Michael's father, Donna descended back to the carpet. She folded her wings back into place, and asked Michael for her B3 Jacket back.

"I had to show him Michael."

"Err . . ."

"I know, Michael. I know. I'll explain it all to you, later."

The kiss was long, and although Michael enjoyed every minute of it, it just felt so final. "Where are you going, Dee?" The tears were already in Michael's eyes.

Donna stuttered with her words, "I have to go now Michael." She looked into his tear filled eyes, "I just have to."

"Go where, girl. What are you talking about?" Michael was now confused and getting angry.

"I will miss you." The words cut Michael's heart in half. "I really will, Michael."

"What are you talking about Dee," pleaded Michael. "I haven't done anything. I haven't cheated on you." Michael was getting sick and tired of decent girls leaving him for some weak and random reason. He lived in a place where he saw the other fellows cheat and beat on their girls, and still kept their harem in tacked. "I love you Dee," he proclaimed!

"I love you also," cried a tearful Donna. "But I have to be near Jay, or I'll perish."

"Perish . . . Dee, what are you talking about? Please." The tears fell freely now, and Michael did nothing to hide them.

"Jay is my life force Michael, and if I stay away from him for too long, I'll just die."

"Die?" Michael could hardly say the three lettered word. They always said that the truth hurts, and he actually believed that Donna was telling the truth, although it didn't make any sense. But did anything make sense around here, especially since Jay and Donna entered his once pathetic life? "Where will you go," he sputtered?

"I will be where Jay is, and Jay will be where you are, Michael. So we will always be with each other!" Now it was Donna's turn to cry uncontrollably, and after the long scene of sobbing between them, Jay decided that it was time to step in. Saying good bye was not easy for anyone, especially himself, but it had to be done – Sometimes.

Jay grunted to get their attention, and then told Donna that it was time for them to leave, and then he took the hysterical Michael to one side. They stood for a while watching the mallards play in the pond, and then he turned to Michael. "This is not going to be easy my friend, but I have to leave." There was a big scream of anguish from Michael's throat, and Jay just held him close to his chest, maybe so Michael could not see the tears in his eyes.

"You have been a very good friend to a stranger Michael, and because of that," stuttered Jay, "I have reserved a place for you in my home." Michael was still trembling in his arms, "I just want you to keep trying to do your best in this iniquitous world you live in, Michael. I want you to keep being kind and caring to others . . ." Jay was choking on his words, but he ploughed on through. "I know it will not be easy for you Michael, but always remember the *Daily Survival Kit* I gave you with the money. Use all of them wisely, and remember that Donna and I will always be watching out for you. We've got ya back, kid."

Michael took his tearful face off of Jay's chest, and looked up into the man's bearded face. It was good to see Jay smiling through his tears.

"I was rubbing off on you Jay, weren't I?"

"Yes you were, Michael. You've taught me a lot."

"Want a 40o/z for your journey?"

"I have my own supply, Michael." They smiled and shook hands like gentlemen, and then Michael saw Donna bow behind Jay giving him the sign to bow in front of the Lord. Michael got on his knees in front of Jay, and bowed his head. "Thank you, Jay. I love you!"

They were both gone in the instant it took for him to raise his head. This time he did not see their backs ascending to the top of Lincoln Terrace, because they were gone in a flash.

"Dear God, please grant me the peace to accept the things I cannot change, the courage to change the things I can, and the wisdom to know the difference! Let me live one day at a time, and enjoy one moment at a time.

Let me accept hardship, as the pathway to peace. Taking as you did, this sinful world as it is, not as I would have it.

I trust that you will make all things right if I surrender to your will, and that I may be reasonably happy in this life and supremely happy with you forever in the next. Amen, Jay!"

He read Jay's letter of Grace each and every morning, before he started each day. He still kept everything that Jay had given him in the extra Jansport together, at the bottom of his bedroom closet. He put the letter of Grace back in its place, with the superfluous amount of money, which Michael had not even bothered to count.

The *Daily Survival Kit* was the only thing that he never put back with the rest of the things he had found in the second Jansport. This he carried in his own Jansport, because he never knew when he will need it, and it was always better to have and not need, than to need and not have.

Jay had said that it will help him in his daily life, so he zip-loc bag filled with toothpick, rubber band, band aid, eraser, Hershey's kiss, mint, bubble gum, pencil, tea bag, and of course God's blessings in one of the many secret zippered compartments of the back pack.

Since then Michael's life has changed, for the better. Not that he had eventually become a successful rock, rap or basketball star. He still lived around the area of Crown Heights with his mother and father, but this time around he had gotten himself a job at the local hospital, and no longer did he waste his life hanging out on "The Block" each precious day.

He did not make great money working at Kings County Hospital, but it was a living, and he enjoyed working with the public. He loved going to work, it was something to look forward to, and it was a reason to get out of bed instead of living for his next hit of crack.

He now had new friends that he worked with, and the patients always made him feel blessed. They constantly told him that they loved his smiling face each morning, and that he was "A ray of sunshine."

Michael could see by the patients that came into the hospital each day that life could be much worse, and yet they amazed him by just getting on with their lives, no matter how bad their ailments and disabilities.

He was also amazed that he worked along vibrant and healthy staff members, a lot of them younger than himself, who constantly complained and cried about how hard their pathetic lives is.

*Truly amazing, Brainz!*

Lightning Source UK Ltd.
Milton Keynes UK
UKOW04f2333090913

216843UK00001B/57/P

A friend named Jay is a book about a young male, who has become a vile product of his sordid surroundings. The once kind, caring, and loving Michael has finally succumbed to the drugs that surround his grotesque world, and is losing himself within.

Alone again, Michael sees an incongruous cloud floating out of the sky toward him. He then meets a stranger with an unshaved face and long hair. Since then, things just have not been the same.

My name is **MICHAEL ATKINSON**, and I was born in London, after a brief intermission of living in Brooklyn New York, I have returned to tell you unbelievable stories.

I am now the proud Author of: "Anthony & Lorraine – Evolution," and "A band of criminals."

This is my third novel and the positive feedback I have received for my two previous novels has my head spinning. I hope you guys will also enjoy this one also. So have a good read, and let me know what you think.

Michael Atkinson
Email:don_mike@blueyonder.co.uk

ISBN 978-1-4836-6234-3
90000

9 781483 662343